"GOOD EVENING. LOVELY NIGHT FOR A STROLL."

"Yes." She slipped her hand into the pocket of her shorts. He saw her hand clench and he wondered what sort of defense she carried in there. A can of Mace, perhaps, or pepper spray. He watched her summon her courage.

"I'm afraid you're trespassing," she said, her tone cool but not unfriendly. "This is a private beach."

"Yes, I know. I have a house nearby."

"Oh, I'm sorry. I didn't know that. I'm new here myself."

He extended his hand. "Dominic St. John."

After a moment's hesitation, she placed her hand in his. "Tracy Warner."

His fingers curled lightly around hers. It was then that he felt it, a sharp jolt of recognition as his essence brushed against hers. A thrill of excitement swept through him. It was she, his soul mate, the woman he had found and lost countless times through the centuries. His beloved one. He had known her in many guises, by many names.

She was staring up at him. It took him a moment to realize he had fallen silent, that he was still holding her hand.

He smiled. "I am pleased to make your acquaintance, Miss Warner."

A WHISPER OF ETERNITY

Amanda Ashley

ZEBRA BOOKS
KENSINGTON PUBLISHING CORP.
http://www.kensingtonbooks.com

ZEBRA BOOKS are published by

Kensington Publishing Corp.
850 Third Avenue
New York, NY 10022

All Kensington titles, imprints, and distributed lines are
available at special quantity discounts for bulk purchases
for sales promotions, premiums, fund-raising, educational
or institutional use.

Special book excerpts or customized printings can also
be created to fit specific needs. For details, write or phone
the office of the Kensington Special Sales Manager: Kensington Publishing Corp., 850 Third Avenue, New York,
NY 10022. Attn: Special Sales Department. Phone: 1-800-
221-2647.

Zebra and the Z logo Reg. U.S. Pat. & TM Off.

First Printing: February 2004
10 9 8 7 6 5 4 3 2 1

Printed in the United States of America

To Jackie Radoumis
because she missed out on the last one

And to Joseph Walsh
and Elizabeth Camp
for enriching my book with their poetry

Nosferatu

Tender are the scars that never heal
Deep are the wounds of the soul
Long is the night that never ends
And false are the tales you've been told. . . .

You have visited me within your dreams
You have seen my shadow upon your wall
You have heard my voice within your mind
And you are helpless to resist my call. . . .

I am the one you hope never to find
Yet I am the one that fills your heart
I am the one whose tender kisses
You long for in the dark. . . .

I could hold you in a lover's embrace
But once would never do
For already you fill my senses
With love and need for you. . . .

I am legend, lore, and myth
I roam the dark of night
I take what I need from the innocent
I flee from dawn's first light. . . .

You ask who and what I am
But in your heart you already know
Though a mortal man I may not be
I am still the one who loves you so.

Elizabeth Camp

Chapter 1

Nightingale House perched near the edge of a high, rocky cliff overlooking the Pacific Ocean. The first time Tracy Warner saw the house, she thought it was the most beautiful place she had ever seen. Sunlight glinted off the arched, leaded windows. Birds sang in the trees. A covered verandah wrapped around three sides of the house; she had imagined herself sitting out there on balmy nights, sipping a tall glass of iced tea while she admired the view of the ocean.

The inside of the house had been equally impressive. The walls and ceilings were freshly painted, the oak floors and banisters gleaming with wax. Though the house was old, it had been remodeled to accommodate all the modern conveniences.

As much as she had loved the big, airy feel of the house, she'd had every intention of asking the realtor to show her something a little less pricey, so she wasn't sure who was more surprised, herself or the realtor, when she said she'd take it. Once the decision was made, she was sure it was the right thing to do, even though it would mean using all of the sizeable inheritance her grandfather had left her, and wiping out most of her savings, as well.

Still, a house by the ocean was bound to be a good investment and she had been pleased with her decision and eager for escrow to be closed.

Now, looking at the place sixty days later, she found herself having second thoughts. The house that had looked so bright and cheerful the morning she had first looked at it seemed somehow ominous with night approaching. Windows that had sparkled in the morning sun now reminded her of dark, soulless eyes staring out at her.

With the sun setting behind the house, it looked like a huge, prehistoric bird about to take flight, or perhaps a cobweb-infested castle that the infamous Count Dracula might have lived in. Glancing around, it occurred to her that the only thing missing was the requisite dark and stormy night. She wouldn't have been at all surprised to see a giant black bat hovering overhead, or to hear the melancholy wail of a wolf in the distance.

For the first time, it occurred to her to wonder why there were two chimneys but only one fireplace.

Climbing the creaky porch steps, she wondered what had possessed her to buy the place. Had she seen it at this time of day instead of early morning, she would certainly have looked elsewhere! Tall trees grew close to both sides of the house. The first time she saw the house, there had been birds singing in the branches; now the birds were silent and the leaves rattled like dry bones in the evening breeze.

Tracy shook her head. Her imagination was really working overtime tonight!

Taking a deep breath, she took the big, old-fashioned brass key from her pocket and slid it into the lock. The door opened with a screech like that of a woman in pain.

How could she have forgotten that awful sound? And why did it sound so ominous?

"First on the list," she muttered, closing the door behind her. "A little WD-40."

Stepping into the entryway, she was overcome by a vague sense of unease. The realtor had warned her that the two previous occupants had moved out because they believed the house was haunted. Tracy had dismissed the notion out of hand. She didn't believe in ghosts but if they existed, this was certainly the kind of house they would be comfortable in.

Searching for the light switch just inside the door, she flicked it on, but the room remained dark. No light penetrated the heavy draperies that covered the windows in the living room.

Tracy sighed in exasperation. The electric company had promised her that the power would be turned on before she arrived.

The thought of walking into that dark, empty house filled her with apprehension. Though she was reluctant to admit it, she had been afraid of the dark ever since she was a little girl.

But, not to worry, she thought with a grin, because there was an oil lamp on the long, low table to the left of the front door. The realtor had warned her that the power was prone to go out during storms and that it might be a good idea to keep a few of the old lamps close at hand, as well as a supply of matches. Being a former Girl Scout, she had come prepared.

Checking to see if the lamp had fuel, she pulled

a book of matches out of her pocket, lifted the chimney, struck a match, and touched the flame to the wick.

The welcome flare of light put her fears to flight.

After adjusting the wick, she replaced the chimney and blew out the match; then, lamp in hand, she moved out of the entryway and into the parlor, her tennis shoes making hardly any noise on the hardwood floor.

The parlor had high ceilings. An enormous stone fireplace with a black marble mantel took up one whole wall. It was the biggest fireplace she had ever seen, easily large enough to hold a horse. And its rider.

Her footsteps echoed off the walls as she walked across the floor to the windows and drew back the heavy draperies, exposing tall, leaded windows. Her mood brightened considerably as the late-afternoon light filtered into the room. The trim around the windows and the doors was also made of oak. The walls, freshly painted, were off-white.

Feeling suddenly lighthearted, she blew out the lamp and put it on the mantel, then went out to the car to get the groceries she had purchased in the quaint little village at the foot of the hill.

The kitchen was large, with windows on three sides. There was a round oak table, cupboards galore, plus a relic of a gas stove and a small refrigerator, both of which she planned to replace in the near future.

After she put the groceries away, she explored the rest of the first floor. She opened the curtains as she wandered from room to room, mentally remodeling each one as she looked around. In addition to the parlor and the kitchen, there was a large library paneled in dark oak and a small room she guessed had been a sewing room at one time.

A winding staircase led to the second floor. She fell in love all over again with the first room at the top of the stairs. It was the master bedroom. Large and square and papered in an old-fashioned dark blue stripe, it featured a corner fireplace and a walk-in closet. One of the windows overlooked the backyard, the other overlooked the ocean. A small sitting room papered in the same dark blue stripe adjoined the bedroom. The bathroom had been recently remodeled. It was powder blue with white trim and contained a new sink and an oval tub.

There were two smaller bedrooms further down the hall, a linen closet, a good-sized bathroom with a pedestal sink and a claw-footed bathtub, and, at the far end of the corridor, a rectangular room with large windows set in three of the walls. One window had an eastern exposure. She nodded as she glanced outside, pleased that this room also offered a view of the ocean. This would be her studio.

Going back downstairs, she began to unload the boxes and suitcases from her car.

By nightfall, she had managed to carry the rest of her things into the house. Her clothes hung in the closet, her underwear and hose were in the dresser, her toiletries were in the bathroom, and she was ready for a hot bath. Holding her breath, she turned on the light switch in the bathroom and murmured, "Hallelujah!" as the light came on over the sink. Silently blessing the electric company for coming through, she turned on the faucet and added some lavender-scented bubble bath to the water.

While the tub filled, she lit a pair of vanilla-scented

candles, pulled a bath towel from one of the boxes, grabbed a paperback from her handbag, and returned to the bathroom. The air was warm now, fragrant with the mingled scents of vanilla and lavender.

Undressing, she turned off the tap, then settled into the tub, book in hand. Scented candles, a froth of warm bubbles, a good book. What could be better?

There was someone in the upper house. Dominic St. John felt the presence of another immediately upon waking. Rising, he took a deep breath, his senses reaching out, testing the night air much the way a nocturnal animal might sniff the wind for danger.

He smiled faintly. He was in no danger from the woman upstairs. He could hear the water draining from the tub, smell the fresh, clean scent of her as she moved into her bedroom and slipped something silky over her head. A nightgown, perhaps?

A wave of his hand and half a dozen candles sprang to life, casting flickering yellow shadows on the gray stone walls. No one living knew that there was another house beneath the one above, a rather cozy place if one didn't mind cold stone floors and walls without windows.

Rising, he laid out a change of clothes, all the while following the woman's movements.

He wondered who she was and what had prompted her to buy a house that had been empty for more than five years. Many people had come to look at the place in the last decade. A few had attempted to live there, but he had not wanted their company and it had been an easy thing to drive them away. Dark thoughts planted in their minds, objects that moved or disappeared completely, the whisper of a cool wind down the back of a neck when the air was warm and the night was calm. He grinned faintly. It was all so easy.

Donning a clean black silk shirt, a pair of black trousers, and a pair of soft black leather boots, he followed the narrow passageway that led to the back of the fireplace in the parlor. There were many such walkways in the old house. A wave of his hand and the hidden passageway opened.

Dissolving into a fine gray mist, he drifted through the parlor and down the hallway to the kitchen. The smell of roasting meat made his stomach clench even as the scent of animal blood stirred a hunger deep within him.

The woman stood at the stove with her back toward him. She stirred something with a long, wooden spoon, then lifted it to her lips for a taste.

"Hmm, not too bad, if I do say so myself," she murmured. Laying the spoon aside, she sprinkled salt and pepper into the pot.

The woman glanced over her shoulder as he floated into the kitchen. Had she sensed his presence? Such a thing seemed unlikely. Few humans had the ability to detect his nearness when he was in an incorporeal form.

She was not classically beautiful, but she was a remarkably pretty woman, with delicate features and fine, unblemished skin. Her honey-colored hair fell in a thick braid past her waist. Her eyes were brown with tiny gold flecks, fringed by long, dark lashes. Her slender figure was clad in something long and silky and pink. Not a nightgown, as he had thought, but some sort of lounge-around-the-house dress.

Dominic grinned as he drifted out of the room.

He had not wanted anyone to occupy the house in the past, but this one could stay. There was something about her . . . something he would pursue at a later date, when his hellish hunger had been appeased. Perhaps one day he would even introduce himself to her, but not now. Now he needed to feed and as handy as it might have been to use the woman, he didn't want to scare her away just yet. It might be amusing, even entertaining, to have company for a while.

Taking on his own shape once again, he made his way to the city located some thirty miles past the quaint village where most of the local people did their business. He never hunted in the village. Not only was it too close to his lair, but the inhabitants all knew each other. If one of them went missing, everyone would know about it in a matter of hours. He had ever been discreet in his choice of hunting grounds.

Walking down one of the crowded cobblestone streets, surrounded by warm, mortal flesh and beating hearts, he again felt the hunger rise up within him, growing stronger, more demanding. It was a need that could not be denied, a thirst that could be quelled but never quenched. The beast that dwelled within him had an insatiable appetite, one that could not for long be ignored.

His footsteps quickened as his hunger mounted, and then he saw his prey. She was a few yards ahead, a young woman with short brown hair. He watched the subtle sway of her hips, lifted his head and sniffed the air, sorting her distinct scent from all the others that surrounded him.

She looked up at him in alarm as he glided up beside her. Her eyes were gray and clear. He gazed into them, his mind speaking to hers, assuring her that he meant her no harm, and when he was certain she would offer no resistance, he slipped his arm around her waist and led her away from the crowds into a dark alley.

Lost in the shadows, he took her into his arms. For a moment, he simply held her, absorbing her warmth, listening to the whisper of the red tide running through her veins. His fangs lengthened in response to the sound of it, the warm, sweet coppery scent of it.

With a low growl, he bent her back over his arm and lowered his head.

Dominic could hear the woman moving about in the house above when he returned to his lair. Her presence unsettled him in a way he didn't understand and he paced the floor restlessly, all his senses focused on the woman. He had fed earlier and fed well. Why, then, did this woman's blood call to him so strongly? Even now, the beast within was urging him to go to her, to bend her to his will, to sample the sweet elixir running through her veins. No other woman had ever tempted him so save for one.

He glanced upward, his gaze tracking her footsteps. He had to meet her and soon, had to hear the sound of his name on her lips, taste the nectar of life that thrummed through her veins in a warm, rich river of crimson.

He ran a hand through his hair. How best to accomplish such a meeting? He did not want to appear out of nowhere and frighten her. A chance meeting, then. Perhaps she would take a walk along the beach some evening after sundown, when the air was cool. Yes, that would afford the perfect opportunity.

Smiling at the prospect, he picked up a book of Shakespeare's plays and settled down to pass a quiet evening at home.

The perfect opportunity presented itself two evenings later, shortly after sunset. Dominic was returning from the city, walking along the shore, when he saw the woman who had haunted his every waking moment jogging toward him.

He spent a pleasant few minutes admiring her long, shapely legs, the smooth, golden tan of her skin, the way her ponytail swished back and forth. Her cheeks were flushed with exertion. Her blood was warm from the run, the smell of it stronger than the faint scent of her perspiration, the ocean, or the salty air.

When she was only a few yards away, she slowed to a walk. He sensed her trepidation at finding herself alone on a deserted stretch of beach at night with a strange man. As far as she knew, he didn't belong here. This part of the beach was private, reserved for the few homes spread out on the cliff above.

As he drew nearer, she stopped walking. He could hear the fierce pounding of her heart as she looked him over, trying to decide whether or not she was in danger.

"Good evening." He offered her a benign smile. "Lovely night for a stroll."

"Yes." She slipped her hand into the pocket of her shorts. He saw her hand clench and he wondered what sort of defense she carried in there. A can of Mace, perhaps, or pepper spray. He watched her summon her courage.

"I'm afraid you're trespassing," she said, her tone cool but not unfriendly. "This is a private beach."

"Yes, I know. I have a house nearby."

"Oh, I'm sorry, I didn't know that. I'm new here myself."

He extended his hand. "Dominic St. John."

After a moment's hesitation, she placed her hand in his. "Tracy Warner."

His fingers curled lightly around hers. It was then that he felt it, a sharp jolt of recognition as his essence brushed against hers. A thrill of excitement swept through him. It was she, his soul mate, the woman he had found and lost countless times through the centuries. His beloved one. He had known her in many guises, by many names.

She was staring up at him. It took him a moment to realize he had fallen silent, that he was still holding her hand.

He smiled. "I am pleased to make your acquaintance, Miss Warner."

"Thank you." She withdrew her hand from his and glanced back the way she had come. "I should go."

"May I walk with you?"

He could easily read her thoughts by the expressions that flitted over her face. He was a stranger. It was dark. The beach was deserted. For all she knew, he could be the next Cliffside Strangler.

"Perhaps another time," he suggested, fully aware of her apprehension.

She hesitated briefly, then said, "I'd be glad for the company, actually."

"Afraid of the dark, are you?" He asked the question lightly even though he already knew the answer. She had feared the dark in every life.

"Just a little," she admitted.

She turned and started walking back the way she had come. He fell into step beside her, aware of the subtle warmth radiating from her body, the floral scent rising from her hair and skin, the slow, steady beat of her heart. He drank in the sight of her, the line of her throat, the delicate shape of her ear, the faint flush that lingered in her cheeks.

"Have you lived in Sea Cliff long?" she asked.

"Yes, for years." More years than she had been alive in this body.

"It's lovely here. I couldn't believe my luck in finding a house near the beach, even though it was quite a bit more than I planned to spend."

"Nightingale House has been for sale for quite some time."

Startled, she looked up at him. "How do you know that's where I live?"

He smiled to put her at ease. "It's the only house that's been up for sale recently."

"Oh." She laughed self-consciously. "Of course."

"What do you do for a living?" he asked.

"I paint. Landscapes and seascapes, mostly. What about you?"

"I'm retired."

"Retired?" She looked up at him and frowned. "You don't look old enough to be retired."

You would be surprised, he thought. Aloud, he said, "I made some good investments when I was very young. Now I live off the interest."

"Must be nice."

"Very."

They stopped side by side when they reached

the long flight of wooden steps that led up to Night-ingale House.

"Thank you for walking me home," she said.

"Shall I see you to your door?"

"No, that won't be necessary."

"Good night, then."

"Good night." She started up the steps, paused, and turned around to face him again. "Would you like to come to dinner tomorrow night at, say, five o'clock?"

"That is a bit early for me," he replied. "How about a movie later instead?"

"All right. What time?"

"I will call for you at seven-thirty."

"I'll be ready." She smiled. "See you then." With a wave of her hand, she turned and started up the stairs again.

He watched her go, admiring the gentle sway of her hips, the graceful way she moved. When she was out of sight, he dissolved into mist and followed her home.

Materializing in his basement lair, he dropped into his favorite chair. A wave of his hand started a fire in the hearth. Sitting back, he grinned in mild amusement as he stared at the dancing flames.

He had a date for tomorrow night.

Chapter 2

Tracy hummed softly as she plugged in the blow dryer. She couldn't help noticing that her hand was shaking, or deny the butterflies in her stomach. She told herself it was just a case of nerves. After all, she hadn't had a date in the last five months, not since she'd broken up with that creep, Richard. She'd had plenty of offers, but until she met Dominic St. John, she hadn't been ready to get on the dating merry-go-round again.

Even as she tried to convince herself it was perfectly normal to be excited at the prospect of going out on a date with someone new, and a wickedly handsome someone at that, she knew she was just kidding herself.

There was something intriguing about Dominic St. John, something she couldn't quite put her finger on, something that made her skin tingle with both anticipation and trepidation when he was near. She still didn't understand what it was that had possessed her to ask a complete stranger to come for dinner. She had never done anything like that before and had had no intention of doing so last night. She supposed it was the same sudden impulse that had made her accept his invitation when he suggested going out to a movie instead of dinner.

Thinking of him now, she realized that he looked vaguely familiar but try as she might, she couldn't recall ever meeting him before. And a man like that would not be easily forgotten.

When her hair was dry, she did it up in a French braid, carefully applied her makeup, and then pulled on a lavender sweater and a pair of white slacks. And all the while, she wondered if she was making a mistake in going out with him. He seemed nice enough, but then, wasn't that what friends and neighbors always said about the boy next door who turned out to be a serial killer? *He was such a nice boy. Never caused any trouble.*

Tracy shook her head. She was really letting her imagination run wild this time! She hated this part of dating, hated the "getting to know you" stage. Some of her girlfriends thought that was the fun part, but not Tracy. She had only had three serious relationships since she graduated from college and each one had lasted just over a year.

Danny had been a great guy, but the longer they went out together, the more obvious it was that they had nothing on which to build a lasting relationship.

Joe had also been a great guy, warm and sensitive and easy to love. She should have known he was too good to last. Just when she had been expecting a marriage proposal, he had entered the priesthood.

And then there had been Richard. He had wined

her and dined her and made her feel like the most wonderful, beautiful woman in the world. Unfortunately, she discovered that he was feeding the same line to her best friend and four other girls.

Leaving the bathroom, she glanced at the clock on the small antique oak table beside her bed. Only time would tell whether Dominic was saint or sinner, but whichever he was, he was going to be here in less than ten minutes.

Slipping on a pair of low-heeled white sandals, she went downstairs into the living room. She turned on the stereo, flicked on the porch light.

She loved this room, she thought, glancing around. Her furniture had arrived yesterday morning and she had spent the day arranging it. The white wicker sofa and chair brightened up the room considerably. The pillows were covered in a variegated blue print. An antique oak bookcase held a number of books and videos. Several dragons—some she had bought for herself, some that had been gifts—decorated the mantel. Her entertainment center took up most of one corner. The next time she went into the village, she would look for an area rug to put in front of the fireplace, and another one for her bedroom.

A knock at the door sent her stomach plummeting down to her toes. He was here.

Standing on the front porch, Dominic sensed the woman's inner tension even before she opened the door.

"Hi," she said, smiling.

"Good evening." He handed her a bouquet of two dozen long-stemmed, blood-red roses.

She looked up at him, unable to hide her surprise, or her pleasure. "They're lovely," she murmured. "Thank you."

She turned and started toward the living room. Noticing he wasn't behind her, she said, "Please, come in."

Stepping over the threshold, he followed her down a short hallway into a large, well-lit room.

She gestured at the sofa. "Make yourself at home, won't you, while I put these in water."

He smiled his thanks, then wandered around the room, taking in the changes she had made, and liking them. Perhaps he should ask her to redecorate his underground lair, he mused, running his hand over the back of the white wicker sofa. Her taste in colors and fabrics ran to bright and cheerful, while his seemed to be mostly dark and dreary.

He turned as she entered the room and placed a crystal vase on the mantel. The scent of roses filled the air.

"They're beautiful," she said again.

"They pale next to you," he replied, and meant it.

The flush that rose in her cheeks at his compliment was most becoming.

She was exquisitely lovely in a lavender sweater and white slacks. Her hair was again in a long braid down her back, which afforded him a delicious view of her slender neck.

The blush in her cheeks deepened under his warm regard.

"Shall we go?" she asked.

With a nod, he moved to the front door and opened it for her, then followed her out of the house.

Tracy's eyes widened when she saw the sleek

black convertible parked in the driveway. "This is yours?"

He glanced at the car. "Is it not to your liking?"

"No, no, it's . . . it's gorgeous."

"I have another if you don't care for the color, or the make."

She looked up at him, wondering if he was serious. His face gave nothing away.

"What color is the other one?"

"Red."

"This one is fine."

He opened the door for her, closed it when she was comfortably seated, and walked around to the driver's side.

Tracy watched him slide behind the wheel. He moved like no other man she had ever seen, his every movement fluid.

He slid the key in the ignition and the engine came to life with a low purr, like that of a jungle cat.

Tracy looked out the window. Small talk. She had never been any good at it. She glanced at Dominic out of the corner of her eye. He was not a handsome man, at least not in the Hollywood pretty-boy sort of way, but he was still gorgeous, with his long black hair, finely sculpted features, and intense gray eyes. He wore a black sweater that emphasized the width of his shoulders and a pair of black jeans that accented his long legs. He exuded an aura of strength that she found both comforting and intimidating.

"You said you were an artist," he remarked. "Are you working on anything now?"

"A rather large landscape for the reception area of a law firm." She studied his profile, thinking she would like to paint it.

The thought had no sooner crossed her mind than he asked, "Do you also paint portraits?"

She shivered. Was he reading her mind? But that was impossible—it was merely a coincidence. "I do portraits occasionally. Dogs and cats, too, when I need the money," she said with a smile. "You said you were retired. What line of work were you in?"

"I have tried my hand at many things over the years," he said evasively.

"Like what?"

He plucked one from memory. "I was a night watchman for a while." He didn't tell her it had been during the reign of a king now long forgotten, or that he had been charged with keeping watch over the queen's chamber.

"You didn't get rich being a night watchman," she retorted with a grin.

"Didn't I?"

"Did you?"

He smiled faintly. "Not in the way you mean."

"What else have you done?"

"Many things, but I would rather talk about you."

"There's not much to tell," she said with a shrug. "I graduated from college, I have a job that I love."

"But no husband," he said quietly. "No children."

"Not yet. I don't seem to be very lucky at love."

"So you wish to marry?"

"Of course. Don't you?"

His gaze lingered on her face. "When she says yes, I will marry her."

"Are you engaged?" she asked, clearly alarmed to think she might be out with another woman's fiancé.

"No."

He stilled the other questions in her mind with a thought. Now was not the time for her to delve into his love life, or ask questions he did not yet wish to answer.

He pulled into the parking lot behind the theater a few minutes later and switched off the ignition. Exiting the car, he came around to open the door for her. She put her hand into his and slid out of the car. Her skin was warm against his.

He locked the car and they walked around the corner to the theater. He bought two tickets and they entered the lobby.

His nostrils were immediately assaulted by myriad smells: buttered popcorn, candy, lemonade, cheese, hot dogs, onions, mustard and ketchup, the overwhelming scents and emotions that clung to the people milling in front of the counter, making him wonder why he had ever suggested a movie. It had been years since he had been to one; now he remembered why.

He reminded himself to ask her if she wanted something to eat, was grateful when she declined.

Entering the theater, they found two seats near the back. Moments later, the theater went dark and the previews came on.

Dominic concentrated on blocking everything from his mind save for the woman beside him. In moments, his senses were swimming with her essence. The scent of her hair and perfume teased his nostrils, the heat radiating from her body chased away the coldness that was ever a part of him, and the touch of her arm against his . . . ah, just that mere touch thrilled him beyond measure. Tracy. He closed his eyes, reveling in her nearness.

"Hey, did you fall asleep already?" she asked, a smile in her voice. "The movie hasn't even started yet."

The sound of her voice warmed him like the sunshine he had not felt in a hundred lifetimes. Opening his eyes, he smiled at her. "No, I was only . . . enjoying the moment."

"Oh." It was obvious she did not understand, could never understand.

The movie started a few moments later.

She watched the film.

He watched her. She had a very old soul. His mind touched hers and in doing so, he found memories of other times and other places buried deeply in her subconscious, memories of lives she had known and forgotten. She had been a dancer in Jerusalem when Herod was king, a queen in an ancient land during the Crusades, a member of a sultan's harem, a witch in Old Salem. She had lived as a slave in the days of the Roman Empire, been a schoolteacher in the Old West, a doctor in a small African village, a freedom fighter in Israel. He glimpsed images of her as a widowed mother sending her only son off to fight in the War Between the States.

He saw it all clearly in her mind, and in his own. Time after time, he had found her throughout the ages. In each life, he had been at her side when death was imminent.

Time after time, he had offered to give her the Dark Gift.

Time after time, she had refused.

Tracy was fully aware of Dominic's scrutiny. She felt his gaze resting on her face, felt almost as if his eyes were burning into her heart, piercing her very soul. Once, foolish as it sounded, it seemed as though she felt his mind inside her own. But that was ridiculous. Impossible.

Frightening beyond words.

And yet, for a short space of time, her mind had been filled with strange images of distant lands. Even more inexplicable was that she had seen herself in a number of foreign places. She tried to remember each one, but it was like trying to hold on to a handful of water—as soon as she got close, the image trickled through her fingers.

But the most frightening thing of all was the last image she had seen, the only one she clearly recalled. She had seen Dominic lying in what looked very much like a crypt of some kind, a tomb lined with cold gray stones.

With a shake of her head, she thrust the disquieting images away. When the lights came on a short time later, she realized she had missed most of the movie.

Dominic rose and offered her his hand in a courtly manner. When she took it, he drew her gently to her feet and they followed the crowd out of the theater into the lobby.

He was still holding her hand as they walked to the parking lot.

"Did you enjoy the film?" he asked.

She nodded, hoping he wouldn't want to discuss it, since she had little recollection of the plot.

He held the door open for her, then walked around to the driver's side and slid behind the wheel.

She was not in the mood for small talk as they drove home and neither, it seemed, was Dominic.

She stared out the window, her thoughts turned inward as she tried to remember the images that had flashed through her mind. Whatever had prompted such bizarre memories? Memories! That was impossible. She had never been a queen, yet she clearly remembered the huge old castle, the stone floors covered with rushes, the faded tapestries hanging on the walls, the long trestle tables laden with meat and cheese and hard brown bread, the knights who had carried her colors in the lists. She remembered being waited upon, her every wish a command. She placed one hand on her stomach. She had never had a child, yet she remembered the excruciating pain of childbirth, of lying at death's door. And Dominic had been there! He had knelt at her side, clinging to her hand as he offered to give her life . . .

She shook the thought from her mind. What foolishness was this? She didn't believe in reincarnation or ghosts or . . . vampires.

A chill ran down her spine.

She was glad when Nightingale House came into view. This was reality. And yet, looking at it, she thought again that it looked like a place where Dracula might comfortably reside, and hard on the heels of that thought came the notion that the house seemed far more suited to Dominic than to herself.

Dominic pulled up to the front of the house and cut the engine. Getting out of the car, he walked around to her side, opened the door and helped her out, then walked her up the stairs.

With a hand that trembled, Tracy unlocked the front door. "Would you care to come in for a cup of coffee?" The question was more of a polite gesture than because she wanted company, and yet, to be honest, she was somehow reluctant to go into the house alone.

"I think not." He, too, seemed distracted. Taking

her hand in his, he bowed over it, his lips brushing lightly over her skin. "Thank you for this evening. I hope to see you again soon."

She nodded, felt an odd tingle as his gaze met hers.

Murmuring good night, she crossed the threshold and closed the door. Going to the front window, she watched him slide behind the wheel of the sleek black car and drive away.

The next afternoon Dominic sent her a dozen blood-red roses with a card that read:

> *Would you like to go walking on the beach this evening? If so, meet me at the foot of the stairs at sundown.*

He had a thing for red roses, she thought, smiling, as she arranged the flowers in a blue-and-white ceramic vase and placed them on the mantel near the others.

That day, as never before, she was aware of time passing as she waited for sundown. Dominic was unlike any man she had ever dated before. Though he looked to be in his early thirties, he seemed older, somehow. Perhaps it was his bearing, or perhaps it was his courtly, Old World manner and speech.

She completed the landscape she had been working on before she moved. When it was dry, she would frame it, then wrap it and ship it to her client in Virginia. Like most artists, she usually had more than one painting in the works at a time. She currently had a seascape, a still life, and a floral in various stages of completion.

She ate a quick lunch, threw a load of laundry in the washer, and changed the sheets on her bed, always watching the clock.

Finally it was time to get ready. She chose a yellow flowered sundress and sandals, tied her hair back in a ponytail, and spritzed herself with cologne. Grabbing a warm sweater, she slipped it on, then left the house.

It was a lovely evening with a touch of a sea breeze. She paused at the top of the stairs that led to the beach to admire the sunset, which was breathtaking. The blue-sky canvas was awash with flaming red and orange, highlighted with brilliant splashes of ochre and darkening shades of purple and indigo.

With a sigh of appreciation for the work of the Master Painter, she started down the stairs.

Dominic was waiting for her at the bottom. He wore a white shirt open at the throat, white trousers, and sandals. The contrast with his black hair and dark skin was striking and she felt her breath catch in her throat when he offered her his hand. "Good evening."

"Hi."

His skin was cool, his fingers long and strong as they folded over hers. His touch sent a shiver of anticipation down her spine.

"How was your day?"

"Busy," she replied. "Yours?"

A faint smile touched his lips. "Peaceful."

"You're lucky." She glanced at the horizon. "That's a beautiful sky."

"Indeed."

"I love painting sunrises and sunsets," she remarked as they walked toward the water. The tide was out and the ocean was calm, a green mirror that reflected the sun's dying rays.

"I have not seen a sunrise in many years," he said.

"You need to get up earlier."

"Would that I could."

"Why can't you?"

He squeezed her hand. "I tend to stay up late, and sleep late."

"Well, sunsets are beautiful, too."

"As are you." His gaze moved over her. "You grow more lovely each time I see you."

A blush warmed her cheeks. "Thank you. And thank you for the roses."

"You are most welcome."

They walked in silence for a time. Her hand fit comfortably in his and she had the inexplicable feeling that they had walked this way many times before, which was impossible, she thought, since they had just met.

When they reached a sheltered cove, they stopped of one accord. Out of sight of passersby, Dominic drew her close, his arms loosely locked around her waist.

He looked into her eyes, an unspoken question in his gaze.

Tracy's heartbeat quickened as she put her arms around his neck and lifted her face for his kiss.

His kiss. Her eyelids fluttered down. How to describe the indescribable? His lips were firm and cool and yet heat flowed through her at their touch, a warm, sweet fire that threatened to engulf her until only ashes remained. His arms tightened around her, crushing her breasts against the solid wall of his chest. His desire was obvious as he drew her body closer to his.

She was breathing heavily when they parted. "I think we'd better go."

"As you wish," he replied, his voice rough with need.

They strolled hand in hand back the way they had come, pausing now and then to share a kiss when no one was looking.

When they reached her door, he kissed her yet again, a kiss of such passion and possession that it frightened her even as it left her aching and yearning for more.

Chapter 3

Dominic sent her red roses every day for the next two weeks, took her out every night. They went to the theater to see *The Phantom of the Opera*. Tracy cried unashamedly at the end, moved to tears by the sad plight of the Phantom, at the soul-deep note of despair in his voice as he bid farewell to Christine, and then watched her go away with Raoul to live a life of ease and luxury that he could never give her.

They went to the movies again, he took her dancing at a swanky nightclub in the city, to the opening of an art gallery. They walked along the beach a few times. A couple of nights they stayed at home and watched videos or played chess, a game she thought she played rather well until she played against Dominic. He beat her every time.

Tonight, because she had loved it so much the first time, he had taken her to see *The Phantom* again. She cried just as hard the second time, her heart aching for the Phantom's loneliness.

"Would you have stayed with him?" Dominic asked as they made their way to the parking lot.

She started to say yes, of course, then paused. "I don't know. I'd like to think so."

"And could you live with his ugliness and his foul moods?" he asked, his gaze intent upon her face. "Could you be happy living with a man who had committed murder? A man who could never share all of your life?"

She thought about it a moment. "I don't know. But I think I would have tried. He loved her so much, loved her in a way that that wimp, Raoul, never would. Loved her enough to give her up."

"Indeed," Dominic murmured. His life paralleled that of the Phantom in many ways, he thought. He dwelled in an underground lair and lived in the shadows. Those who saw him for what he was shrank from him in fear. He had killed to preserve his life. He had given up the woman he adored countless times. But she was here now, and he had another chance to win her love.

He thought about that as they drove home. Perhaps this time, he thought, perhaps this time she would be his.

And now they were standing in the entryway of Nightingale House and Dominic was holding her in his arms, his gaze burning into hers.

She closed her eyes as his mouth claimed her own in a searing kiss that seemed to last forever and end too soon.

Releasing her, he turned toward the door. "I should go."

"So soon?" She placed her hand on his back. His muscles were tense, his stance rigid.

"It is for the best." His voice was gruff and unsteady.

"One more kiss?" she begged shamelessly.

Turning, he pulled her quickly into his arms and kissed her, his lips hard and demanding, bruising hers. His tongue plundered her mouth. His hands delved into her hair, loving the touch of it, alive and silky against his skin.

With a hoarse cry, he let her go and left the house, not bothering to close the door behind him.

Tracy followed him. Standing in the doorway, she stared after him, bemused. His footsteps made no sound on the pavement. He seemed almost to float above the ground as he made his way to his car. He slid behind the wheel; a moment later, the car growled to life, the headlights cutting through the darkness as he gunned the engine and raced away.

Tracy frowned, puzzled by his abrupt departure and then, overcome with a sudden, overwhelming need to paint, she ran up the stairs.

In her bedroom, she threw off her chic black dress, kicked off her heels, and peeled off her nylons. Slipping on a pair of faded jeans and an old T-shirt, she walked down the hallway to her studio, tying her hair back in a ponytail as she went.

She grabbed her smock and put it on, then took a fresh canvas out of the closet and placed it on an easel.

She had intended to start the Old English castle one of her clients had requested but her hand refused to paint the image in her mind. Instead of rough-hewn stones and parapets, her brush strokes took on the shape of a man—a tall man with hair as black as a midnight sky and mysterious gray eyes. A man whose full lips were drawn back to reveal sharp white fangs. Clad all in black, he stood alone on a high cliff that looked very much like the one upon which Nightingale House now stood. A long black cloak billowed from his broad shoulders. The ocean stretched away behind him, the waves tossed by a cold winter wind. Overhead, turbulent clouds chased each other across an indigo sky.

She worked like a woman possessed throughout the rest of the night, never stopping for rest or refreshment. The first faint light of dawn was brightening the eastern sky when she stepped away from the canvas.

It was easily the most unsettling piece she had ever done. The image in the painting looked frighteningly alive as it stared back at her, his face half in shadow, half in winter-cold moonlight. His eyes, as turbulent as the clouds overhead, held a wealth of closely guarded secrets and a whisper of eternity.

She took a step to the left and felt a chill run down her spine when his eyes seemed to follow her.

Overcome with a sudden sense of uneasiness, she quickly cleaned her brushes and threw off her smock.

Hurrying out of the room, she slammed the door behind her, then stood in the hallway, one hand pressed over her heart, feeling utterly foolish. It was only a painting, after all.

There was nothing to be afraid of.

He moved through the dark of the night, silent as a shadow, more deadly than the weapon his prey carried concealed inside his jacket.

The man he pursued knew something was wrong. He turned his head this way and that constantly, his hooded gaze searching the darkness, looking for the danger he sensed but could not see. Panic rose within him and he began to walk faster and faster, until he was running down the street, his heart pounding with terror. The stink of his sweat and fear trailed behind him like smoke.

A sob rose in the man's throat as he turned down a narrow alley, only to discover it was a dead end. Turning around, his back pressed against the wall, he reached inside his jacket.

"Who's there?" He withdrew his weapon, held it out in front of him in hands that trembled. Eyes narrowed, his gaze swept the darkness, widened in terror as a dark shape materialized out of the shadows. "Go away!" He cocked the pistol in his hand. "Don't make me shoot!"

"Do as you wish." There was a hint of amusement in the deep voice, but none in the deep gray eyes that regarded him without blinking.

Beyond panic, the man fired. He knew a fleeting moment of relief as the bullet struck his pursuer full in the chest. But his pursuer did not fall, and he did not stop. Relentless as death, the other glided toward him on soundless feet.

Frozen with horror, the man made no move to resist as the other plucked the weapon from his fist and carelessly tossed it aside.

"Who . . . who . . . ?" He shrieked as the other's hand closed over his shoulder, the fingers grasping his arm in a vise-like hold. "What are you?"

"Does it matter?"

The man was shaking so badly now, he could scarcely speak. "Are you . . . going to . . . to . . . kill me?"

"It depends." He had not killed in years yet some perverse devil made him tease his prey, like a cat with a mouse. He smiled, revealing long white fangs. "On how thirsty I am."

Chapter 4

Tracy woke abruptly, the sound of her own scream lingering in the air. Reaching blindly for the lamp on the table beside her bed, she switched on the light with fingers that trembled.

She sat up, her heart pounding as though she had run a mile down the beach. "Only a dream," she whispered. "It was only a dream."

Clutching the blankets to her chest, she glanced around the room. Everything was as it should be. There were no monsters hiding in the corners, no slitted eyes glowing at her with a fiendish light, no fangs stained and dripping with blood.

"Just a dream." She laughed uneasily. "That's what I get for painting vampires before I go to bed."

Gradually, her heartbeat slowed. Her breathing returned to normal. Slipping out of bed, she pulled on her bathrobe and padded downstairs. She switched on the light at the bottom of the steps, then headed for the kitchen, turning on every light she passed along the way.

Entering the kitchen, she gasped, one hand flying to her throat as she saw a vague shape moving toward her. She opened her mouth to scream then she realized it was merely her own reflection staring back at her from the window over the sink.

Letting out a sigh of relief, she quickly closed the curtains. Lifting the teapot from the counter, she filled it with water and set it on the stove to heat.

Maybe buying a house way out here hadn't been such a good idea. Standing there, waiting for the water to get hot, she was acutely aware of how alone she was. There were no other houses within shouting distance. If she telephoned for help, it would take the police a good ten or fifteen minutes to arrive. She could be a headline in the morning paper by then.

The whistling of the kettle made her jump. Turning, she grabbed the handle and lifted the pot from the stove, only to drop it on the counter when the handle burned her palm.

"Ouch!"

Sucking on her fingers, she turned off the stove. She was as nervous as a hen in a thunderstorm.

Willing herself to calm down, she took a mug from the cupboard, filled it with hot water, dropped a tea bag inside, and added a spoonful of honey.

Standing there, waiting for the tea to steep, she shifted restlessly from one foot to the other. What *was* the matter with her tonight? Whatever had possessed her to paint Dominic as a vampire?

Carrying the cup to the table, she sat down, her gaze darting around the room as if . . . as if what?

She took several deep breaths, admonishing herself to calm down. There was no one there. Nothing to be afraid of. Nothing at all. With a sigh, she went back to bed.

* * *

Deep in the underground lair below the house, Dominic was aware of Tracy's unease. It was impossible for her to know what he was. No one had ever perceived what he was unless he wished it. And yet he sensed her uneasiness, her awareness that something preternatural lurked nearby. It was the same kind of uneasiness his prey experienced when they knew he was close at hand. No doubt she would be shocked to discover that there was a vampire dwelling below Nightingale House, that it was his presence she found so disturbing.

If he told her what he was, if he told her that he had known her in many lifetimes before this one, would she believe him, or think him mad? He had followed her through the centuries, sometimes loving her from afar but always waiting, always hoping she would accept the Dark Gift and take her rightful place at his side.

Perhaps this time.

It was his last thought before the darkness dragged him down into oblivion.

She paced the floor of her bedchamber, too restless to sleep, grateful, once again, that the king found no pleasure in her company now that she was carrying the heir to the throne. No doubt her husband was curled up in the arms of his latest mistress. If the fates smiled on her, she would not have to take him to her bed again until this child was weaned.

She walked to the door and placed her hand upon the richly carved wood. Dared she call for him? What excuse could she use this time? Did she even need an excuse? Surely he knew that she called for him to relieve her loneliness.

Sitting down on the edge of her bed, she smoothed her gown, lifted a hand to her hair, and then called his name.

"Dominic!"

He answered her summons immediately, his dark gray eyes sweeping over her as if to assure himself that she was well. "What is it you wish, my lady?"

She waved her hand toward the pitcher. "A drink, please."

He bowed his head in acknowledgement and moved to fulfill her request, though they both knew it was not water she craved, but his presence at her side; his touch, which he bestowed upon her whenever she desired.

Her gaze met his as he handed her a goblet encrusted with sapphires the color of her gown. But for him, for the hours he spent at her side, life within the castle would have been unbearable.

"Jocelyn." His voice was filled with respect, and the longing of a thousand years.

It pleased her that he did not find her unattractive even though her belly was swollen with the king's child. There was no accusation in his eyes, no hint of revulsion, only the same sweet expression of love and desire she had seen there since the night he was assigned to guard her quarters.

"Dominic." His name was a sigh upon her lips. Putting the goblet aside, she held out her arms. He went to her gladly, willingly. She gloried in his nearness, in the husky sound of his voice as he crushed her close. He whispered to her, telling her she was beautiful, desirable, that he loved her beyond life, beyond death. . . .

She fell back on the bed and he followed her down, then drew her into his arms, cradling her to his side. She rested her head on his broad chest, her fingers splayed over his heart.

"Jocelyn," he implored. "Come away with me."

It was the same request he made of her every time they were together. More and more, she yearned to leave the cold walls of the castle, the cold comfort of her husband's arms, and fly away with the man who kissed her so tenderly, who gazed deep into her eyes and promised to love her forevermore.

"Dominic . . ."

"You do not love the king!" he exclaimed, his voice rising in frustration. "Why do you stay in this place? What ties you to him?"

"He is my husband! I carry his child! It is my duty to stay and give him an heir." Tears welled in her eyes as she spoke, tears of bitter regret, of hopelessness. She had been born to be queen. It was in her blood. Her child would be the heir to the throne. How could she deny her own child its destiny? But, oh, how could she stay with a man she despised when the one she loved with her whole heart and soul held her so tenderly, loved her so completely?

"Come away with me, Jocelyn," he begged. "Now, tonight."

She looked up at him and knew she could refuse him no longer. "Yes," she whispered. "Yes, now, tonight. Take me away from this place."

"Jocelyn!" His arms tightened around her shoulders. He kissed her long and lovingly, then gained his feet. "Come," he said, taking her by the hand. "We must hurry."

She rose to her feet, then doubled over as pain knifed through her. He was at her side in an instant.

"What is it, my lady?" he asked anxiously.

She wrapped her arm over her swollen womb.

"The babe," she gasped. "It comes."

He swept her into his arms and placed her gently on the bed. "Do not be afraid," he said. "I will summon the midwife."

"Do not leave me!" She grabbed for his hand, cried out as another pain caught her.

"I will not be gone long, my lady." His hand caressed her cheek. "Be brave, my best beloved one."

"Hurry!"

Her hands clutched at the bedclothes, a sob rising in her throat as the pains grew worse. It was too early, she thought frantically, too early for the child to be born.

It seemed like hours passed before the door opened and the midwife hurried in, her brow furrowed with concern.

Dominic entered the room behind the midwife, only to be told, rather brusquely, that his presence was neither welcome nor desired. As the king's guard, he could not argue, could only do as he was told.

She cried out when he left the room, then fell back on the pillows, weak and afraid. And alone. So alone.

It was late the next night when she was finally delivered of the infant. A boy, who took only a few short breaths and then lay still in the midwife's arms.

She knew, from the looks that passed between her ladies and the midwife, that she would soon be joining her child. She heard them whispering when they thought she was asleep. Something had gone terribly wrong. The bleeding would not stop.

Lost in grief and pain, she called for the only man she had ever loved, called for him over and over again, much to the horror and astonishment of her ladies, but she was past caring. Past caring that her husband did not bother to visit her.

"Dominic." She sobbed his name weakly. "Dominic, please come to me."

He appeared at her side in the last hour before dawn. Clad all in black, for a moment she thought he was the Angel of Death come for her. In her fevered state, she imagined that his eyes were red and glowing, that his teeth, always whiter than new-fallen snow, were growing longer, becoming fangs.

Kneeling beside her bed, he took her hand in his. His gaze burned into hers with an intensity she had never seen before.

"Join me, Jocelyn," he begged. "Only say the word, and I will bring you to my side. We will be together for eternity—only say the word."

"What is it you are asking of me?" she murmured. "How can we be together when I am dying?"

"You need not die, my best beloved one. You have but to ask, and I will make you as I am."

"And what are you?" It was a question she had ever harbored in the back of her mind but never dared ask.

"I am vampire," he replied quietly. "Look at me, and see me for what I am."

Vampire . . . it was the answer she had long suspected and feared, the reason she had not asked before. He was truly a creature of the night. Forever lost, forever damned. If she joined him of her own free will, she would forfeit all hope of heaven.

"No." She shook her head weakly. "I cannot . . . not even for . . . you."

Tears filled his eyes. Crimson tears. "I love you," he said, his voice thick. "I will find you again, I promise, no matter how many lifetimes it takes. . . ."

She woke with a start, one hand spread over her stomach, her eyes damp with tears. Never had she had a dream like that before, a dream so vivid, so real, that she had felt the pain. What was happening to her?

Flinging the covers aside, she slipped out of bed, padded barefoot across the floor and drew back the curtains, then opened the window. With a sigh, she lifted her face toward the heavens, basking in the sunlight, reveling in the warmth of it against her skin.

The light of a new day, the sound of the waves dancing cheerfully on the shore below, banished the last remnants of the dream from her mind. This was reality! And she had work to do.

After taking a quick shower, she dressed in a faded pair of paint-stained denims and an old shirt, then went downstairs to make a pot of coffee. Pouring herself a cup, she carried it upstairs.

When she opened the door to her studio, the first thing she saw was the painting she had done. It was just as unsettling in the bright light of day as it had been the night before. She couldn't help the shiver that ran down her spine as she moved into the room. Couldn't shake the feeling that the painting was somehow alive. It was disconcerting, the way the eyes seemed to follow her.

With a huff of annoyance, she lifted the canvas from the easel and put it on the floor, facing the wall. Feeling better, she drained her cup, then put on her smock, grabbed a fresh canvas, and placed it on the easel. She had no time to waste. She still had to paint that English castle, and she had a seascape that had to be finished for a new client by next week. If the buyer, Mr. Petersen, liked it, he had promised to purchase a dozen similar paintings for all the offices in his bank.

She studied the numerous snapshots of the ocean she had taken a few days earlier—pictures of the ocean when it was calm, photos of the waves crashing against the shore, pictures taken at all hours of the day and night.

She closed her mind to everything else and lost herself in her art. She loved the smell of the paint, the sense of creativity, of accomplishment, that flowed through her as the scene she saw in her mind took on depth and color and life on the canvas.

She took a short break to get another cup of coffee and something to eat, and then spent the rest of the day in the studio.

She quit when she lost the light. After cleaning

her brushes and tidying up the studio, she went into the bathroom, filled the tub, lit a couple of candles, and took a long, hot bubble bath. Lying there with her eyes closed, she decided that cooking didn't sound appealing, so when the water cooled, she stepped out of the tub, pulled on a pair of gray slacks and a white sweater, and drove down to the village.

Dominic rose with the setting of the sun, his preternatural senses immediately probing the upper level of the house. He had no sense of her presence. Where had she gone?

He dressed quickly in a pair of black trousers and a shirt and willed himself into the upper house. He walked quickly from room to room until he reached her studio.

He paused in the doorway. There were several lamps located around the room. He supposed they were to provide light when the skies were overcast or when she felt the urge to work after dark. An overstuffed chair took up most of one corner. A couple of paint-stained smocks hung from hooks near the door.

Stepping inside, he moved slowly around the room. Her scent was strong in here, as was the odor of paint and turpentine. There were several blank canvases stacked in a corner. Three easels, each holding paintings in various stages of completion, stood several feet apart along one wall. Though all three were exceptional, he preferred the seascape. It was done mostly in shades of blue and green save for a splash of crimson and gold left behind as the sun sank in the distance. So long since he had seen a sunrise.

Drawing his gaze from the painting, he continued his perusal of the room. A round, wooden piano stool on casters sat in front of the painting in the middle. An oblong table held an assortment of paints, a box of rags, a palette, a can of turpentine, half a dozen bottles and cans, a sketch pad. An old ceramic flower pot held an assortment of brushes. Several photos of the ocean were tacked to a bulletin board. A closet contained an assortment of wooden frames in various sizes and styles.

He was about to leave the room when a canvas turned toward the wall caught his attention. Curious, he walked across the floor and turned it around.

And found himself staring at his own likeness. It took him quite by surprise. He had not seen his own face in centuries. He had almost forgotten what he looked like.

If she had painted him as he truly appeared, then his physical appearance had changed little since Kitana had bestowed the Dark Gift upon him so many centuries ago. He wondered what had prompted Tracy to paint him as a vampire. Was it possible she suspected his true nature?

He studied the painting for several minutes. Forgetting for the moment that he was the subject, he found himself admiring her work. She was a truly talented artist. The lines were bold and confident, the colors well chosen, the balance of light and shadow just right.

Lost in thought, he left the house. Where would she have gone? A look in the garage showed that it was empty. Had she perhaps driven down to the village? It was as good a place as any to start.

Backing his car out of the underground garage, he drove down the hill. He could have willed himself into the village with a thought, but he enjoyed the simple act of driving, enjoyed the feel of the wind in his face, the low purr of the engine. But tonight, even that paled in the anticipation of seeing her again.

He found her car parked in front of Sea Cliff's only restaurant. After locating a parking place over on the next block, he walked back to the restaurant. The dinner rush was over and after a few words with the hostess, Dominic made his way to Tracy's table.

She looked up, obviously surprised to see him standing there.

"Good evening."

She smiled, though it was tentative at best. "Hello."

He returned her smile. "Would you mind if I joined you?"

She wanted to refuse. It was evident in every line of her body, in the look on her face. It was just as evident that she couldn't think of any way to refuse without appearing rude, and so she murmured, "No, please do."

He slid into the seat across from her. "Nice place," he remarked after noting that there were no mirrors in this section of the restaurant.

"Yes, it is," she agreed. "Do you come here often?"

"No."

A waitress appeared at their table. "Are you ready to order?" she asked without much enthusiasm.

"Yes," Tracy said. "I'll have a bacon, lettuce, and tomato on sourdough bread and a glass of iced tea, please."

"Yes, ma'am." The waitress made a note on her pad, then glanced at Dominic. Her attitude underwent an immediate change. She straightened up, brushed a lock of hair out of her eyes, thrust out her ample chest. And smiled. "And what can I bring you, sir?"

"A glass of red wine."

"Will that be all?"

Dominic nodded.

"Are you sure? Our apple pie is the best in two counties."

"Quite sure."

"Well, let me know if you change your mind," the waitress purred, and with a last toothy smile, she left the table.

Tracy took a sip of water, then unfolded her napkin and placed it in her lap. "You're not eating?"

"Not now. Later, perhaps."

"So, you just came in here for a glass of wine?"

"You've caught me out," he replied. "I saw your car out front and thought I would see if I could entice you to let me share your table."

Her cheeks grew pink under his blatantly sensual regard.

"Have you plans for tonight?"

"Yes. No, not really . . . that is . . . no."

"You seem flustered this evening. Is something amiss?"

"No. It's just . . ." She lifted a hand and let it fall. "I stayed up very late last night, painting. I'm afraid I haven't caught up on my lost sleep yet."

He leaned forward. "Were you working on a new canvas?"

The blush in her cheeks deepened. "Yes."

"Perhaps you would show it to me later."

"It's nothing, really. Just a seascape. If my client likes it, he's promised to order a dozen or so for the offices in his building."

He knew it was not the seascape that had put

that becoming blush in her cheeks, but the painting she had done of him.

"I should still like to see it," he remarked. "If you have no other plans, perhaps you would show it to me after you've had your dinner."

Tracy nodded. Why was it so difficult to tell him no?

A moment later, the waitress arrived with their order.

Dominic sat back and sipped his wine. Time and again, his gaze moved to her neck, to the pulse beating steadily in the hollow of her throat. Thinking of the rich red blood that flowed through her veins made the wine in his glass taste like water. He licked his lips as he thought of running his hands over the mortal heat of her skin, tasting the warm, sweet essence of her life on his tongue.

Clenching one hand into a fist, he thrust such thoughts from his mind lest she see them mirrored in his eyes.

Tracy found it difficult to enjoy her meal with Dominic sitting across from her. It was terribly disconcerting to know he was watching her every move. If only he would eat something, too! But he simply sat there, occasionally sipping his drink, his gaze intent upon her face.

She looked up, her meal momentarily forgotten, when he asked her if she believed in reincarnation.

"No, I don't," she replied firmly. "Do you?"

He nodded slowly. "I sense that you have a very old soul."

"Me?" Her voice emerged in a high-pitched squeak. "Why would you think that?"

His eyes darkened as he leaned across the table. "Have you had dreams of things you could not possibly know? Remembered people or places where you know you have never been?"

"Of course," she said. "Who hasn't? But it doesn't mean anything."

"Have you ever dreamed of being a doctor? Or of being a queen during the Crusades? A witch in Old Salem?"

"Stop it!"

He drew back and took a sip of his wine. "Forgive me. I did not mean to upset you."

She stared at him, remembering the dream that she'd had the night before. She had been a queen then. And Dominic had been her bodyguard. . . .

With a start, she realized that she had dreamed of him in the past, dreamed of him even before they met. That was why she had thought he looked familiar when she met him on the beach.

A cold chill ran down her spine. How was it possible to dream of someone she had never met?

She pushed her plate away, her appetite gone. "I . . . I've got to go."

"Is something wrong?"

"I . . . I have . . . uh . . . an appointment with a future client, and I'm . . . I'm late . . . and . . ." Grabbing her handbag, she quickly slid out of the booth. "I'm sorry."

He watched her hurry toward the cash register. She didn't look back.

Chapter 5

The schoolhouse was located in a small, square building at the end of the street. It was painted red with white trim, and boasted a bell tower on the roof. There were windows in the east and west walls for cross ventilation. She had fifteen students in her class—nine girls and six boys—ranging in age from five to sixteen.

Books were scarce and she had to rely on her wits and imagination to keep her pupils interested, especially the older boys. Reading, writing, spelling, grammar, and arithmetic were expected; geography and history and geometry were a plus. The school term was erratic, as children were not expected to come to school when they were needed at home for spring and summer planting and fall harvesting.

She was expected to fill the lamps and clean the chimneys every day, to bring a bucket of water and a scuttle of coal, to provide pens and wipers for the students. She was also expected to enforce discipline but was cautioned not to go overboard.

She loved her position, though she found some of the rules she was expected to follow a trifle stifling. She was *expected to be a model of deportment both in the school-house and in the community. It was taken for granted that she would attend church each week and sing in the choir. She was not to smoke or use liquor in any form.*

She was not allowed to live in a house by herself but was expected to board with the families of her students. She would have preferred to live alone but that left too much room for scandal. Of course, living with her students did give her a valuable insight into their behavior. She had been informed that, should she decide to marry, her tenure would end immediately.

Still, in spite of all the restrictions, she loved teaching, and she loved the town. She was thinking about the next day's lessons as she made her way toward home that evening. Lost in thought, she didn't see the man striding toward her until it was too late. She barreled into him, would have fallen if he had not caught her shoulders to steady her.

"Oh, excuse me," *she exclaimed.* "I'm so sorry."

"No harm done."

His voice was deep and richly textured and it seemed to seep into the farthest reaches of her soul. She looked up quickly, her gaze meeting his. Dark gray eyes looked back at her; they, too, seemed to delve into her very soul.

His brow furrowed as he stared into her eyes. "Is it you?"

"I beg your pardon? Have we met before?"

"Yes," *he said,* "though I fear you do not remember me." *He swept off his hat with a flourish and bowed.* "Dominic St. John, at your service."

"Annie Williams," *she replied.* "I'm sorry, I don't recall meeting you before, Mr. St. John. Was it here, in town?"

"No. Might I inquire as to where you were going in such a hurry, Miss Williams?"

"I was just on my way home." *She smiled self-consciously.* "I'm afraid my mind was not on where I was going."

He smiled, revealing remarkably white teeth. "Might I accompany you the rest of the way?"

She glanced over her shoulder. Old Man Peters was sitting in front of the barber shop, pretending he wasn't listening to every word. Mrs. Peabody was sweeping the boardwalk in front of her shop, watching avidly.

"I'm not sure that's a good idea," she replied. "I can't afford the gossip."

Dominic followed her gaze, his eyes narrowed. Abruptly, Old Man Peters got up and hurried down the street. Mrs. Peabody shook the dirt from her broom and went into her shop.

"Change your mind," Dominic urged softly.

She knew she should refuse, but she couldn't resist the sweet, pleading tone of his voice, or refuse the urgings of her own heart. When he offered her his arm, she took it.

"I don't remember seeing you around before," she remarked.

"I've only just arrived."

"Will you be staying long?"

His gaze rested on her face, his dark gray eyes filled with an intensity that was both frightening and somehow tantalizing. "I will be now . . ."

"Dominic." She woke with his name on her lips, the memory of her dream still vivid. Was it only a dream?

Sitting up in bed, she stared out the window. Where were these dreams—she refused to call them memories—coming from? Was it just the power of suggestion? That would have been the easy answer, she thought, if she hadn't had them before she met Dominic on the beach.

With a sigh, she turned onto her stomach and closed her eyes.

She saw him every night for the next three months and each night saw her falling more deeply in love with him. He treated her with such gentleness. There was an Old World courtliness about him that was charming and ut-

terly appealing. The only thing she found odd was that he never sought her out during the day.

On All Hallows Eve, just before midnight, he asked her to marry him and she accepted, even though it would mean losing her position with the school. She knew she would miss teaching, but looked forward to the time when she would be able to teach her own children. He wanted to wed the next evening, but she couldn't go off and leave the children with no one to teach them.

"As soon as my replacement arrives," she promised. "We'll be married that night if you wish."

He had not been happy with her decision, but, knowing how she loved teaching and how much she loved the children, he reluctantly agreed.

It was the week before Christmas when she came down with a headache that sent her home early from school. When she woke the next morning, she was burning with fever, then shaking with chills.

Dominic came to her late that night.

"Annie?" She heard the anxiety in his voice as he smoothed her hair from her brow.

"Dominic? Is that you?" She opened her eyes but saw only darkness.

"I'm here, sweeting," he replied softly.

She reached for his hand, clutched it to her breast. "I love you."

"And I love you, *querida*."

"Have you talked to the doctor?"

He nodded.

"Then you know I'm . . ." She couldn't say the word. How could she be dying? She had never been sick a day in her life until now.

"Annie, please do not leave me."

"I don't want to."

"Then stay. Trust me to help you."

"What can you do that the doctor cannot?" she asked,

and listened in growing horror as he told her a tale she could not believe.

"No." She shook her head weakly. "Even if what you're saying is true, I can't live like that."

"Annie, it is the only way!" He caught her up in his arms and buried his face in her hair. "Please, my best beloved one, please do not leave me again!"

She clutched at his shoulders as she felt the life fading from her body. "I think I shall miss you, Dominic, even in heaven."

His voice, calling her name, was the last thing she remembered. . . .

"No!" Tracy woke abruptly, her body bathed in sweat. She glanced at the window, relieved to see that night was withdrawing her cloak from the face of the land.

On the brink of the dark sleep of his kind, he stared into the darkness, his senses filled with Tracy. The scent of her perfume lingered in his nostrils. The memory of her voice whispered in his ear. Her smile warmed his heart. He closed his eyes and images from the past flooded his mind.

He saw a scantily clad Tracy dancing in front of a tent full of men, holding them spellbound as she moved in sinuous grace, her long golden hair falling like a veil of silk past her waist. Her hips moved in slow, sensual allure, the hint of a smile promising to fulfill the fantasy of every man in the place. Only she wasn't Tracy then—she was Kiya, the enchantress.

He stood near the back of the tent, his hands fisted at his sides, his jaw clenched. The scent of unbridled lust filled the evening air.

He took a step forward, anger surging through him when one of the men tried to grab hold of her arm. With *a laugh, Kiya twirled out of the man's reach, her diaphanous skirts swirling around her ankles, flying up to offer a glimpse of her long, shapely legs. The jeweled bracelets on her wrists winked in the candlelight.*

Men tossed gold coins at her feet when the music ended. She quickly scooped up the money and with a last seductive smile, ran out of the tent.

Dominic followed her outside. Keeping to the shadows, he ghosted after her as she made her way toward her lodgings.

Though his feet made no sound as he moved over the sand, she paused and glanced over her shoulder.

"Who's there?"

"A friend," he replied.

Lifting her skirt, she drew a wicked-looking knife from a sheath strapped high on her thigh. "What kind of friend hides in the darkness?"

"One who would like to know you better."

"Then show yourself."

He walked slowly toward her, stopping an arm's length away.

"Why are you following me?" she demanded.

"I merely wanted to make sure you arrived at your destination safely."

"Oh? And why is that?"

"I would not wish to see any harm befall one so lovely, so talented."

She studied his face as if judging his sincerity, then nodded. "You were watching me tonight."

"I have watched you every night."

"And followed me home!" she exclaimed.

"Yes."

She studied him a moment longer, then sheathed her weapon, uncaring that she exposed a long, slender leg to do so.

"Come," she invited, "walk with me."

He walked her home every night after that, often staying with her until the hour before dawn, when he left to seek his lair. She was a wild girl, filled with the fire of youth and an inexhaustible passion for living. Her laughter was like the tinkling of temple bells, her hair like fine black silk, her skin smooth and without blemish.

In time, she took him into her heart, and then into her bed. And when, at last, he told her what he was, she did not turn away in disgust or look at him with revulsion, or banish him from her presence. And for that he had vowed to love her as long as she lived, to grant her any wish that was within his power to give.

They spent three years together. She became famous throughout all the known land. She danced for kings and princes, for sultans and sheiks. And always he stood in the shadows, watching over her.

As her fame grew, he warned her to be careful of her associations, never to go anywhere alone. There were many men, both old and young, who tried to gain her favor. Some offered marriage, some offered wealth, a few offered both. And there were those who tried to take by force that which she would not willingly give. His wrath was their reward.

But he was not there the day she needed him most. Ignoring his advice, she had gone out to wander through the marketplace in the late afternoon. On her way home, she had been attacked. She had fought off her attacker but not before the man stabbed her several times. Badly wounded, she had tried to make it back to her lodgings and when she realized she wasn't going to make it, she had crawled into the underbrush alongside the road.

He had found her there shortly after sunset. Her face had been as pale as fine white linen, her garments soaked with her life's blood. For once, the sight and the scent of blood had no effect on his inhuman hunger. He had gathered her into his arms and held her close.

"Kiya." He called her name again and again, willing her spirit to return, until, at last, her eyelids fluttered open.

"Dominic." Her lips formed his name but no sound emerged.

"Do not leave me!" Using his teeth, he ripped open his wrist and held it to her mouth. *"Drink!"*

But it was too late. She was too weak to fight for her life, too weak to swallow the life-giving liquid.

Her eyelids fluttered down.

He held her in his arms, rocking her back and forth, as she breathed her last. *"Kiya, my best beloved one, I will find you again, I swear it."*

And he had found her, again and again and again, only to lose her when death took her beyond his reach.

But no more.

"No more." He murmured the words as the sun climbed high in the sky, dragging him down into the dreamless depths of that sleep that was like death itself.

It was late afternoon when Tracy laid her brush aside and stood to stretch her back and shoulders. She had risen with the dawn, eager to put her dreams behind her, to lose herself in her painting. Her art had always been an escape from whatever problems were worrying her. She was in control at the canvas, her whole being focused on the intimate act of creation. This morning, she had not painted from any sketches or photographs; she had simply stood in front of a blank square of canvas and let her imagination take flight.

Now, she stared at her work in wonder. A tall, dusky-skinned woman danced across the canvas, her long hair shimmering around her shoulders. Her colorful skirts swirled around her ankles, revealing shapely calves. A bracelet of rubies and emeralds reflected the light of the candles that lit the tent. Men of all ages sat in a wide circle around her, staring avidly. And in the background, blending in with the shadows, stood a tall, dark man.

A man who looked very much like Dominic St. John.

But it was the woman who held her gaze. It was the woman she had dreamed of the night before. It seemed she was no longer able to separate her troublesome thoughts from her work, after all.

Pulling off her smock, she tossed it over the back of a chair and hurried from the room, her thoughts on Dominic. For the first time in two weeks, he hadn't sent her flowers with a note telling her where to meet him. Perhaps he had been called away on business, she thought, though she couldn't believe he would have gone anywhere without telling her beforehand. They had spent every night together since he sent her flowers the first time. Occasionally, she found herself wondering what he did during the day, why he never called her on the phone, why they never went out to lunch or dinner. After all, he had told her he was retired, so it couldn't be a job that kept him occupied during the daylight hours. Next time she saw him, maybe she would ask him to come over for lunch.

Needing to feel the sunlight on her face, she left the house and went down the long, winding stairs that led to the beach. Kicking off her shoes, she walked along the shore, enjoying the sound of the waves. Seagulls flew overhead, wheeling and diving. She saw a couple of seals frolicking out past the breakers.

She stopped to watch them for a few minutes. But even the antics of the seals couldn't keep her troublesome thoughts at bay for long. Why was she having those disturbing dreams? Why had she felt compelled to paint Dominic as a vampire? Who was the dancing woman, and why did she have the feeling that she knew her? Was it just stress? That seemed like the obvious answer, but she didn't feel stressed. She loved the house. Her painting was going well. Maybe she had just been working too hard.

With a shake of her head, she started walking again. She wouldn't think of it now. The day was too beautiful, the sky too blue.

The beach was crowded today. Teenage girls in brightly-colored bikinis lounged on blankets, working on their tans, while their boyfriends showed off playing volleyball. Mothers helped their kids build castles in the sand. A father perched his young son on his shoulders and waded into the shallows. Further down the beach, an old man and woman were fishing. A lifeguard sat on tower number ten some distance away. She had waved to him from time to time when she passed by.

Finding a quiet place on a patch of sand, Tracy sat down, her arms resting on her bent knees. There was something mesmerizing about staring at the ocean, watching the endless cycle of the waves as they washed in to kiss the shore, then rolled back out to sea.

She lost track of time as she sat there, lost in the infinite rhythm of the waves, the quiet beauty of the ocean that stretched away as far as the eye could see. This was reality. Not the bizarre dreams that troubled her sleep. Not memories of past lives that she didn't believe were possible in the first place.

Certainly not vampires with glowing red eyes and fangs dripping with blood, or mysterious raven-haired dancing girls.

"Are you all right?"

"What?" She looked up to find a tall, blond man wearing a pair of red trunks staring at her through the bluest eyes she had ever seen.

"You've been sitting here for a long time. I . . . I just wanted to make sure you were okay." He looked suddenly embarrassed. "I know you're not drowning, but . . ."

It took Tracy a moment to realize he was the lifeguard. "I'm fine," she said, smiling. "Just lost in thought, I guess."

He nodded. "You might want to get out of the sun for a while," he said. "You're getting a heck of a sunburn."

Tracy glanced at her arms and legs, which were indeed very, very pink. "I think you're right." When she started to rise, he offered her his hand. She took it without a second thought and let him pull her to her feet. "Thank you."

"My pleasure, Miss . . . ?"

"Warner. Tracy."

"Bryan Longstreet."

"Nice to meet you, Bryan."

"Likewise."

She walked over to a shady place beneath a tree and sat on a rock, somewhat surprised when Bryan followed her.

"Have you lived in this area long?" he asked.

"No. Actually, I just recently bought a house here. Why?"

"I'm new here myself. Kind of a strange town, don't you think?"

"What do you mean?"

"Have you been to the village? You hardly see any-body on the streets during the day, but at night . . ." He shrugged. "It's like the place comes alive after dark. Seems like most of the residents are night people. Some of them seem kind of . . . weird."

"I hadn't noticed, but it's kind of an artsy town, isn't it? You know, lots of musicians and painters and writers, actors hiding out."

"Yeah, I guess that could be it." Bryan glanced at his tower, then back at Tracy. "I don't suppose you'd like to go over to the Driftwood for a drink later? I'll be through here in another hour or so."

Her first thought was to say no. He was younger than she was, after all. And then she thought, why not? The Driftwood was a local bar not far from the beach, and it was just for a drink, nothing more. "I'd like that."

"Great!"

She couldn't help being flattered by his exuber-ance. "I'll go home and change and meet you there."

"Terrific. See you then." He smiled, revealing a dimple in his left cheek, then ran down the beach toward tower number ten.

Chapter 6

Returning home, Tracy went upstairs and took a quick shower. Humming softly, she brushed out her hair and tied it back in a ponytail, then changed into a sleeveless flowered sundress, slipped on a pair of strappy gold sandals, and drove to the Driftwood. She parked in the lot in the back, grabbed her handbag, and walked around the corner to the entrance.

Bryan Longstreet was waiting for her on the sidewalk in front of the bar. He was dressed in a green shirt, a pair of beige Dockers, and tan loafers.

"Am I late?" she asked.

"No." He smiled a little sheepishly as he took her arm. "I was early."

He was a handsome young man, tall and lean with a great tan. It didn't take more than a few minutes in his presence to realize he was just what the doctor ordered.

The Driftwood was a nice place. Catering mostly to tourists, it was decorated with seashells, pieces of the wood from which it derived its name, and colorful paper lanterns.

Sitting in a booth sharing a Mai Tai with Bryan, Tracy learned that he loved movies and that he was a big *Star Wars* fan, as was she. He liked Elvis and rock and roll, his favorite color was red, and he confessed that, if he had to, he could live on pizza and Coke forever. His father was a police officer in Washington, D.C, and his mother was an accountant. He had four brothers—all older and all cops— and an older sister who was in the Air Force. He had just turned twenty-one to her twenty-six.

"Does it bother you?" he asked. "My being younger?"

"I guess not. It's only five years." She grinned at him. "When I'm eighty and you're seventy-five, it will hardly matter."

There was a pause in their conversation while the waitress brought them another drink. Tracy glanced out the window. The street was crowded with men and women. She thought it odd that most of them wore black, then shrugged. Maybe they were into the Goth thing. She saw very few teenagers, practically no children. But, as she had told Bryan earlier, this was an artsy town, not a family community, so maybe it wasn't so strange after all.

As the evening wore on, Tracy found herself liking Bryan Longstreet more and more. He was easy to be with, easy to talk to. Not like Dominic, she thought. There was something about Dominic that bothered her, and it was more than the strong sexual attraction that sizzled between them. It was unsettling, the way he sometimes went still, his gaze resting on her face, his dark eyes hot. At such times, she felt like a very small mouse being stalked by a very large, very hungry cat.

But there was nothing about Bryan to arouse either fear or suspicion. He was as open and outgoing as a puppy. She couldn't remember when she'd had a more pleasant evening.

Later, they went to an outdoor café and ordered cheeseburgers and French fries and talked about their favorite movies.

He liked *Bullitt* and *Airplane* and *Rambo*. And *Star Wars*, of course.

She liked *Ladyhawke* and *The Princess Bride* and *Gladiator*. And *Star Wars*, of course.

"All right," he said, waving a French fry in the air. "Who's your favorite character?"

"Han Solo, of course," she replied, wiggling her eyebrows. "What a silly question."

"Figures," he muttered.

"Who's yours?"

"Obi-Wan."

"In which episode?"

"All of them," he said with a wide grin. He swung an imaginary light saber over his head. "You have much to learn, young Jedi."

"So tell me, oh wise one, how do we get rid of Jar Jar?"

"Any way we can!"

She laughed at that and so did he.

Later, they went window shopping, stopping to point out which things they would buy if they had a million dollars.

They were nearing the end of the block when Tracy felt a prickling down her spine. Someone was watching her! Casually, she glanced up and down both sides of the street, but saw no one. Still, the feeling persisted.

Bryan took her arm as they crossed the street.

The feeling of being watched grew stronger.

And then Dominic materialized out of the shadows. "Good evening," he murmured. He spoke to Tracy but his gaze was fixed on Bryan, and there was nothing friendly in it.

Tracy swallowed a sudden sense of guilt, though she had no idea why she should feel guilty. She wasn't doing anything wrong. "Hi."

She glanced from Dominic to Bryan and back again. The tension between the two men was thick enough to cut. "Dominic, this is Bryan Longstreet. Bryan, this is Dominic St. John."

Bryan stuck his hand out. "Pleased to meet you, Mr. St. John."

"Indeed." Dominic hesitated only briefly before taking the other man's hand.

"Bryan's a lifeguard," Tracy said. "I met him on the beach this afternoon."

"How fortunate." There was no mistaking the sarcasm in Dominic's voice, or the fact that he was making an effort to control his anger. "I went by your house earlier."

She didn't miss the accusation in his tone. "I didn't know you were coming."

He lifted one black brow, then bowed his head in a gesture of contrition. "Forgive me. I did not have time to contact you earlier."

She told herself there was no reason to feel guilty because she hadn't stayed home waiting for him. Just because he had come to see her every night for the past two weeks didn't mean she couldn't see anyone else, or that she had to sit around waiting for Dominic, wondering if he was going to show up.

"I'm sorry," she murmured. "It was nice seeing you, Dominic. Good night."

He was not accustomed to being dismissed. It

was obvious in the tightening of his lips, the narrowing of his eyes.

"Good night." He inclined his head in her direction, but his gaze never left Longstreet's.

Bryan cleared his throat, clearly disturbed by Dominic's scrutiny. Tracy couldn't blame him. The look in Dominic's eyes was cold enough to freeze boiling water.

"Good night. Sir." Taking Tracy by the hand, Bryan hurried her down the sidewalk. "Who is that guy?"

"Just an acquaintance."

"He's spooky as hell."

"What do you mean?"

"His eyes! I felt like he could see clear through me. How well do you know him?"

She shrugged. "Like I said, he's just an acquaintance." *Acquaintance* was hardly an adequate description, she thought, remembering the passionate kisses and intimate embraces she and Dominic had shared.

"Does he know that? He looked mighty jealous to me."

Was that it? Was Dominic jealous? She was surprised to find herself pleased by the idea. And now that she thought about it, she decided Bryan was right. Dominic had looked jealous. And angry.

Glancing over her shoulder, she saw he was standing where they had left him. Even from this distance, she could feel his gaze burning into her.

Come to me.

She took one step toward him and then another and then stopped abruptly. What was she doing?

"Tracy, hey, Tracy, are you okay?"

She glanced over her shoulder. "Yes, why?"

"You looked kind of funny there for a minute."

"I'm fine. Let's go have a nightcap, shall we?"

* * *

A shiver of unease slithered down Tracy's spine as she climbed the porch steps. Why hadn't she left a light on? Why hadn't she ever noticed how ominous the house looked at night with the lights out and the moon shining down on it? The thought that it resembled one of Count Dracula's domains crossed her mind yet again. Maybe Dominic was really the infamous Count. Maybe he had decided to leave the mountains of Translyvania and take a vacation on the coast of California.

Shaking off her foolish thoughts, she unlocked the door and stepped into the entryway.

The words, dark as a tomb, leaped to the forefront of her mind.

"Enough!"

The word seemed to echo off the walls . . . *enough . . . enough . . . enough.*

She flipped on the light switch. Hurrying into the living room, she turned on all the lights, then went into the kitchen, turning lights on as she went.

She paused at the foot of the stairway, her heart pounding as she stared at the darkness at the top of the second floor landing.

Blowing out a deep breath, she turned and went back into the kitchen. A cup of peppermint tea was just what she needed to settle her nerves. She filled the pot with water and put it on the stove, then closed the curtains on the window over the sink.

Sitting down at the table, she crossed her arms over her chest and tried not to listen to the small, creaky sounds the house made. Instead, she thought about Bryan and what a good time she'd had with him. He had asked for her phone number, promising to call her in the next couple of days. She looked forward to going out with him again. . . .

You will not, my best beloved one. You are mine.

My best beloved one. Why did those words sound so familiar, so welcome? Dominic had never said them to her, and yet it was his voice she heard in the back of her mind, so loud and clear that she turned around, expecting to see him standing there behind her.

But there was no one else in the room.

Or was there?

As strange as it seemed, she no longer felt as though she was alone in the house.

Rising, she opened a drawer and pulled out a butcher knife. "Is someone there?"

She practically jumped out of her skin when the shrill whistle of the teakettle sounded behind her.

Muttering an oath, she dropped the knife on the counter and turned off the stove, then sagged back against the countertop. When her breathing returned to normal, she put the knife back in the drawer, dropped a tea bag in a cup, and filled it with hot water.

"Geez, girl, get a grip," she muttered as she stirred a spoonful of honey into her cup. "There's nothing to be afraid of."

But she couldn't shake the feeling that there was someone else in the house. Someone else in the kitchen.

Standing with her back to the counter, she slowly perused the room. Was that something there, near the doorway? She turned her head slightly to the right and from the corner of her eye, she seemed to see something shimmery, something in the vague shape of a man.

Fear congealed in the pit of her stomach. Her mouth went dry. She reached for the knife again, even though she knew that it would be useless against anything that wasn't flesh and blood. And that strange, shimmering, silvery image was definitely not human.

A ghost, perhaps? That seemed the most obvious. This was an old house. It was entirely possible that someone had died here, that some restless spirit haunted the rooms. Previous occupants had sworn the place was haunted. Tracy didn't believe in ghosts or goblins, but there was definitely an unseen presence in the room. The certainty of it shivered over her.

"Who are you?" she asked, her voice shaking so badly she hardly recognized it. "*What* are you?"

There was no answer, of course.

And then it—whatever *it* was—was gone.

Dominic materialized in his rooms below the house. She had been aware of his presence, had known he was in the kitchen, but how? If he had taken her blood, they would have shared a telepathic bond, but he had never taken her blood. Time after time, in every life, he had ignored his ever-growing need and respected her wishes in that regard.

He paced the floor, his long, restless strides carrying him swiftly from one end of the room to the other. So, how had she known he was there? Did she possess psychic powers in this life? Or was it because their souls had been forged together in so many lifetimes through the ages? Perhaps now, at last, they shared a bond that not even her death could break.

Tracy. Her scent still filled his nostrils—warm and sweetly feminine. His hands clenched at his sides as he caught the faint scent of the boy she had been out with earlier. It would be so easy to dispose of the competition. So easy and so tempting. He could break the interloper in half with one hand, crush the life from his frail mortal body with nothing more than a thought.

But he would not. Closing his eyes, Dominic took a deep, calming breath. He was a civilized vampire now. He no longer killed indiscriminately or merely for the sheer pleasure of draining the thoughts, the wishes, and the life's blood of a mere mortal. These days, he drank no more than he required. He left his victims alive, though he wiped his memory from their minds.

Oh, yes, he mused, he was a civilized vampire now. But now and then he missed the old days, when he had been a young vampire, new in the life, when he had gloried in his newfound strength and preternatural power, when every night had been a new adventure and every mortal a feast for his relentless thirst.

Ah, for those nights when he had hunted at Kitana's side. They had swept through the tiny villages and hamlets of the Old Country like an invisible plague, glutting themselves on the warm, rich crimson that fell on the tongue like the finest of wines, smooth and intoxicating.

They had hunted throughout the cities and towns of England and France, Italy and Spain, sweeping through docks and dark alleyways, charming their way into fancy balls and masquerades, always leaving death behind. Kitana. That she had looked at him twice had been a miracle to him. Her body was as supple and slender as a willow tree, her dusky skin smooth and unblemished, her hair a cloud of thick auburn silk, and her lips . . . ah, her lips were like wild, sweet honey. She had fascinated him from the moment they met, captivating him, enchanting him, until he was hopelessly caught in the web of her supernatural power, and happy to have it so. When she promised him a way to stay forever young, forever at her side, he had agreed without a second thought. The loss of the sun had seemed a small price to pay for eternity in her arms.

The transformation had been nothing like he expected. When he had seen her in her true form, her eyes red with hunger, her fangs like white ice, he had tried to run, but he was no match for her preternatural speed and she had caught him easily. She had held him in her arms, her eyes glowing like hellfire as she bent over his neck. He had struggled in her embrace, but she had held him effortlessly, his strength like that of a newborn babe compared to her supernatural power.

Surprisingly, there had been no pain as she sank her fangs into his throat, only warm, sensual pleasure. When she drew back, he had whimpered like a child taken from its mother's breast and begged her not to stop. Instead, she had opened a gash in her own wrist and pressed it to his lips.

You must drink now.

Mesmerized by her gaze, he had opened his mouth and swallowed the thick, red fluid, felt it burn a path down his throat, felt it spread through his body like liquid fire. He had grasped her wrist and sucked greedily, hissed at her when she tore her arm free.

He remembered little else of that night. She had carried him to her lair, let him spend the day in death-like sleep at her side.

When next he opened his eyes, the land lay shrouded in darkness and he was a full-fledged vampire.

Chapter 7

Tracy woke slowly, the memory of last night's dream still vivid in her mind. She had been a slave in a grand house in ancient Rome. Her master had been a senator, his wife a stern woman with no compassion for those beneath her. It had seemed so real, not like a dream at all. She had felt the cold tiles beneath her feet, smelled the scents of food and wine at the marketplace, felt the sting of the whip on her flesh. Her name had been Nysa back then.

She whispered the name aloud, shivering because it sounded so familiar on her tongue. She had dreamed of the days Nysa had spent avoiding the wrath of her mistress, the nights when she had used her wiles to avoid the advances of her master. In many ways, it had been a good life. Unlike the poor citizens of Rome, she'd had a roof over her head, enough food to eat, a soft bed to sleep in. Still, it was hard to be grateful when she had no life of her own, when her every moment was spent in servitude to a cruel mistress.

She had been in her early twenties when her master decided to breed her to one of the other house slaves.

Tracy shuddered with the memory. When she refused to cooperate, she had been beaten by her mistress. She had run away that night.

It had been a man who looked very much like Dominic who had found her cowering in the ruins of an old burned-out barn. Could it have been Dominic? His name had been the same. He had taken her to his home and given her shelter. Her new owner had kept strange hours, never rising until after sunset, always disappearing before the dawn. He made no demands on her save that she be in the house when he arrived. He provided her with the best food the city had to offer, though she never saw him eat. He clothed her in silks and fine linen, treated her as the mistress of his house rather than a runaway slave. And when he took her in his arms, she offered no resistance.

Days became weeks, weeks became months, the months became a year. And in that year, she convinced herself that there was nothing odd about him, that he simply preferred to sleep during the day and pursue his life in the evening.

It was during that year that she fell madly, desperately, in love with him.

It was during that year that she discovered what he was. . . .

Feeling a sudden chill, Tracy wrapped her arms around her middle. Was it possible that she was truly dreaming about past lives? Was reincarnation a reality even though she didn't believe in it? And if her dreams were truly recollections of the past surfacing from the depths of her subconscious memory, if they were indeed true, then it stood to reason that she had known Dominic before, and that he really was a . . .

Swallowing, she forced the word past her lips. "Vampire."

Oh, but that was impossible, almost as impossible as the notion that she had known him in countless lives before.

The ringing of the doorbell interrupted her reverie. Swinging her legs over the side of the bed, she grabbed her robe and hurried downstairs.

She opened the door and exclaimed, "Oh, my!" at the sight that met her eyes. Her front porch was covered with red roses. In vases. In baskets. In boxes. And amid the flowers were stuffed animals and balloons, all bearing notes that said the same thing. *"My heart beats only to see you again."*

She picked a rose from one of the vases and inhaled the heady fragrance. "Oh, Dominic," she murmured. "This must have cost you a fortune."

It took several trips to carry it all into the house. When she was finished, her living room, bedroom, and kitchen looked like a florist shop. There were cute little stuffed bears and bunnies and puppies on every chair and on her bed. Vases and drinking glasses and pitchers were filled with roses that were beautiful and smelled divine.

She found herself smiling all through the day, whether she was painting a new seascape, watering the grass, or fixing dinner . . . she frowned as she tossed the salad. She had never seen Dominic eat, never seen him drink anything other than an occasional glass of wine. She never saw him during the day. . . .

With a shake of her head, she pulled a bottle of bleu cheese dressing out of the fridge. Just because she hadn't seen him in the daytime and hadn't seen him eat didn't mean he was a vampire. Vampires were ugly, disgusting creatures with long fangs and hairy hands and foul breath who skulked in the shadows of the night preying on the innocent and unsuspecting, and . . .

"Stop it!"

Leaving the salad on the counter, untouched, she went upstairs to look at the painting she had done of him, noticing, for the first time, that it was no longer facing the wall, as she had left it. Who had turned it around? Why hadn't she noticed that before?

She stared at the painting, thinking again that it was the best, most lifelike portrait that she had ever done. His hair gleamed inky black in the light of the moon, his eyes seemed to follow her around the room; she could almost hear her name on his lips.

Turning the painting toward the wall, she left the room, and closed the door behind her.

He was at her door with the setting of the sun. He filled his eyes with the sight of her, his need to make her his almost overpowering. He had followed her through the centuries, never able to make her fully his, waiting impatiently for her soul to be born again, searching, always searching, until at last he found her again.

But this time she had found him. Had some deep inner need she was unaware of led her to this place, this house? To him? Had her soul been searching for him even as he had been searching for her?

Her smile looked strained when she opened the door. "Hi, Dominic."

He frowned, aware of her nervousness. "Is something wrong?"

"No, why?" She stepped back, allowing him entrance to the house. Closing the door, she went into the living room, very much aware of the man behind her.

A faint smile curved his lips when they entered the living room. "I see you got the flowers."

She laughed softly. "Really, Dominic, you didn't have to send so many. They must love you at the flower shop."

"You should always be surrounded by roses," he said, moving toward her.

"Who are you?" The words slipped out, unbidden.

"You know who I am."

"*What* are you?"

"Search your mind, your heart. You know what I am."

"It's impossible. I don't believe it."

"The painting you did of me is most accurate."

She shook her head in denial. "No."

"I have followed you through the centuries. Always I have found you. But this time, you found me."

"What are you talking about?"

"This house. Why did you buy it?"

She frowned. "Why? Because I liked it, of course. It was just what I was looking for. What other reason could there be?"

"I live below this house."

"Below it? Like in the basement?"

"No. There is another house beneath this one."

"And you live there?"

He nodded.

"That doesn't mean you're a vampire."

"You know it is true."

"No." She didn't believe in vampires or ghosts or reincarnation. "If you're a vampire, prove it."

She had no sooner spoken the words than the air around her grew thick, charged with energy, like the buildup before a storm. Dominic's dark eyes blazed with an unholy light, his lips drew back to reveal his fangs. Preternatural power danced over her skin, raising the hair along her arms and at her nape.

"Now," he said, his voice smooth and silky. "Now do you believe?"

A wordless cry erupted from her lips, and then she fainted.

When she came to, she was lying on the sofa. Dominic stood at the window, looking out at the night. She noted that he was wearing black again, and that it suited him perfectly. She wondered if he owned a long ebony cloak, or if that was just a Hollywood affectation. Her heart pounded in her ears as she stared at his broad back. She had asked for proof, and she'd gotten it, in spades!

As though sensing she had regained consciousness, he turned slowly to face her. "Now," he repeated, his voice low and mesmerizing. "Now do you believe?"

She did, but she refused to admit it, even to herself. If she accepted the fact that he was a vampire, she would have to accept all of it, and she just couldn't. To do so would shake the foundations of everything she believed in. There had to be some other explanation. If there wasn't, if he was indeed a vampire, as he said, then everything else he had told her was probably true, as well. She had been a queen, a slave, a dancer, a teacher, a doctor, and all the other things he had said. Her dreams were not really dreams at all, but actual memories of past lives. Her past lives. She had been Jocelyn and Kiya and Annie Williams and Nysa and who knew how many others. If she accepted it, if she admitted it was true, it would change her whole life, change everything she believed in.

Dominic took a step toward her, paused when she recoiled.

"Are you afraid of me now?" he asked quietly.

"Yes. No. I don't know."

"I will not hurt you, my best beloved one. I have searched for you, followed you, throughout time."

"Why, when I've rejected you at every turn?"

"Do you not know that we are destined to be together, *querida*? Our souls were mated long ago."

"You want to make me a vampire."

"Only if it is your wish. Many times in the past I have offered you the Dark Gift to save your life."

"And I've always refused." That much was obvious, she thought, since she was still mortal.

"Yes."

"And still you persist."

"I will have you for my own, my best beloved one, if I have to follow you into eternity."

"I don't want to be a vampire."

"Then I will love you as you are. We will be together in this life, as we have been together in your past lives. I will be at your side when death claims you, and I will find you when your soul is born again."

Talking of her own death sent a shiver down Tracy's spine. She had always been afraid of dying. Was it because she had experienced it so many times? Or because so many of her deaths had been violent or premature?

"How long have you been a vampire?"

"Two thousand and twenty-three years."

She stared at him in amazement. What would it be like to live for more than two thousand years? Never to grow old? Never to be sick? Never to see the sun . . . to watch your friends grow old and die while you stayed forever the same.

"It must be a lonely life," she remarked.

"It can be."

"Have you been lonely?"

His gaze rested gently on her face. "Only when I could not find you."

His words, low and from the heart, obliterated whatever fear of him remained, though she was still wary. He was, after all, a vampire, and whatever memories of him she might have from past lives, she was no longer Nysa or Kiya or any of the others. She was Tracy Warner now, a twenty-first-century woman with a life and a career of her own. If, as he said, she had loved him in the past, it seemed she would have to learn to love him all over again in the present. And what if she didn't? She stared up at him, thinking he looked like an immense dark cloud looming over her. He didn't seem like the type of man who would just let her go if she decided she didn't want him around.

"Do we start over every time we meet?" It was one of a thousand questions churning in her mind.

He sat down in the chair across from her. "Yes."

"And do I always die in your arms?"

"Yes."

"Have you ever . . . drunk my blood?"

He shook his head. "No."

She saw the yearning in his eyes as he said, "I have been tempted, many times, but, no."

"Why not? Isn't that what vampires do?"

"You have never wished for it."

"Why haven't you just taken it by force?" She lifted a hand to her throat, probing softly. "Or when I'm asleep?"

"Is that what you want?" He didn't move, didn't alter his tone or expression, yet something she didn't comprehend changed in the air between them. Though he remained where he was, it seemed as if he was leaning toward her, waiting.

"No!"

"You would find it most pleasant."

"Never mind. I want to see where you live."

If he thought her request odd at such a moment, he didn't say so. Instead, he held out his hand. "Come."

He led her out the door that led to the backyard. Turning right, she followed him down a narrow path that seemed to end in a tangle of trees and shrubs that she had planned to clear away when she found the time. Just beyond the shrubbery was a narrow iron door that, as far as she could see, had no handle or latch of any kind.

Dominic put his hand on the door and it swung open on well-oiled hinges. Beyond the door, she saw nothing but blackness.

Dominic crossed the threshold, pulling her along behind him.

Tracy jerked her hand from his. "I'm not going down there. It's dark."

A wave of his hand brought several candles to life.

The passageway led steadily downward, not leveling out until they came to another door. Dominic opened this one as he had the other, revealing a large, square, windowless room. The walls, floor, and ceiling were of stone. A large fireplace took up most of one wall, accounting for the house's second chimney. Bookshelves lined another wall, a third was covered with drawings of a woman. Stepping farther into the room, Tracy studied the pictures. She was not surprised at what she saw. A queen in a long gown; a dancer clad in a provocative costume reminiscent of Salome; a schoolmarm clad in a long-sleeved, high-necked dress; a young woman wearing a veil and flowing robes.

Looking at the drawings made her uncomfortable and she turned away. The room was sparsely furnished. An easy chair faced the hearth. There was a large ottoman on one side of the chair, a small table on the other. A sofa stood at a right angle to the chair.

Opening a door, Dominic beckoned for her to follow. "My bedroom," he said.

There were no windows in this room, either, of course. Windows would be impossible so far underground. There were paintings of all shapes and sizes on all four walls—paintings of sunrises, nothing but sunrises. An armoire of dark cherrywood stood in one corner. There was a small desk and matching chair.

And in the center of the room, a sleek black casket lined with rich black satin.

She stared at the coffin, stared at Dominic, and then at the casket once again.

She blinked as the room went out of focus, spinning around her faster and faster, sucking her down, down, into blessed oblivion.

He caught her before she hit the floor.

Chapter 8

She woke cradled in Dominic's arms and knew, on some subconscious level of awareness, that he had held her this same way many times in the past. A fire burned in the hearth, providing the only light in the room.

He smiled faintly when he saw she was awake.

"I don't remember ever fainting before I met you." She had an almost irresistible urge to laugh out loud as she muttered, "At least not in this life."

"Are you all right now?"

She nodded. "I think so."

But he made no move to let her go, and she made no attempt to rise. Somehow, the effort seemed too great. Or maybe it was just that she was numb inside, overwhelmed by what he had told her and what she had seen. Maybe she was dreaming again.

He was a vampire.

He was over two thousand years old.

She had lived before, many times.

She shook her head to clear it, and shook off

her lethargy at the same time. It didn't matter who she had been before, only who she was now.

As for Dominic . . . she looked up and met his gaze. "Where do we go from here?"

"Wherever you wish."

"And if I wish to go upstairs?"

Sitting back, he took his arms from around her. "You are free to go, as always."

Not sure that she trusted him, she scooted off his lap. For a moment, she stood looking down at him, waiting. When he made no move to stop her, she walked toward the door and left him sitting there on the sofa, staring after her.

Upstairs, she thought of all he had told her. How did it feel to live such a long life, even if it was only half a life? Did one get tired of living? Oh, but how could that be? He had seen the history of the world unfold, seen mankind evolve, been there throughout the ages. How wonderful it must have been, to have seen so much, learned so much. And yet, how lonely, to have no one his own age to reminisce with, no one to grow old with, no one who shared his past, his memories. How sad, to fall in love with someone and lose them over and over again. As he had lost her . . . as she had lost him.

No! Whatever her past lives had been, they were gone now. She couldn't spend this life thinking of the ones before. She would go crazy if she did. She was Tracy Warner now. Not Kiya. Not Jocelyn. Not Nysa, or Annie Williams or any of the hundreds of other women she might have been.

She moved through the house, drawing the curtains over every window, locking every door, even though she knew nothing would keep him out.

Vampire.

Undead.

She changed into her nightgown and climbed under the covers. She didn't turn out the light.

He didn't have to be with her to know what she was doing. If he opened his mind, let his senses expand, he could read her thoughts. Tempting as it was, he wasn't sure he wanted to know what she was thinking. Not now.

He stared into the fire, his preternatural sight showing him colors that mortals never saw. He saw each flame in vivid detail, each wisp of smoke, each ash that fell. The fire burned brighter, its energy fed by his rising frustration. Stubborn woman! Would she never give in? Was he fated to follow her forever, always watching her, always loving her and yet always losing her?

He was the most powerful creature on the face of the earth. He could destroy life with a thought, bend mortals to his will. He could change his appearance, control the elements, bring this house down with a wave of his hand. Had he wished, he could supplant her will with his own. But he did not want to force her to come to him. He wanted her love, freely given.

And he would have it, sooner or later.

She woke in the morning feeling foolish. No matter what she had said last night, in spite of everything Dominic had told her, in spite of her own vivid dreams, she didn't truly believe in reincarnation. One birth, one life, and one death—that was what she believed in. And she didn't believe in vampires, either. She did believe in the power of suggestion and in hypnotism and both of those

possibilities made more sense than believing she
had lived a hundred other lives or that Dominic
was a two-thousand-year-old vampire. She knew there
were people who believed they were vampires. They
engaged in role-playing games online, wore nothing but black clothing, and only came out at night.
Some claimed to be immortal. Some claimed to
drink blood. But, no matter what they pretended
to be, they were just people acting out some bizarre
fantasy. And no matter what Dominic said, what he
tried to make her believe, she wasn't Annie Williams.
She wasn't Kiya or Nysa or Jocelyn. She had never
been a queen or an exotic dancer. She was just
plain old Tracy Ann Warner, artist, and happy to
be so.

As for Dominic . . . well, he was just too weird.
She'd be better off if she never saw him again.

After breakfast, she put on her bathing suit.
Glancing in the mirror, she resolved to lose ten
pounds before summer's end, and then blew out a
sigh. She made the same resolution every year.

Grabbing her beach bag, she tossed in an orange,
a bottle of water, her suntan lotion, and a paperback novel. She found a blanket and a towel and
went down to the beach to work on her tan.

Hoping to see Bryan, she gravitated toward Tower
Ten. She felt a moment of disappointment when
she saw another lifeguard on duty. With a shrug,
she spread her blanket on the sand, slathered herself with suntan lotion, put on her dark glasses,
and lost herself in her book.

After an hour, she put the book aside, took off
her sunglasses, and waded into the surf. She yelped
as the water swirled around her ankles. Gee, but it
was cold.

Determined, she waded deeper into the water, then dove under a wave and began swimming.

She let out a shriek when something came up behind her and brushed against her arm.

"Hey, it's only me."

"Bryan!"

"Sorry, I didn't mean to scare you."

"Well, you did." Treading water, she turned to face him. "What are you doing out here?"

"I always come out for a swim before I go to work. When I saw you . . ." He shrugged. "Hope you don't mind a little company."

"No, but I was just about to go back in."

"I'll race you."

She made a face at him. "Like I have a chance of beating a lifeguard."

"Well, because I'm a lifeguard, I'll give you a head start."

"Well, because I'm out of practice, I'll take it."

She struck out for shore, her adrenaline pumping. She had been on the swim teams in high school and college, but that had been a few years ago. She hadn't had a chance to get in much practice since college. Now, it felt good to be in competition again, even if she didn't have a hope of winning.

She risked a glance over her shoulder to see Bryan coming up behind her. He swam with seemingly effortless ease. And he was gaining on her.

And then he passed her.

He was standing on the shore, grinning, when she emerged from the water. "You could have been a gentleman and let me win," she said, shaking the water out of her hair.

"I thought about it," he said, "but then I decided you'd rather lose honestly."

"You were right." She walked up the beach toward her blanket, and he followed her. "How soon do you have to go to work?"

He glanced at his watch. "I've got a few minutes."

She plopped down on the blanket. "Want to keep me company until then?"

"Sure." He dropped down beside her. "Are you doing anything tonight?"

"Not really."

"Wanna go to the movies?"

"I'd like that."

"Great! Pick you up at seven?"

"All right. How long have you been a lifeguard?"

"Since I got out of high school. I'd do it all year, if they'd let me."

"What do you do in the winter?"

"I work over at the Y. I teach kids how to swim, hold classes in self-defense, and if there's enough interest, I teach tai chi."

"You look like you lift weights."

A faint flush colored his cheeks. "Yeah, well, I do that, too."

"So, why don't you live in D.C. with your folks?"

"They expect too much of me, you know? I mean, I think it's great that my brothers all followed in the old man's footsteps, but I'm just not cut out to be a cop. Or an accountant, for that matter. I'm afraid I'm a big disappointment to both of them."

She laughed. "I'm a big disappointment to my folks, too. They were hoping I'd marry a doctor or a lawyer and give them a dozen grandchildren."

"How about a lifeguard?"

She laughed again, only to break off abruptly when he didn't join in. "You're not serious?"

He nodded. "'Fraid so."

"But we just met, and . . ."

"And I'm too young for you. Does age really matter? Would you be happier if I was older?"

"No," she said, thinking of Dominic, "I wouldn't be happier. But, Bryan, we hardly know each other."

"I'm hoping to remedy that." Leaning forward, he kissed her on the cheek. "I've gotta go. See you tonight." Rising, he took a few steps, then turned back. "Hey, where do you live?"

"Up there," she said, pointing. "The big house that looks like Dracula lives there." She said the words without thinking, and then shuddered. Dracula *did* live there.

"Gotcha. See you at seven."

Tracy stared after him, bemused. She hadn't had a date in months. Now she had a too-young lifeguard on one hand and a too-old vampire on the other. Given a choice . . . but she didn't have to decide, she thought, applying a fresh coat of suntan lotion. She could date anyone she wanted.

But right now, she just wanted to soak up some sun.

Bryan arrived at her door promptly at seven. He wore jeans, a T-shirt, and boots and it occurred to her that, with his blond hair and blue eyes, he looked an awful lot like Brad Pitt.

"Ready?" he asked.

"Yep, just let me get my jacket."

"Jacket?"

"It gets mighty cold in the theater sometimes. Come on in. I won't be a minute."

She left Bryan in the living room while she ran upstairs to her bedroom to get her jacket.

And almost ran into Dominic. She looked up at

him, one hand pressed to her heart. "Dominic! What are you doing here?"

"What is *he* doing here?"

"Who? Oh, Bryan. We're going to the movies."

"You're dating that boy?" he asked incredulously.

She lifted her chin defiantly, though she was trembling inwardly, frightened by the intensity in his eyes. "Yes."

He took a step forward. "You are mine. I will not share you with another."

"I am not yours." Anger replaced her earlier fear.

He took another step forward, and now he was towering over her, his hands clenched into tight fists at his sides, his gray eyes smoldering with barely suppressed rage.

"Listen, Dominic, I know you think you have some sort of prior claim on me or something, but you're wrong. I don't believe all that reincarnation mumbo jumbo. And even if I did, none of that matters now. I'm not any of those other people, not anymore. Now, if you'll excuse me, Bryan is waiting."

Gathering her courage, she grabbed her jacket off the bed and swept past him. She could feel his eyes burning into her back as she left the room.

Bryan was waiting for her on the sofa downstairs. Grabbing him by the hand, she pulled him to his feet.

"Come on," she said, "we don't want to be late."

Dominic stared after her. She had ever been a fiery wench, but never before had she defied him so openly. He was tempted to go downstairs and let her see the full force of his wrath; instead, he took a deep breath and let it out in a heavy sigh. He could always kill the boy later, if necessary.

Gathering his power around him like a cloak, he vanished from the house. He was sorely tempted to follow Tracy, to torment himself by watching her laugh and smile at another man, but to do so would only add fuel to the rage seething inside. Better to take himself far away from her before his jealousy got the best of him, before the beast that dwelled deep within him escaped his control. Should that happen, the boy would surely die.

A thought took him into the city where he prowled the streets, feeding the hunger that would not be ignored. But there was no relief from the jealousy that plagued him, no respite from the anger churning in his gut.

He slammed his hand against a wall, watched the stones turn to dust beneath the force of his blow. She was his! What right did she have to turn her back on him for some foolish mortal boy? He had followed her throughout time, waiting, always waiting, for her to realize that they were meant to be together.

This time, he vowed, this time he would not lose her.

"Well, that was one of the worst movies I've ever seen," Tracy said as they left the theater. "Who would have thought that a brilliant director and two sexy actors could turn out such junk?"

"I guess you didn't like it," Bryan said dryly.

"Did you?"

"Well . . . I didn't think it was all that bad. The car chases were great. Do you want to go have some coffee?"

"Sure."

They walked across the street to a small café and ordered coffee and apple pie.

"Car chases," Tracy said with a huff of annoyance. "That's all movies are these days, car chases and special effects and remakes of stupid TV shows."

Bryan laughed. "Come on, they're not all bad."

They discussed movies over pie and coffee, and then Bryan drove her home.

"I had a good time tonight," Bryan said as he walked her to her door.

"Me, too." She looked up at him, thinking what a handsome young man he was, wishing he were older, more settled, wondering if he would kiss her. She had truly enjoyed being out with him. Unlike Dominic, Bryan had no dark secrets. He was honest and open.

His gaze met hers. Whispering her name, he lowered his head and kissed her.

It was a chaste kiss, warm and sweet, one with no demands, no expectations. She thought of Dominic's kisses, filled with fire and passion, then thrust the thought away.

"I'll call you tomorrow, okay?" Bryan asked.

"Okay."

He smiled at her, revealing the dimple in his cheek. "Good night, Tracy."

"Nite, Bry."

She watched him walk down the steps and open the car door. He blew her a kiss before sliding behind the wheel.

He really was a nice boy.

She was smiling when she unlocked the door and went into the living room.

She stopped smiling when she saw Dominic standing in front of the fireplace, his arms folded across his chest, his face like something set in stone.

"Am I late, Dad?" She forced a teasing note into her voice, hoping he wouldn't hear the fear beneath.

"He kissed you."

She tilted her head to one side. "So?"

"You are mine, Tracy. I do not want another man's hands on you. I do not want to smell his touch on your skin."

"Then don't." She stared at him, her heart pounding. Was she mad to defy him like this? Anger radiated from him like heat from a forest fire. She didn't believe for a minute that he was actually a vampire, but he was a man, a big man, one capable of doing her great bodily harm if she pushed him too far. "I'm sorry," she said contritely. "Would you like a cup of coffee?"

"I do not drink coffee."

"Milk? Tea? Hot chocolate?"

"No."

"Well, I'm sorry, but I'm all out of fresh blood."

"Do not mock me."

His eyes narrowed as his gaze moved to the pulse throbbing in her throat. Maybe it was only her imagination, but she would have sworn she could feel his fingertips caressing her neck, feel his breath on her cheek, followed by the heat of his mouth and the sharp prick of his teeth. . . .

She jerked her head up and the sensation disappeared. "I think you'd better go."

"Do not see that boy again."

"Don't tell me what to do!" So much for being meek and lowly. "I'll see whoever I wish, whenever I wish."

He took a step forward. "If you see him again, I will not be responsible for what happens."

"Is that a threat?"

"No, my best beloved one, it is a warning. If you care for the boy, you would be wise to listen."

The look in his eyes, the soft menace in his voice, sent a shiver of unease down her spine. Even though he wasn't a vampire, it occurred to her that he would be a very dangerous man to run afoul of.

"You still do not believe me," he murmured. "Perhaps this will convince you."

Before she could ask what he meant, he was engulfed in a sort of silvery haze and then, between one heartbeat and the next, he was gone and in his place she saw a fine gray mist.

She felt the blood drain from her face. This was not some hypnotic suggestion, not some magician's trick done with mirrors. It was the same silvery haze she had seen that night in the kitchen.

The mist swirled around her ankles, drifted upward until it surrounded her like a cold gray fog.

"Stop it!"

The sound of her voice had barely died away when he stood before her once more.

With a bravado she did not truly feel, she said, "Can you turn into a bat, too?"

"You still do not believe?" he murmured, and before she knew what he was doing, he had pulled her against him.

The next thing she knew, she was standing in a dark alley watching Dominic. Watching him lift a homeless man out of his ragged blankets and into his arms. Watching his fangs lengthen. The man struggled a moment, then went limp. Dominic bent over the man's neck and when he lifted his head, his fangs were stained with blood.

"Now?" he asked quietly. "Now do you believe?"

She stared at him in horror and then, for the third time in her life, she fainted.

Chapter 9

Dominic caught her in his arms and willed them back to Nightingale House. Upstairs, he sat on the edge of her bed and cradled her against his chest. Amazing, he thought. No matter her shape or form, she always fit in his embrace as if she had been made for him, as if she were the other half of his body, the missing half of his soul.

He studied her face, the gentle arch of her brows, the dark sweep of her lashes against her cheeks, the tempting shape of her lips, the slight cleft in her chin, the slender column of her neck.

The pulse beating there. Though he had fed earlier, the hunger stirred within him, stretching like a big cat awaking from sleep, its claws raking his insides.

He took a deep breath and his nostrils filled with her scent—perfume and shampoo and toothpaste. He could detect the boy's touch on her skin. And, over all, the tantalizing smell of her blood, rich and red, flowing through her veins.

His fangs lengthened.

His arms tightened around her as he lowered his head.

Just one taste. Surely, after so many centuries, he deserved just one taste.

He ran his tongue over the skin below her ear, growled low in his throat as he jerked his head up. He had vowed he would never take her by force, never take her unawares. He swore softly. Whether he took a single sip of her blood or brought her into his world, it had to be her decision, her choice.

Rising, he pulled back the covers and laid her down on the mattress. After drawing the blankets up over her, he smoothed a lock of hair from her brow, then bent and brushed a kiss across her lips.

Murmuring, "Sweet dreams, my best beloved one," he vanished from the room.

She woke to the ringing of the phone beside the bed. Still groggy, she grabbed the receiver to make the ringing stop. "Hello?"

"Hi, Tracy, it's Bryan. Did I wake you?"

"Uh-huh."

"Oh, sorry. I thought you'd be up by now. I was wondering if you'd be coming down to the beach today?"

She blinked the sleep from her eyes and tried to focus on the clock. Noon! She never slept this long.

She was about to tell him she would meet him there in an hour when Dominic's warning rippled through her mind. *If you see him again, I will not be responsible for what happens.* She wasn't sure if Dominic would actually carry out his threat, but she wasn't willing to find out.

"Tracy?"

"I don't think so. I've got some work to do."

"All right," he said, the disappointment evident in his tone, "maybe some other time."

"Have a good day, Bryan."

"Yeah, thanks—you, too."

Feeling like she'd just ripped the wings off of a baby bird, Tracy hung up the receiver.

Feeling numb, she stared up at the ceiling. Dominic was a vampire. She couldn't deny it any longer, not after what she had seen last night.

There was only one thing to do, and now was the time to do it. Scrambling out of bed, she took a quick shower. After dressing in a pair of jeans and a T-shirt, she threw some clothes in a suitcase, packed up her toiletries, then gathered up her paints, an easel, and several blank canvases. It took several trips to carry everything down to her car. Going back to the house, she filled an ice chest with ice, then loaded it with the perishables from the fridge. She dropped a loaf of bread, a box of crackers, a box of cereal, some canned goods and a couple of candy bars into a grocery sack, then carried the ice chest and the sack out to the car, as well.

She walked through the house one last time. Seeing her laptop, she decided to take it along. After making sure everything was turned off, she locked the place up and drove away. Her first instinct was to go home to her folks, but after a moment's thought, she knew she couldn't go there, couldn't take a chance that Dominic would follow her. She couldn't put the lives of her parents at risk. So, she just drove away, heading north. She wasn't sure where she was going, just some place far, far away, some place where he would never find her.

By late afternoon, she had left her house, the ocean, and, hopefully, Dominic, far behind.

At dusk, she pulled into a restaurant for dinner, then found a nearby motel where she could spend the night.

Inside, she locked the door behind her, then dropped her suitcase on one of the twin beds. There was something about motel rooms that she found depressing. This one was no different from most: twin beds covered with dark green spreads, drapes heavily lined for those who wanted to sleep during the day, a TV set bolted to the wall, an ugly, nondescript carpet on the floor.

She switched on the TV, flipped through the channels until she found an old Tom Hanks movie, and turned the sound down low. *The Money Pit* had always been one of her favorites and she sat down on the edge of the bed and lost herself in the antics of Hanks and Shelley Long. She even found herself laughing out loud once or twice.

When the movie was over, she went into the bathroom and turned on the tap in the bathtub. She felt a shiver of unease when she looked out the bathroom window and saw that it was dark out. Dominic would be stirring now. How long until he discovered she wasn't home? How long before he realized she wasn't coming back?

She put her hair into a ponytail, tossed her clothes on the floor, and stepped into the tub. Lying back, with her eyes closed, she let her mind drift.

She tried to blink back her tears as she smoothed the collar of her son's uniform. He was so young, barely sixteen.

He smiled at her and for a moment it wasn't her

grown son looking at her, but the little boy he had once been. "How do I look, Ma?"

"Mighty handsome." She stroked his cheek. "Mighty handsome. Promise me you'll be careful."

"Ma . . ."

"Promise me, Jacob. Indulge your poor old mother."

"I'll be careful, Ma, don't worry. We'll whip those Yanks in a week, you'll see.""

She could hear the eagerness in his voice, see it in his eyes. "I've gotta go, Ma. Tom's waiting."

Tom Myles was Jacob's best friend. They had grown up together, played together. It was only fitting that they would go off to war together.

She followed him out onto the verandah, blinked back her tears as he mounted his grandfather's horse.

"Make us proud, son," his grandfather said, handing Jacob the reins.

"I will, Gramps."

Charles shook hands with his grandson and with Tom, then climbed the steps to stand beside her, one arm draped across her shoulders.

Forcing a smile, she waved to her son, unable to shake the awful foreboding that she would never see him again this side of heaven.

They stood there until the boys were out of sight, then Charles went inside, leaving her to stand there alone, her heart breaking.

Dominic came to her that night. Knowing that there were no words that would comfort her, he took her into his arms and held her close, one hand stroking her hair. The tears came then, flooding her eyes, soaking his ruffled shirt front. She cried until she felt hollow inside, until there were no tears left.

"Libby, come away with me," he said. "We can go north. You'll be safe there, with me."

*She shook her head. "I can't. I have to be here when . . ."
She swallowed hard. "I have to be here when Jacob comes
home."*

*He didn't argue; instead, he took her by the hand and
they walked down the tree-lined path that circled the
main house. The air was heavy with the scent of honey-
suckle and magnolias. If she tried hard enough, she
could pretend that nothing had changed, that there was
no war.*

*When they were out of sight of the house, Dominic
drew her into his embrace again, not as a friend this
time, but as the man who loved her. To her shame, she
went into his arms willingly. He was her only comfort,
the only security in a world gone mad, and she clung to
him with mindless desperation while he held her and stroked
her. It was wrong, so wrong. Her husband, Warren, had
been dead less than two years and now her son had gone
to war. But, right or wrong, she needed Dominic, needed
his strength.*

*She rested her cheek against his chest, remembering the
night they had met three years ago. She had been at a
cotillion with her husband when she looked up and saw
a tall, dark stranger with piercing gray eyes watching her.
She had stared at him, bemused by the feeling that she
had met him before—though of course that was impossible. She would never have forgotten a man like that. He
lifted one dark brow under her frank regard, then sketched
a bow in her direction.*

*She had been appalled when he asked her to dance.
She was a married woman. He was a stranger. Warren
had started to protest but she had waved off his objections, saying they must make the newcomer welcome in
their midst.*

*They danced together as though they had done it for
years, fit together as though they had been molded one for
the other.*

They had said little but there was no need for words. When the music ended he had escorted her back to her husband, bowed over her hand, and bid her good evening. They had both known they would meet again. And they had. He seemed always to know when Warren was away from the plantation. He came to her always in the dark of night, appearing out of the shadows as if he were a part of the darkness itself. He spoke to her of faraway places, read poetry to her, brought her gifts—a hat from Paris, a bit of silk from the Orient, a pair of tortoiseshell combs for her hair, a book of Shakespeare's plays, a silver-backed comb and brush, a gold heart on a fine gold chain. She felt guilty for accepting his gifts, yet she could not refuse.

He was there to comfort her when her mother passed away from a fever. He was there to hold her when Warren was swept away while trying to save one of the Negro children from drowning in the river.

And he was here tonight, when she needed him most.

"I'll never see Jacob again."

"Libby, you cannot know that. Even I cannot foretell the future."

"I know." She lifted a hand to her heart, a heart that was slowly breaking. "In here."

"Then come away with me, my best beloved one. Now. Tonight. Charles can run the plantation. There is no need for you to stay."

She looked up at him, tears stinging her eyes once again. "Don't you understand? I have to be here for . . . for Jacob when he . . . when he comes home. Later, when he doesn't need me anymore, then . . ." She looked up at Dominic and dissolved into tears.

"As you wish," he said, drawing her body close to his. "I will not force you, or rush you." He stroked her cheek with his knuckles. "I will wait as long as it takes, my best beloved one, should it take a year or an eternity."

They had neither. The war grew more intense. Times grew hard, but not for Libby or those she was responsible for. Dominic managed to find food and fuel and clothing. More than once, he was there to defend them against the enemy.

But he wasn't there the afternoon the raiders came. They stormed through the house, carrying away the silver, Warren's rifle, and whatever else caught their fancy.

Libby drew back in horror as one of the raiders burst into her bedroom, his intent clear in his eyes. She had fought him with all her strength but it had not been enough and when she knew he meant to defile her, she made a frantic grab for the gun holstered at his side. They struggled over the weapon and somehow the gun went off.

The pain was like being hit by a sledge hammer. It drove her backward, knocking the breath from her lungs. At first, she hadn't known what it meant. And then she had seen the horror in the raider's eyes as he scuttled off the bed and stared down at her.

"I'm sorry," he mumbled drunkenly. "I never . . . I didn't mean to . . ." Face pale, he had run out of the room and left her there.

Staring at the blood slowly spreading over her bodice, she had called for Charles, for Pansy, for Bedelia, but no one answered her call. Murmuring Jacob's name, she slid into oblivion.

When she woke, Dominic was holding her in his arms. In her weakened state, she had imagined that his eyes were red. She tried to say his name, but she was too weak.

"Libby. Can you hear me? Libby!"

She wanted to comfort him. His voice was filled with such pain, such grief, but she was too weak to lift her hand, too weak even to say his name.

"Come to me," he said.

She stared at him, not comprehending.

With a low growl, his lips drew back.

She stared at him in helpless horror as he ripped open his wrist and held it toward her.

"Drink," he said. "It will preserve your life until I can bring you across."

"No." She mouthed the word but no sound emerged from her lips.

"Drink." It was a command now. "Drink, Libby. I cannot lose you again!"

Somehow, she found the strength to murmur, "What are you?"

"I will explain it all to you later," he said urgently. "Now you must drink before it is too late.!"

But she had lost too much blood. "It wasn't Jacob's death I saw," she said, her voice tinged with wonder. "It was my own. . . ."

She stared up at Dominic, no longer frightened by his dark mien, no longer frightened of anything. His image paled, the room faded as she stared toward a light that grew brighter, brighter.

His voice, crying her name, was the last thing she heard. . . .

She woke to the echo of her own voice crying his name. She shivered, and not just because the water had grown cold.

Stepping out of the tub, she dried off quickly, pulled on her nightgown, and crawled into bed, only to lie there awake, afraid to close her eyes, afraid to sleep, afraid to dream.

What if it was true? Oh lord, what if it was all true?

Chapter 10

He knew she wasn't at home as soon as he woke from the dark sleep. He could feel the house's emptiness, the lack of life. Where was she?

Fueled by anger and jealousy, Dominic surged to his feet. If she had defied him, if she had dared to go out with that boy again . . . what would he do? Much as it might please him to do so, killing the young upstart would not win Tracy's affection.

After changing his clothes, he went into the city to satisfy his thirst. It wouldn't do to approach Tracy when the urge to feed was clawing at him.

It was Friday night and the streets were crowded with tourists taking in the sights, young lovers holding hands, teenagers with spiked hair and trendy clothes. Dominic shook his head. How times and fashions had changed!

He took a deep breath, his senses quickening when he scented his prey, a pretty young girl hurrying down the street, a bag from a popular clothing store swinging from her arm.

He moved up beside her, measuring his steps to hers.

She glanced at him, her eyes widening in alarm.

"Do not be afraid," he said, his voice low and hypnotic. "I am not going to hurt you."

"You're not?"

"No." He put his hand on her arm and guided her down a dimly lit side street.

"Where are we going?"

"Right here," he said. "There is nothing for you to be afraid of."

"Nothing to be afraid of," she repeated dully.

He tightened his grip on her arm, bringing her to a stop. "Close your eyes."

Mesmerized by his voice and the look in his eyes, she did as she was told.

Taking the bag from her arm, he placed it on the ground, then drew her into his arms, his embrace gentle. Humans were so very fragile, one had to be careful not to crush them, not to bruise them.

He drew a deep breath, breathing in her scent, letting it flow through him. An appetizer, so to speak. With his preternatural sense of smell, he caught every nuance—the lavender soap she had washed with, peppermint toothpaste, a slight hint of starch in her clothes mingled with a faint odor of cologne from the man she had been with earlier.

His fangs lengthened in response to her nearness, the pounding of her heart, the whisper of blood moving through her veins. Gently, he brushed her hair away from her neck.

And then he drank.

It was a pleasure like no other.

Warmth suffused him, spreading through him

like liquid sunshine, filling him with strength and power.

Even after all these centuries, the urge to take it all was strong but he was no longer a slave to his hunger, no longer helpless to resist the beast within. He took only what he needed, what he required to survive.

Five minutes later, the woman was back on the street with no memory of what had happened.

With preternatural speed, Dominic returned to Nightingale House.

The boy was standing on the front porch, a box of candy in one hand, the other raised to knock on the door, when Dominic arrived.

Slowing, Dominic walked up the driveway toward him.

The boy—Bryan—turned at his approach. "I don't think she's home."

"Did you have an appointment?"

"No." Bryan shook his head. "I was just hoping to see her." His eyes widened. "Damn, did you two have a date for tonight?"

"Not exactly."

"Well, I've been knocking for five minutes," Bryan said. "If she's here, she's not answering the door. Maybe she just doesn't want to see me."

Dominic closed his eyes, let his preternatural senses explore the house. A fine anger rose within him when he opened his eyes to find the boy still there. "Go home. She is not here."

"Oh. Well." The boy cleared his throat. "I guess I'll go then. If you see her, tell her I'll call her to-morrow."

"I will see her," Dominic said, and there was no room for doubt in his tone.

"Yeah. Well." The boy cleared his throat again, then rushed down the stairs.

Dominic watched him toss the box of candy into the back seat, then climb into an old Chevy convertible and drive away far faster than was safe. But he had no thought for the boy's welfare. His every thought was for Tracy.

Where was she?

Chapter 11

Tracy rose after a restless night. If she dreamed, she didn't remember doing so. Dressing quickly, she checked out of the motel, then stopped at a nearby café for breakfast.

She felt more relaxed this morning. Fears were always less scary in the light of day; there was comfort in the presence of other people. And, if Dominic was really a vampire, he wouldn't come out during the day. She blew out a sigh. There was no *if*. She'd seen too much to deny the truth any longer.

She ate a leisurely breakfast—hot cakes smothered in butter and syrup, bacon and scrambled eggs. She didn't often indulge in such things but this morning, it seemed right.

After leaving the café, she stopped at the grocery store to pick up a few snacks and sodas for the road, filled up the gas tank, then turned onto the freeway, heading north. She turned the radio on to her favorite country station and settled back for a day of driving. Perhaps she'd go to Canada, she thought. Maybe she would meet one of those sexy Mounties and settle down and raise a family in the great northwest.

Dominic rose the instant the sun slid behind the horizon. Dressing quickly, he materialized in the house above.

Standing in the center of the living room floor, he let his senses sweep through the house. She wasn't home. He sniffed the air. She had not come home last night.

Where was she? He cursed softly. Had he not respected her wishes all these centuries, had he taken her blood as he so longed to do, there would now be a bond between them, a connection that would lead him to her with no more than a thought.

Going upstairs, he went into her bedroom. Her closet door was open. Most of her clothing was gone.

Jaw clenched, he went to her studio. If he needed further proof that she was gone, he found it here. Though several canvases remained, including the painting she had done of him, her painting supplies were missing.

She had run away. Run away from him. Anger burned through him as he flew down the stairs and out of the house.

Standing in the driveway, he unleashed his senses. It was easy to pluck her scent from the air, to follow the near invisible tracks of her car's tires.

"You will not escape me so easily," he murmured.

And dissolving into a fine gray mist, he followed her trail.

To the freeway.

To the motel where she had spent the night.

To the café where she had eaten breakfast.

To the grocery store, the gas station, and back to the freeway.

And, at last, to the motel where she slept, unaware that he watched her.

Tracy woke slowly. Eyes closed, she stretched her arms and legs; then, with a yawn, she sat up. Time to hit the road again. She had covered several hundred miles before she stopped for the night. At this rate, she'd soon be crossing the Canadian border.

She frowned as she swung her legs over the edge of the bed. Something wasn't right.

The room wasn't right.

Rising, she padded across the floor and opened the drapes.

And looked out over a huge yard surrounded by an enormous wall.

Was she dreaming again? It was a silly question, and she knew it, but she pinched herself anyway. Ouch! She was definitely awake.

Fear was a cold, hard knot in her belly as she slowly turned and glanced around the room. It was large and square. There were tall, narrow windows set in three of the walls; the bed she had slept in took up most of the fourth. Several thick rugs covered the hardwood floor. There was an armoire in one corner, a small cherrywood dressing table and matching chair stood between one pair of windows. Her suitcase sat on the floor near the door.

Where was she?

And how had she gotten here?

She didn't like the answer that quickly came to mind.

She put on a pair of jeans and a sweater over her

nightgown, then went to the door and tried the latch, surprised when it opened. Stepping through the doorway, she found herself in a long, dark corridor. Her bare feet made no sound on the dark red runner as she tiptoed toward the head of the stairs and peered over the railing. She listened for a moment and then, convinced there was no one there, she tiptoed down the winding staircase and hurried toward the front door.

It didn't appear to be locked, but it wouldn't open.

Frowning, she wandered from room to room, opening the draperies as she went.

The house was bigger than any she had ever seen, including her own. There was a living room with a big stone fireplace, a huge dining room, a library whose walls were lined with shelves filled with books, a large room with a polished oak floor—a ballroom, perhaps? She wandered through the kitchen and pantry, noting they were both stocked with food. There was a music room that held a very old piano, a violin, and a harp. There was another room she thought might be the solarium.

She tried every door, every window—they refused to open. Were they locked from the outside?

Was this place some sort of *Twilight Zone* bed and breakfast?

Going back upstairs, she poked her head into the rooms that lined the corridor. They were all bedrooms or sitting rooms furnished with antique oak furniture. She was glad to see that the house seemed to have all the modern conveniences, except a telephone. And mirrors, she thought, frowning. She didn't recall seeing a single mirror in the whole place.

The last room she looked into seemed very much

like her studio at home. It contained a long table, a half-dozen empty jars and cans, a small box of rags, a couple of easels, and several blank canvases in a variety of sizes. The case that held her paints and brushes sat just inside the door, along with the blank canvases and the easel she had brought from home.

Returning to the room she had awakened in, she sat on the edge of the bed. How was she going to get out of here? She hit her head with the heel of her hand. Her cell phone! Why hadn't she thought of it sooner?

Grabbing her bag, she rummaged inside, only it wasn't there. Whoever had brought her here must have taken it.

With a sigh, she tossed her bag aside and glanced at her surroundings. It was a pretty room. The walls were covered in old-fashioned paper with pink cabbage roses. The ceiling was high; painted angels and nymphs smiled down at her. There were wrought-iron candelabras on the walls, a small Tiffany lamp on the cherrywood table beside the bed. The bedspread was a deep, dusky rose, as were the heavy draperies at the windows.

Hunger drove her downstairs once again. In the kitchen, she went through the cupboards. They were fully stocked with canned goods, bread, crackers, Jell-O, cake mix, a dozen brands of cereal, hot fudge, marshmallows, flour, sugar, salt and pepper, spices and condiments, a wide variety of candy bars, and practically anything else she could possibly want, including the items she'd had in her car.

The refrigerator held milk, cream, butter, sodas, lunch meat, and several kinds of cheese; the freezer was filled with meat, frozen vegetables, and three kinds of ice cream.

At least she wouldn't starve to death.

But where the devil was she?

And who had brought her here?

She couldn't believe that someone could have taken her out of the motel room and transported her here without waking her. Nevertheless, here she was. Which brought her back to her original question.

Where was she?

After eating a bowl of cereal and sliced peaches, she went through the house once again, trying every door and window, but to no avail. In the living room, she picked up an iron poker, turned her face away, and swung the poker at the window. The glass should have shattered, but nothing happened.

She stood there for several minutes and then, resigned to the fact that there was no way out, she went into the library, found a copy of *Wuthering Heights,* and curled up in a chair. She spent the rest of the morning reading the bittersweet love story of Cathy and Heathcliff.

After lunch, she went upstairs, laid out her paint brushes, set up a canvas, and spent the rest of the afternoon painting the view out her bedroom window.

It was only when the sun began to set that fear once again began to make itself known.

She wasn't surprised when Dominic appeared in the doorway. He wore a long black cloak over a black shirt and black trousers. His feet were encased in soft black leather boots. Though she had refused to admit it, she had known, on some deep level of awareness, that this was his house.

He inclined his head in her direction. "Good evening. I trust you found everything you needed."

"Yes." Her fingers clenched around the brush. It

was hard to speak past the lump of fear in her throat. "Thank you." Though why she should thank him was beyond her. He had brought her here without her consent, after all.

He took a step into the room.

She took a step back.

He lifted one brow. "Are you afraid of me now?"

"How did I get here? Why am I here?"

"I brought you here because I wanted you here."

"Why didn't I wake up?"

"Because I did not wish you to."

The fear in her throat moved downward and congealed in her stomach. She started to ask another question, but before she could form the words, he was standing in front of her, only inches away. She gasped, startled. She hadn't seen him move.

"I will not hurt you, my best beloved one."

"Where are we?"

"This is my house."

"But where are we?"

"Ah. We are in a distant corner of Maine."

"So, I'm your prisoner now."

"You are my guest."

"A guest who can't leave. Sounds like prison to me."

"We need time to get to know each other again. I will not be shut out of your life this time. I will not share you with another. This time, you will believe. This time, you will be mine."

"So you're going to keep me locked up inside this house?" She stared down at her hands, noticing, for the first time, that she was holding the brush so tightly, her knuckles were white. "And what if I believe and I still don't want you? Still don't want to be what you say you are?"

"Then I will let you go."

"Why won't the doors or windows open?"

"Because I did not wish them to, but they will open for you now."

"Did you take my phone?"

"Yes."

There was no need to ask why.

She glared at him, angry and more than a little frightened.

Gently, he took the paint brush from her hand and dropped it into a can of turpentine. "Come," he said quietly, "walk with me."

Though it sounded like an invitation, she knew she had no choice. When he offered her his hand, she took it. Together, they walked down the stairs. The front door opened at a wave of his hand and they stepped outside.

The night was cool and clear. A full moon hung low in the sky, bathing the trees and flowers in a wash of silver. Electric lights illuminated a flagstone path that led around the side of the house and through a wrought iron gate that opened into an enormous yard. Tall trees grew in the distance. Closer at hand were flower beds filled with roses and shrubs. There were trees cut into a variety of shapes: a bear standing with one paw raised, a unicorn looking over its shoulder, an elephant standing on its hind legs, a giraffe, a whale, a seal, a dragon. There were a number of fruit trees and, further down the path, a small natural pond. A large gazebo stood in the middle of the yard, surrounded by rose bushes. A high wall surrounded the yard and the house. She made note of the trees that grew near the wall. It wouldn't be too difficult to shinny up one of the trees and climb over the wall.

Dominic's hand tightened on hers. "The wall is electrified. To discourage vandals."

Tracy looked at him sharply. Was he reading her mind?

"There is nothing beyond the wall save a large forest," Dominic went on. "The nearest house is thirty miles away."

"If you live here, why were you staying at Nightingale House?"

"I did not say I lived here. Only that it belongs to me."

"And what am I supposed to do here? Oh! The seascape! I'm supposed to ship it to Mr. Petersen next week."

"I will take care of it."

"But . . ."

"I will take care of it."

"His address is in my book."

He nodded.

"How long are you going to keep me here?"

He shrugged. "That remains to be seen."

She looked up at him and their gazes met and locked. A shiver of anticipation ran down her spine as he moved toward her, one arm curling around her waist to draw her up against him. He was going to kiss her—she knew it. Well, she had no intention of kissing him, not while he was keeping her here against her will. No way!

She put her hands against his chest to push him away, but it was like trying to move a block of granite.

Gently, he caught both her hands in his, and then he placed one finger beneath her chin and tilted her head back to give him better access to her lips. She started to object but before she could form the words, he kissed her, driving all thought of protest from her mind.

Tracy's eyelids fluttered down as his mouth covered hers. Whatever else he might be, the man knew how to kiss. Had she always responded like this, always felt as if her bones were melting, as if her blood was on fire? She pressed herself against him, a sense of feminine satisfaction flowing through her when she felt his response to her nearness.

He broke the kiss briefly, then claimed her lips once again, more aggressively this time. His tongue teased the seam of her lips until, with a sigh, she opened for him.

She moaned softly, all thought fleeing her mind. There was only Dominic, his tongue exploring her mouth, his hands moving over her back, her breasts, lightly massaging her belly, making her burn like a fire out of control. He released her hands and she wrapped her arms around him, her body intimately molded to his, certain she would fall if he let her go.

Faint images whispered through her mind. It took her a moment to realize they were fragments of his life. She saw him as a young boy tending sheep on the side of a grassy hill. He was tall, even then, his skin dark, his hair long. He sat on a rock holding a small black lamb in his arms. In the distance, she saw a hut with a thatched roof. The scene changed and he was strolling down a cobblestone street with two other young men. They were laughing as they walked along. The scene changed yet again, and Dominic was seated at a small table in what looked like an inn. A woman sat beside him, a beautiful woman with long red hair and skin that was almost translucent. The woman smiled at him, a come-hither look in her dark eyes, and Dominic followed her out of the inn. The scene changed yet again and she saw the two of them sharing an embrace in a dimly lit room, saw the woman's lips draw back to reveal a pair of small white fangs. . . .

Startled by what she saw, Tracy drew back, frowning.

Dominic looked down at her, askance.

She shook her head in wonder. "I . . . I saw you . . ."

He lifted one brow. "Saw me? Where?"

"You were a little boy holding a lamb . . . a young man laughing with two other men." She swallowed hard. "I saw you with a woman. A beautiful woman with red hair . . ."

"Kitana."

"She bit you."

"Aye, she did indeed."

"She was a vampire?"

There was a wrought iron bench under one of the trees. Dominic sat down, and after a moment, Tracy sat beside him.

"I had just turned twenty-five when I met her," he said. "Until then, I had done little, seen little. I knew nothing of the world beyond our little village, had no ambition other than to tend the sheep with my father. It was not a bad life. I had a few friends, and I had met a woman I planned to marry. And then I met Kitana. She was a wild Gypsy woman, more beautiful than any creature I had ever seen. She tempted me beyond all reason and I was suddenly filled with a restlessness I did not understand. And then one night she asked me to go away with her. She said she could arrange it so that I could be what she was, promised that I could live with her forever, if that was what I desired. I said yes without a moment's thought. Naïve as I was, I thought she meant I would be as wild and free-spirited as she. I had no idea then what she really was, or what being like her entailed."

"So, you're saying she was a vampire?"

He nodded. "Yes. She was very old, and very powerful."

"Did it hurt? Becoming a vampire?"

"The bite did not hurt. What came later was . . . frightening, more than anything else, though she could have made it easier for me."

"What came later?"

"What difference does it make, if you do not believe?"

"What happened to her? To Kitana?"

"We spent many years together and then one night I woke up and she was gone. It was while I was looking for her that I found you the first time. I knew the moment I saw you that we were fated to be together."

"How did you find me in all those other lives you claim I've had?"

"I do not know how to explain it, but somehow, sooner or later, I am drawn to where you are." He smiled faintly. "But this time, it seems, you were drawn to me."

She didn't want to think about what that might mean. "Did you ever see Kitana again?"

"From time to time."

"Why did she leave you?"

"She found another young man. I imagine the world is filled with those she has brought over and abandoned." He did not tell her that once Kitana had tired of her young man, she had come to him again, wanting to take up where they had left off. They had not parted on the best of terms. He had told her it was over between them. She had vowed that one day she would bring him to his knees.

"You're saying there are hundreds of vampires running around sucking people dry and no one knows?"

He laughed softly. "It is easy to pass among mortals. They do not want to believe vampires exist and so they dismiss the little things they see that are beyond their comprehension. As for sucking people dry, that is rarely done these days except by overeager fledglings who cannot control their hunger."

"Did you . . . have you ever . . . done that?"

"Not for many years."

Tracy gazed out over the gardens. They were beautiful, even in the moonlight. The air was fragrant with the scents of earth and grass, trees and flowers. It was beyond bizarre to be sitting here having such an outlandish conversation. With a vampire.

"Where do you sleep?"

He pressed a kiss to her palm. "That is one question I cannot answer."

She regarded him curiously. "Why not?"

"There is no need for you to know."

"Don't you trust me?"

"Should I?"

"I don't see why not. I knew where you . . . where you slept at Nightingale House."

"Indeed."

"Are you afraid I might . . . let's see, what are the ways to destroy a vampire?" She frowned, trying to remember how it was done in the movies. "You can cut out its heart, or chop off its head, or burn it up. Isn't that right?"

"It?" he asked with a wounded expression. "Do I look like an 'it' to you?"

He didn't kiss like an 'it'! Oh, no, he was all man

in that regard. "Don't change the subject," she admonished. "Let's see, what am I forgetting? Oh, the ever popular stake through the heart."

"Shall I hide the axe and the matches?"

"No need," she said, laughing in spite of herself. "I couldn't dissect a frog in biology class. I think you're safe from me."

He laughed with her.

Warmth passed between them, bringing with it a sense of camaraderie from shared laughter.

His gaze rested on her lips again.

Her heart seemed to skip a beat.

Before she succumbed to the look in his eyes and the yearning of her own heart, she said, "What's it like for you, during the day? What happens when the sun comes up?"

"The sun steals a vampire's strength. We are overcome with a lethargy that is, in the beginning, impossible to resist. We sleep the sleep of, you will pardon the expression, the dead."

"And if someone found you while you were asleep, what then?"

"Very young vampires are totally helpless when the sun is up. After many centuries, some vampires are able to stay up after sunrise and rise before sunset."

"Can you?"

"Yes, though my powers are weak until after dark."

"And if someone invaded your resting place, would you know? Would you be able to protect yourself?"

He nodded. "Self-preservation is as strong with us as with anyone."

"Has anyone ever tried to . . . to destroy you while you were at rest?"

"Yes."

"What did you do to them?"

He did not answer, only gazed at her through fathomless gray eyes.

"You killed them, didn't you?"

"Should I have let them destroy me?"

"No, of course not." She smiled faintly. "It was self-defense, after all." She didn't ask how many times he had defended himself, didn't want to know how many men or women he had killed to defend his life or to satisfy his thirst.

Silence settled between them. Tracy was keenly aware of Dominic's presence beside her. Their conversation, while interesting, had been quite disconcerting. Feeling a sudden need to change the subject, she asked him how she was supposed to pass the time.

"In any way you wish. Paint. Read. Walk in the gardens. If there is anything you want or need, you have only to let me know."

"And you'll get it for me? Kind of like my own personal Santa Claus?"

"If you wish to think of it like that, yes."

Tracy smothered a yawn behind her hand. Though it was still early, she was suddenly sleepy.

Dominic stood and offered her his hand. "Come. You've had a long day, and much to think about."

Chapter 12

Much to think about was putting it mildly, Tracy mused as she lay in bed with the covers pulled up to her chin later that night. She had locked her door even though she knew it would not keep Dominic out. She was completely at his mercy here, in this house. He could take her blood or her virtue and she would be helpless to stop him. He could keep her here for as long as she lived, and no one would ever know what had happened to her. It surprised her that she wasn't afraid of him, but then, he had never done her any harm.

Still, she couldn't stop tossing and turning. She didn't know whether it was the strange house, the strange bed, or the fact that there was a vampire downstairs, but sleep eluded her.

Finally, she slipped out of bed, drew a comforter around her shoulders, and curled up in the window-seat. She stared out the window, her mind replaying the conversation she'd had with Dominic earlier. It was beyond belief that he had existed for so long, or that she had lived many lives.

So, if he was truly a vampire, and she had little doubt now that he was, what was it like for him never to grow old, to watch the world change and evolve while he always stayed the same? What had it been like to watch her die in his arms time after time? For the first time, she considered how awful it must have been for him. If he loved her as he said he did, it must have been painful to tell her goodbye over and over again, unsettling to wonder if he would be able to find her when she was re-born. What had he done while waiting for her return? How much time passed between one lifetime and the next?

Questions, and each one more eerily weird than the last. Were the answers as bizarre?

A movement outside caught her eye and she lean-ed forward to get a better look. At first, she wasn't sure what she was looking at and then, when he moved out of the shadows, she realized that it was Dominic walking in the moonlight. His cloak bil-lowed behind him, stirred by the same breeze that whispered through the trees.

He moved fluidly, lightly, as though his feet barely touched the ground. And when he passed under one of the lamps, she saw that he cast no shadow. She rubbed her eyes and looked again. Everything in the yard cast a shadow on the ground, save Dominic.

After everything he had told her, after every-thing she had seen, it was that fact that convinced her of the truth once and for all.

* * *

He came to her the next night as soon as the sun was down. One minute she was alone and the next he was there, standing in the kitchen doorway, watching her dry the dishes.

She pressed a hand to her heart. "You startled me!"

"Forgive me."

She wiped the last dish and put it away; then, feeling slightly self-conscious for no reason that she could discern, she slipped past him and went into the living room. She sat down on the sofa, her heart skipping a beat when he sat beside her, close enough to touch.

"How did you spend your day?" he asked.

She shrugged. "I painted a little. I wandered around the yard. I finished reading *Wuthering Heights*. She regarded him for a moment. "I wondered where you were . . . sleeping. Is it like sleeping? Do you dream?"

"It is like death," he replied quietly. "There are no dreams. And yet . . ." And now it was his turn to regard her through narrowed eyes. "Back in Nightingale House, I dreamed of you."

"I saw you last night. You were walking in the gardens."

"Indeed?"

She nodded. "You had no shadow."

"Perhaps, like Peter Pan, I have merely lost it."

Tracy stared at him, then burst out laughing. Peter Pan! Now that was funny! And yet, they were very much alike. Like Pan, Dominic never aged.

"It's true, isn't it?" she said. "You really are a vampire."

He nodded.

"What did you do all those years when I was between lives and you were waiting for me to be . . . to be reborn?"

"I educated myself," he said, "over and over again. I traveled the world, learning to speak other languages so that I would be able to speak your language, whatever it might be. It was no easy thing, keeping up with the world. Vampires are reluctant to change. We try and cling to the life we knew before the change came upon us. But those who do not change do not endure. So many new inventions with every century. New languages. New countries. New ways of life. I came from a poor village. We raised sheep for a living." He laughed softly. "In my day, people rarely traveled beyond the place where they were born. Today, you can be across the world in a matter of hours. It is a remarkable time."

"You're the one who's remarkable. Don't you ever get tired of, well, of living?"

"Only when you are not in the world with me."

Sincere words, quietly spoken. They went straight to her heart.

"Dominic . . ." She lifted a hand to his cheek. His skin was cool beneath her fingertips.

He went utterly still at her touch. His eyes were focused on her face, his breathing suddenly shallow.

Slowly, she leaned forward and pressed her lips to his. Perhaps she could learn to love him as he deserved. One thing was certain—no man she had ever known had affected her the way he did. Never had she responded so quickly to another man's touch, or another man's kiss. Had her subconscious remembered him from the past even though she had not? Did her body yearn toward his because they had made love in other lives?

His arm slid around her waist to draw her closer and when she didn't resist, he deepened the kiss, stealing her breath away until all she could do was cling to him as the world slipped away and there was nothing left but Dominic's mouth on hers, his body pressing intimately against hers, his hand caressing her back, lightly skimming the outer curve of her breast.

His touch filled her with such pleasure it was almost painful and she moaned softly, a wordless plea for more, or less.

Dominic drew back, his gaze burning into hers, his body trembling with a deep-seated desire that was far more than the yearning for physical fulfillment.

Muttering an oath, he gained his feet. He stood there staring down at her, his eyes blazing. And then he was gone.

Tracy stared at the floor where he had been standing, flabbergasted by his sudden disappearance.

She took a deep breath. My, oh my, but that man knew how to kiss! If he had kissed her like that in any of her previous lives, it was no wonder she hadn't been able to resist his advances. To tell the truth, she was glad he had vanished when he did because she wasn't sure she would have been able to tell him no if things had gone any further. One thing was for certain—if any of her boyfriends in this lifetime had kissed her like that, she would have lost her virginity long ago.

Which left her wondering if she had said no to all the others just to surrender her virtue to a vampire. She shook her head in bewilderment, not certain if she felt like laughing or crying. She had refused to let him make her a vampire in all her past lives, and she wasn't about to let him make her one now, either. She really didn't know anything about vampires other than what she had seen in movies and the little Dominic had told her. Knowing Hollywood, she doubted if their portrayals of vampires were any more accurate than their portrayals of cowboys and Indians in the Old West.

So, where to find out the truth? Would Dominic answer her questions? If she had access to a telephone, she could hook up her laptop and do some research online, but for now that was out of the question.

Books? She thought of the library with its shelves and shelves of books. Would a vampire have research books on vampires? There was only one way to find out.

She went to the library first thing in the morning. The door opened on well-oiled hinges. Stepping inside, she opened the curtains wide. Sunlight poured into the room.

She had never before seen so many books, except in a library. A sliding ladder provided access to books on the top shelves.

She started in one corner of the room. There was no rhyme or reason to the arrangement of the books. Paperbacks were tucked in beside expensive volumes bound in leather. His taste in reading was varied, from Shakespeare and Steinbeck to Chaucer and Dickens, as well as novels by more contemporary authors. She found encyclopedias, dictionaries, books of poetry and limericks, and novels in just about every genre imaginable, from westerns to horror.

She was about to give up when she hit the jackpot. Located at the top of the last shelf were three rows of books, all of them having to do with vampires. Some were novels by Elrod, Huff, Yarbro, Hamilton, and Herter; some were research. She glanced over the titles: *The Complete Book of Vampires, V is for Vampire: An A to Z Guide to Everything Undead, The Vampire Encyclopedia, The Vampire Gallery,* and *Vampires, Restless Creatures of the Night.*

There were also a couple of books on Transylvanian-born Vlad Dracula, also known as Vlad the Impaler, who had killed thousands of people by impaling them on wooden poles, surely one of the most horrible deaths imaginable. In spite of his cruelty, he was hailed as a hero in Romania for defeating the Ottoman Turks.

She also found several editions of Bram Stoker's *Dracula.* It was said that while trying to find a model for his vampire, Stoker had come across the history of Vlad Dracula, who fit Stoker's vampire perfectly. Vlad had died under mysterious circumstances; he had been decapitated, and it was rumored that his body had never been found. She recalled hearing somewhere that Stoker's novel had never been out of print since it was first published in 1897.

Whether vampires were real or not, they certainly garnered their share of literature. Plucking several books from the shelf, she curled up on the sofa and began to read.

In the next few hours she discovered that, according to the books, a true vampire was a dead body. It wasn't a spirit or a ghost or a demon from hell. Some believed that vampires weren't human at all, but a separate and distinct species. Unless they met with some sort of fatal accident, like a stake through the heart, they were immortal. They needed the blood of the living to survive. They had superhuman strength and while they were helpless during the day, they were practically unstoppable at night. Of course, since they were already dead, they were naturally hard to kill. They lived in graves. They had the power to control animals and could even turn into bats or wolves or dissolve into mist. . . .

She shivered. She had seen that firsthand.

Around noon, she went into the kitchen and made herself a sandwich. She chewed thoughtfully, enjoying the taste of mayonnaise, tuna, tomato, and whole wheat bread. Did Dominic ever miss chewing? Did he miss the taste of solid food? Did he even remember what it had been like to sit at a table and eat a meal? Did he ever get tired of a warm liquid diet?

The thought soured her appetite and she threw the remaining few bites of her sandwich in the trash. After tidying up the kitchen, she went back to the library.

She supposed it was to be expected that the authors couldn't agree on vampire characteristics. Some books said that vampires had no reflection. Some said they did.

She tried to remember if she had ever seen Dominic's reflection in a mirror or window.

One book said vampires could not be active during the day. Another book said they could move about during the day or the night. The books also mentioned contemporary men and women who took on vampire characteristics—sleeping during the day, always wearing black, claiming to drink blood, and, in some cases, actually doing so.

She knew the books she was reading were based on conjecture and old myths and ancient tales; still, the more she read, the more fascinated she became. One book said that in Eastern Europe it was believed that vampires had two hearts or two souls and since one heart or one soul never died, the vampire was immortal. Other beliefs were that if a vampire wasn't found and killed immediately, it would first kill the members of its family, then kill the people in the town or village where he lived, and finally kill the animals. Another belief was that if a vampire could go undetected for seven years, it could travel to another country and become human again. It could marry and even have children, though the children were all doomed to become vampires when they died.

Closing the last book, she put it on the table, then leaned back in the chair and closed her eyes and tried to remember what she knew to be true about her own personal vampire. She never saw him during the day. He could dissolve into mist. He had transported her across country without her being aware of it. He seemed able to appear and disappear at will. He had put some sort of spell on the doors and windows. He cast no shadow. For some reason, that was the most disturbing thing of all.

It was a small house set deep in a dark wood. She lived there alone save for a gray cat and a one-legged crow. The townspeople were afraid of her, yet they came to her when they needed help, for her power to heal was known throughout the countryside. Some called her a healer. Some called her a witch. And a witch she was. It was a craft she had learned at her mother's knee. Some came to her seeking power or vengeance or riches, but those she turned away. Her magic was only for good, for finding that which was lost, for healing, for hope.

She had been alone the night he came to her, a tall,

dark man with piercing gray eyes. A man who was not a man at all. She had known that the moment her eyes met his, known that, whoever he was, he possessed an other-worldly power far beyond her own.

Frightened of that which she did not understand, she had sent him away, and he had left without protest, only to return again the next night, and the next. Each night he brought her a gift: a bouquet of wildflowers, a cat carved of jade, a ruby necklace, a seashell.

Gradually, her curiosity overcame her fears and she invited him into her home, only to listen with growing disbelief to the tale he told her. She had heard of vampires, of course, but never believed such creatures existed. And then he told her another tale, of a man who loved a woman so much that he followed her through time. He told her stories of past lives and as he related each one, she knew deep in her soul that he spoke the truth.

And she loved him again. He begged her to join him, to accept the Dark Gift so that they might be together for-ever, never more to be parted. At first, the thought was re-pugnant, but as time passed, she began to relent.

"On All Hallows Eve," she said, "on that night, I will become as you are."

With a glad cry, he swept her into his arms. "At last, my best beloved one," he had shouted exultantly. "At last you will be mine!"

But it was not to be. Unbeknownst to her, people from the town had been spying on her. They had seen Dominic, for that was his name, coming to her in the dark hours of the night. Foolish, superstitious folk, they believed him to be the devil, believed that she was in league with him. Just after midday on All Hallows Eve, they came for her, to accuse her. In spite of her protests, in spite of those who spoke in her behalf, saying that her magic had only been used for good, they had declared her guilty of witchcraft and sentenced her to hang as the sun went down.

And once again she had died in his arms. She had not died instantly when they slapped the horse out from under her. She was still fighting for breath when he came for her. She heard his wild cry of rage and disbelief, the terrified screams and shouts of the townsfolk as he sent them scattering like sheep from a wolf.

But he was too late. Too late. Gazing up into his tormented gray eyes, she whispered his name with her last breath. . . .

Tracy woke with a cry. Once again, his face had been the last thing she had seen. Was she fated to die in his arms in this life, as well?

And that was the first thing she said to him when he appeared at sundown.

"Will I die in your arms again?"

"I believe you are fated to do so," he replied, his voice calm and unruffled, as if she asked him such odd questions every night. "Until . . ."

"Until what?" It was a foolish question. She already knew the answer.

His gaze moved over her face, lingering on her lips. "Until you accept your destiny."

The touch of his gaze was like a physical caress, reminding her of the kiss they had shared the night before.

Rising, she took a step toward him only to find that he was moving toward her as well. There was no need for words, neither question nor answer. He wrapped his arms around her. She rose on her tiptoes and their lips fused, drawn together like a honeybee to a flower, like a moth to the brightest flame.

He deepened the kiss, and she felt his longing, his hunger, his need, not just for the relief of his physical desire but to ease his hunger. It was a huge and painful thing, one he had learned to control but could never conquer, a thirst he could satisfy but never fully quench.

She moaned softly, aching for his need, hating herself because she could not give him that which he most desired.

His eyes were blazing with vampire fire when he broke the kiss and drew back. "Do not blame yourself, my best beloved one," he said, his voice husky, and then, as he had the night before, he vanished from her sight.

Tears stung her eyes, though she wasn't sure if she wept for his pain, or for her own.

The next day, Tracy set about making the house her own. She needed something to do, something to keep her mind from paths she was not ready to travel. On this day, painting was not the answer.

She opened all the windows in the house, then rearranged the furniture in the living room and the dining room, no easy task considering how heavy the pieces were. Her bedroom came next. The physical exertion felt good, freeing somehow.

She paused just after noon for a quick lunch, then went upstairs. She set up the studio to her liking, laying out her paints and brushes, moving the easel here and there until she found just the right place in front of one of the windows. She picked up one of the brushes, and then laid it down again. Perhaps she would paint later, but for now, she wanted to be outside, to smell the earth and the flowers, to see the blue sky.

It was pleasant, walking through the gardens. After a time, she strolled toward the wall, drawn there in spite of herself. She spent several minutes staring at the gnarled old tree that grew nearest the wall. She was certain she could climb the tree without much trouble, but the wall . . . was it really electrified? Or was that merely a threat to keep her from trying to leave?

But Dominic St. John didn't seem like the kind of man who would make empty threats and in the end, she decided not to take the risk. And what would be the point? He would only find her again.

Returning to the gardens, she picked a huge bouquet of roses and carried them into the house. She arranged the flowers in a large jar—there were no vases to be found—and placed the jar on the mantel.

Humming softly, she went into the kitchen to fix dinner. She had never liked cooking so her meals tended to be quick and simple, running more to sandwiches and salads than anything else. Tonight it was a ham and cheese sandwich on wheat bread, a green apple cut into quarters, some cottage cheese, and a frosty glass of iced tea.

She felt a growing sense of anticipation as she sat at the table, watching the shadows outside the window grow long. He would be waking soon, rising from wherever it was that he slept away the hours of daylight. Did he ever miss the sun? Was he ever sorry he had accepted the Dark Gift from Kitana? What was it like, to live for hundreds and hundreds of years, never to be sick, never to grow old? Was it a blessing beyond measure, or a curse without end? Why wouldn't he tell her where he slept? He hadn't kept it a secret from her at home.

Rising, she quickly washed and dried her few dishes and then went outside. The setting sun set the sky aflame as it went down in a blaze of fiery reds and ochre and orange.

She sensed his presence behind her and when she turned, he was standing there.

For stretched seconds, they stared at each other, and then Dominic held out his hand. Without hesitation, Tracy put her hand in his. As if by pre-arrangement, they turned and walked along the path that led through the gardens.

"How was your day?" he asked.

She shrugged. "Fine. I spent most of it rearranging the furniture. I hope you don't mind."

"Of course not. My house, like my life, is yours."

She wasn't ready to hear that just yet and because she couldn't think of anything else to say, she asked, "How was your day?"

He looked down at her, one brow arched in wry amusement. "Quiet."

Tracy grinned. "It must be lonely, sleeping alone all the time."

"You could change that."

She stared at him. "You aren't suggesting that I . . ." She swallowed hard. "That I sleep beside you during the day?" The thought of lying next to his cold, unmoving body sent a chill down her spine.

"Of course not. But if you would accept the Dark Gift, we could sleep away our days together."

He stopped walking and drew her into his arms. "Do you know how often I have yearned to succumb to the darkness with you beside me? How often I have wished to wake with you in my arms?" His hand stroked her cheek. "How oft I have wished that your face would be the last thing I see at daybreak and the first at the moon's rising."

"Dominic . . ."

He pressed one finger to her lips, silencing her. "Be mine, my best beloved one. Let us be together in life and death, as we were meant to be."

"But I don't want to be a vampire, Dominic."

"I know." He blew out a sigh that seemed to come from the very depths of his soul. "I know." He had tried to persuade her to join him countless times. Always, she refused, choosing mortal death over sharing his life with him.

Taking her by the hand, he started walking again. "You might enjoy being a vampire," he remarked. "You would see colors and textures as never before. You could paint for hours and never grow weary. Music becomes more than mere sound, sight more than mere vision. You would see the world as never before, experience life as never before. There are so many things I long to show you, to share with you."

He stopped suddenly, his gaze moving over her, lingering at the pulse throbbing slow and steady in the hollow of her throat. "Tracy . . ."

She stared up at him, at the hunger glowing in his eyes. Fear made her heart beat harder, faster.

His hand tightened on hers. He took a step toward her, his gaze fastened on her throat.

"Dominic."

He looked up, his eyes burning into hers. "Tracy, in all the times I have known you, I have never tasted you. Let me now," he pleaded softly. "Just one taste."

"I'm afraid."

"One small taste, my best beloved one. There is nothing to fear."

"Will it . . . will it hurt?"

"No, I swear it."

She stared up at him, torn by doubt and yet wanting to ease the awful pain she saw in his eyes. How could she refuse him again? How could she not? She put her worst fear into words. "Will it make me what you are?"

"No."

"And you'll only take a little, you promise?"

"I promise."

She lifted a hand to her throat, touched the pulse beating there. To her amazement, she found that her curiosity was stronger than her fear.

"All right, but remember, only a little," she murmured, and wondered if he was as surprised by her answer as she was.

"*Querida!*" He pulled her into his arms and kissed her tenderly.

She pressed herself against him, everything else forgotten in the wonder of his kiss, the pleasure of his touch as his hands moved over her body.

He rained feather-light kisses over her cheeks and brow, kissed the tip of her nose before he claimed her lips once more.

Drowning in waves of pure delight, it took her a moment to realize that he was dropping kisses along her neck, just below her ear. She knew a moment of sharp, primal fear when she felt the touch of his teeth at her throat but it was quickly swallowed up in what came after. As he had promised, there was no pain, only a deep sensual pleasure unlike anything she had ever known.

A soft moan escaped her lips.

At the sound, Dominic lifted his head. He stared down at her, his brow furrowed.

"Are you all right?"

"Oh, yes," she murmured. "Better than all right."

His gaze moved over her face, his expression worried.

She tried to smile reassuringly, but it required too much effort. She was suddenly tired, so tired. . . .

"Tracy!"

He scooped her up into his arms and carried her into the house. Placing her on the sofa, he went into the kitchen and filled a glass with orange juice, which he insisted she drink.

It revived her immediately and she blinked up at him, confused. "What happened?"

His eyes filled with remorse. "Forgive me, my best beloved one, I am afraid one taste was not enough."

Her eyes widened. "Will I become a vampire now?"

He grinned indulgently as he gathered her into his arms. "Did you learn nothing from all those books you read? One does not become a vampire by giving blood, only by drinking from one who is already vampire."

"So, I'd have to . . ."

"Yes, you would have to drink my blood. An exchange, as it were. I would take your blood, a great deal of it, and then give it back to you."

She shuddered. "It sounds . . . gruesome. Don't you ever miss eating real food?"

He grunted softly. "After so many years, I hardly remember what it was like, except . . ." He kissed her again, his tongue sliding over her lips. "Except when I kiss you. You had ham and cheese and tomatoes for dinner." He closed his eyes. "And bread. And tea sweetened with honey." He opened his eyes again, his gaze moving to her lips. "The flavors linger ever so sweetly on your tongue."

His knuckles caressed her cheek, lightly stroking up and down, up and down. It made her feel like purring.

She was lost in his nearness, drowning in the depths of his eyes.

"Sleep now," he said. "The rest will do you good."

She wanted to tell him she wasn't that tired, but her eyelids were heavy, so heavy. Sleep wrapped her in a warm blanket of darkness.

Dominic's voice was the last thing she heard before she surrendered to the darkness.

"I love you," he said, his voice soft and low, yet brimming with emotion. "I have loved you for centuries. Can you not love me just a little?"

Chapter 13

After tucking Tracy into bed, Dominic wandered through the house. Though Tracy had only been under his roof for a short time, her influence was everywhere—her shoes were on the floor beside the sofa, there was a jar of roses on the mantel. The very air in the house was filled with her scent, along with the odor of food, both cooked and raw.

The bathroom held bottles of peach-scented shampoo and conditioner, lipstick and perfume, and myriad other feminine articles, all with their own unique scents.

He went into her studio, curious to see what she had been working on. To his surprise, he found she had painted his portrait again, not as a vampire this time, but as a mortal man. He moved closer, studying the lines of his face. He looked as he had the last time he had seen himself in a mirror. Kitana had not told him that vampires cast no reflection. Even after all these centuries, he could remember his shock the first time he had looked into a mirror, expecting to see his face looking back at him, and seen only the room behind him. It had made him feel as though he no longer existed.

Kitana had laughed at his chagrin. "Didn't you know?" she replied with a laugh. "Vampires have no souls—therefore, they have no reflection."

"No soul?" The thought had astounded him. Though he had never been a deeply religious man, he was a believer nevertheless. How could a body move and have life when it was nothing but an empty shell? How could he live without a soul?

"But you are not alive," Kitana had said airily. "You are Nosferatu. Not dead and not alive."

"Not dead and not alive?" He had scoffed at her. Of course he was alive! More alive than he had ever been before. His sight was keener, his touch more refined, colors were brighter, textures deeper and richer. His hearing was nothing short of phenomenal. A tear slipping down a cheek, a raindrop sliding down a leaf, the movement of a spider over a web, the delicate flutter of a moth's wings, he could hear them all. He was never sick, never tired, never cold. How could she say he was not alive?

And it had been a good life, when Tracy was there to share it with him. It was only when they were separated, when he was on the earth and she was not, that he felt dead. Dead inside and out. His existence had no meaning without her. In the beginning, he had tried to find fulfillment in the arms of other women, but their beauty paled beside hers. Physical gratification alone was not enough. He needed Tracy, needed her love. It mattered not what body she inhabited, the color of her eyes or her hair, whether she was tall or short, dark or fair, whether she was bound or free. Without her, he was nothing but a dry, empty husk, a shell of a man with no reason to live and nothing to live for.

He left the house and wandered aimlessly through the gardens. For centuries, the moon had been his sun, the night his day. With his preternatural eyesight, he saw everything distinctly—each individual leaf on each tree and flower and shrub, the small creatures of the night scurrying through the dew-damp grass, the thorns on the rose bushes, each crack in the wall that surrounded the house. He heard the distant hooting of an owl, the sighing of the wind through the trees, the ripple of the water in the stream beyond the wall. He had so many wondrous abilities, yet they meant nothing without Tracy.

Tracy. She tasted sweet, so very sweet, like the finest nectar. He had thought one taste might be enough, but now that he had tasted her once, he was eager to do it again. And again. To drink of her sweetness until he was sated, until the taste of her, the very essence of her, filled all the empty places within.

His hands clenched at his sides. It would be so easy to take her, to take her and bring her across. He could cloud her mind, bend her will to his, make her yield to him that which he had so long desired, and yet that was something he would never do. She must come to him willingly, without doubts, without hesitation. He had seen what happened to those who'd had the Dark Gift forced upon them. Some went mad and had to be destroyed. Some became little more than killing machines, slaking their unholy appetite in an endless river of blood, heedless of the misery and suffering they caused. Some refused to accept the gift and destroyed themselves by walking into the sunlight. It was not an easy life, to be a vampire. It took a great deal of courage and strength to live a life against nature. Only those who freely embraced the Dark Gift were able to endure it for more than a century or two.

He wondered if Tracy had any idea of how difficult it was for him to be with her, to kiss and caress her, but never make love to her as he so longed to do. Love and desire were closely intertwined with the hunger that was ever within him, making it both pleasure and pain to hold her in his arms. And always, in the back of his mind, was the memory of other lives, past lives, when she had loved him, when she had made love to him and let him make love to her in return.

He glanced up at the house, his gaze moving instinctively to the window of the room where she lay sleeping. If he touched her mind with his, would he find that she was dreaming of him?

He took a deep breath, blew it out in a long sigh. In this life more than any other, he at least had hope. In this life, she was neither slave nor queen nor wed to another. She was her own woman, free and independent, able to do whatever she wished.

In this life, she could be his.

Tracy woke feeling wonderful. She stretched languidly, then padded downstairs to put the coffee on. Standing at the window, staring out at the yard, she lifted a hand to her neck. She had let Dominic drink her blood. Last night, it had seemed so right. Now, in the cool light of day, she couldn't believe she had actually let him do such a thing.

What had she been thinking?

She shook her head. Obviously, she *hadn't* been thinking, or she never would have agreed to it. But she had been moved by the soulful look in Dominic's eyes, touched by the gentle pleading in his voice.

He had promised it wouldn't hurt, and it hadn't. He had also promised he would take only a taste and she knew, on some deep, primal level, that he had taken more than just a taste. And yet, to tell the truth, his vampire kiss had given her such pleasure, she had not wanted him to stop.

Tracy Ann Warner, vampire blood bank.

She turned away from the window and poured herself a cup of coffee. No matter how pleasurable it had been, it couldn't happen again.

After a quick breakfast of toast and cereal, she went upstairs for a shower, then spent the rest of the morning painting another seascape for Mr. Petersen, deciding that if he didn't like her work, she could always sell it to someone else. There was a small art gallery in Sea Cliff that accepted paintings on consignment.

A little after noon, she went downstairs to fix a sandwich for lunch. She added a slice of watermelon, a handful of chips, and a can of root beer and carried her plate outside.

It was quite pleasant, sitting there with the sun shining down on her. A gentle breeze kept the heat at bay. She stared at the house, wondering how old it was and who had lived there before Dominic bought it. She hadn't thought of it before but now it occurred to her that he must be a wealthy man, which made her wonder why he hadn't bought Nightingale House. It seemed strange that he would live in a house he didn't own, and own a house he didn't live in.

Strange. She laughed at that. With Dominic St. John, everything was strange.

He came to her just before sundown. She was sitting in the living room working a crossword puzzle when he entered the room. Her heart skipped a beat when she looked up and saw him standing there, clad in brown leather boots, buff colored trousers, and a loose-fitting white shirt. He reminded her of a hero out of a Regency novel.

"This came for you." Crossing the floor, he handed her an envelope. It was addressed to her in care of a Maine post office box.

"Thank you." She opened the envelope and withdrew a sheet of paper. It was a letter from Mr. Petersen.

"Good news?" Dominic asked.

"Yes." She glanced down at the letter again. "Mr. Petersen says he's pleased with my work. He wants a dozen seascapes to be delivered within sixty days." She looked up at Dominic. "I don't have that many canvases."

"I will take care of it."

"Thank you."

"I brought you something else, as well," he said.

"Oh? What?"

He left the room, only to return a moment later carrying a huge cardboard box and two smaller ones.

Tracy read the lettering on the cartons. One held a 36-inch television set; the others contained a stand and a combination DVD/VCR player, yet he carried the boxes effortlessly, as though they weighed no more than a pound or two.

Dominic set the boxes down and began opening them. He lifted the TV set out of the carton and put it on the floor. "Where do you want it?"

"Over there, I guess," she said, pointing at the wall across from the sofa. "We can move that table."

They spent the next few minutes assembling the stand and rearranging the furniture. Dominic plugged the set in and after a little trial and error, had the VCR hooked up.

"What made you buy a TV?" Tracy asked.

"You cannot paint or read all day, every day," he replied with a shrug. "I did not want you to get bored."

"Thank you."

"Is there anything else you want?"

"Cable would be nice. Oh, and a stereo."

"I will see what I can do."

"Too bad we don't have any of my DVDs," she remarked.

He smiled a sly smile, then left the room. Moments later he returned with a cardboard box.

"What's that?"

"Your movies," he said, dropping the box on the sofa beside her.

"You never fail to amaze me," she said, grinning.

They spent a pleasant evening watching a DVD of *The Mummy*. Dominic admitted he hadn't watched many movies. Books were more to his liking, but he seemed to get a kick out of watching this one. Tracy had seen it several times before but she never tired of watching Oded Fehr. Or Brendan Fraser, for that matter.

About halfway through the movie, Tracy went into the kitchen and came back with a bowl of popcorn and a can of root beer.

Sitting down, she looked at him and shrugged. "I'm hungry."

His gaze met hers and then he glanced at her throat, his eyes darkening. "So am I."

Tracy stared at him, her mouth suddenly dry. "Dominic . . ."

He didn't say anything, only looked at her, his whole body still, waiting for her decision.

She saw the need in his eyes and while the thought of letting him drink from her was instinctively abhorrent, on some deeper level, she wanted to take him in her arms and ease his pain.

When he stood up, she reached for his hand. "Where are you going?"

"Out."

"Didn't you . . . do that earlier?"

He nodded.

"Then why . . . ?"

"Your nearness arouses me in more ways than one," he said bluntly. "Good night."

And just like that, he was gone.

Tracy blew out a sigh of exasperation. Why should she feel so guilty because she didn't want to let him drink from her? But feeling guilty wasn't the worst of it. Stronger than her guilt was the unexpected surge of jealousy that burned through her at the thought that he might be going out to ease his physical desire with someone else.

"Oh, girl," she muttered, "you're losing it."

She slipped *The Mummy Returns* into the DVD player, put on a fresh pot of coffee to keep her awake, but Dominic didn't come back. She couldn't help wondering where he had gone. Was he prowling the streets here, in Maine, or had he taken off for some distant land?

She stayed awake until she couldn't keep her eyes open any longer; then, filled with resentment and jealousy, she went to bed.

Her dreams were frightening that night, filled

with shadowed images chasing her down unfamiliar paths. She heard distant cries for help, never certain if they were her own or someone else's as she ran through a maze of dark streets. Leering eyes watched her; maniacal laughter filled the air and echoed off the sides of buildings. She felt the hell-hot breath of her pursuer on the back of her neck. Her breathing was labored as she ran across a wobbly wooden bridge, praying she would find refuge on the other side. She screamed when it collapsed beneath her, dropping her into a river that ran red with blood.

She woke with the sound of her own screams ringing in her ears. Sitting up, she switched on the light.

Trembling, she wrapped her arms around her waist.

In the distance, she heard the melancholy howl of a wolf. The sound, filled with the loneliness of eternity, tugged at her heart and brought tears to her eyes.

"Dominic," she whispered. "Where are you?"

Outside, a large gray wolf ceased its restless pacing as the sound of Tracy's voice drifted through the window. He heard the fear and the loneliness in her soft lament, sensed her confusion. She was caught up in a world she did not understand, had questions only he could answer. He knew she was torn between loving him and wishing they had never met. Her life had been peaceful until he found her. He could not fault her for wishing to return to that time, but he could not let her go, not when he had just found her again. But perhaps he could ease her pain, comfort her until the sun chased the moon from the sky.

He was about to change shape and go to her

when a new scent was borne to him on the wings of the night.

Lifting his head, the wolf sniffed the air, hackles rising as the scent of danger filled his nostrils.

After all these centuries, Kitana had found him.

Chapter 14

She glided toward him across the dark green velvet lawn, as regal as any queen who had ever lived. Her waist-length red hair flowed over her shoulders, shimmering like wildfire in the silvery light of a full moon. She had not changed since he had last seen her. Her skin was still pale and perfect, her eyes the deep green of pure jade. She wore a long gown of ruby-red silk that clung to her slender form, emphasizing every voluptuous curve.

"Dominic." She held out a pale, slender hand.

"Kitana." He took her hand in his, noting its warmth as he brushed his lips across her skin, which was almost translucent. "What brings you here?"

She lifted one shoulder in a graceful shrug. "I was bored."

"How did you find me?" A foolish question, but one he could not resist asking.

She looked up at him with an indulgent smile. "Did you think I would not?"

"I did not think you would bother after so many years."

Her laughter was soft, musical, yet he heard the hard edge beneath it. "What is time to us? I have always known where you were, Dominic St. John. How could I not when my blood runs in your veins?"

"Why are you here?"

"I told you. I am bored."

"Surely you do not expect me to entertain you?"

"But of course. I have never been in this part of the world before. It is quite lovely. I should like to see more of it."

"I am afraid I cannot spare the time."

"Really? What is it that keeps you so busy?" She glanced at the house, her gaze resting momentarily on one of the second-story windows. "Is it possible you have found that woman yet again?"

"And if I have?"

Again, the sound of her laughter filled the air. "Really, Dominic, do you never tire of pursuing that little mortal through the ages? It should be obvious, even to you, that she does not want what you have to offer."

"This time she will be mine."

"Really? What makes you think so?"

"Have you come here to make trouble for me?" She pouted prettily. "Is that what you think?"

He grunted softly. "I have not forgotten your last words to me."

"Oh, that." Her laughter fell on his ears like the tinkling of tiny silver bells. "You don't think I came here because of that, do you? I admit I was angry at the time, but even I cannot stay angry forever. You have nothing to fear from me."

"I would like to believe that."

"Then believe it." Rising on tiptoe, she ran her

tongue over his lower lip, then kissed him. It was not the kiss of a friend, but of a lover, and, as she had no doubt intended, it reminded him of the nights they had shared, nights filled with passion and blood.

She smiled a knowing smile. "*Au revoir, mon amour.*"

A wave of a slender hand, and she was gone.

Dominic stared up at Tracy's bedroom window. Had Kitana gone there first? Filled with a growing sense of unease, Dominic hastened to Tracy's side. She was asleep, but tossing restlessly. Bad dreams, perhaps?

Sitting on the edge of the mattress, he took her hand in his. "Rest now, my best beloved one," he murmured. "I will watch over you until the dawn. Nothing will harm you while I am here."

She stilled at the sound of his voice. A sigh escaped her lips as she turned onto her side, slipping deeper into the peaceful abyss of sleep. He listened to the steady beat of her heart, the soft, even sound of her breathing.

Leaning forward, he kissed her cheek, smoothed a lock of hair from her brow. They had shared many lifetimes, each different from the last yet the same in so many ways. Each time he had found her, he had been certain that, at last, she would be his, forever his, yet each time he had lost her before he could bring her across.

"But not this time, *querida*," he murmured. "Come what may, I will not lose you again."

He stayed at her side until the first golden rays of dawn brightened the sky and then, reluctantly, he left the house to seek his lair.

* * *

Tracy woke slowly. Sitting up, she glanced around the sunlit room, expecting to see Dominic there even though she knew it was impossible. She had felt his presence so strongly last night. Had it been a dream, or had he actually been there in her room, sitting on the edge of her bed, holding her hand? She had been having a frightful nightmare when his voice penetrated her dreams, chasing away the horror that had been pursuing her. Had she truly heard his voice, or had it been another dream?

Dominic.

She wished suddenly that he were there, that she could climb into his lap and feel his arms holding her close. Strange, that she should think of his arms as a place of safety when, in reality, he was far more dangerous than anyone else she had ever met. Of course, even though Dominic might be dangerous, she knew that he would never hurt her, and that no one else would ever be able to hurt her, either, so long as she was with him. She knew that he would defend her with his very life, if need be, knew that he had defended her life and her virtue countless times before.

She felt a rush of warmth in the region of her heart.

He loved her beyond her ability to comprehend and with that realization came a truth she had thus far refused to acknowledge.

She was in love with him. Loved him in this life as surely as she had loved him in all the others. The thought made her giddy with excitement, and filled her with a sudden sense of dread. She had died in his arms in all her previous lives. Was she destined to die in his arms this time, as well? If so, was it possible to change her fate?

Throwing back the covers, she slid out of bed and headed for the kitchen. She couldn't be expected to think clearly without her morning jolt of caffeine.

She stared out the window while she waited for the coffee to perk.

She loved Dominic.

The thought lingered in the back of her mind the rest of the day. She thought of him while she showered, while she painted, while she ate lunch, while she walked in the gardens, while she counted the hours until sunset when she would see him again. And each time she thought of him, happiness welled within her, bringing a smile to her face.

She loved Dominic.

And then, as the sun began to sink behind the wall, she was overcome with nervousness. Did she dare admit she loved him? If she confessed how she felt, would he ever let her go? Did she want to be free of him? What sort of future could a mortal have with a vampire? Was it possible for him to become mortal again? Could she . . . she thrust the thought away. She had refused to accept the Dark Gift in every past life. That, at least, had not changed. She could not imagine herself as a vampire, forever doomed to dwell in darkness, never to see the light of day again, forced to drink blood for eternity. How could she face the future if she knew she would never again be able to satisfy her craving for dark chocolate, or enjoy a milk shake on a hot summer day, or indulge in a piece of lemon meringue pie?

She sensed his presence before he appeared. There was a familiar tremor in the air and suddenly he was standing beside her. Tall and dark and more handsome than the law allowed. Black jeans hugged his long legs, a black sweater emphasized the width of his shoulders.

His nearness made her tremble.

Bemused, Dominic lifted one brow. "Surely, after all this time, you cannot be afraid of me?"

"No. I'm not afraid. Not anymore."

"What is it, then?"

"I'm just happy to see you. I missed you today."

"Indeed?"

She nodded, her heart pounding with happiness and anticipation. What would he say when she told him how she felt?

"Tracy?"

She moved toward him. Standing on tiptoe, she wrapped her arms around his neck. "I love you."

He stared down at her, his eyes filled with hope. "Can it be true?"

"Yes, but I'm not ready . . . I can't, you know? Not yet . . ."

"Hush." He placed his fingertips over her lips, stilling her words. "It is enough that you are mine."

Their relationship changed after that. Tracy no longer felt like a prisoner in his house and when she expressed a yearning to go back to Nightingale House, he made no objection.

She packed her things the next day and as she did so, she realized she would miss this house. Perhaps, later, they could visit here again.

She wandered through the rooms while waiting for Dominic, mentally redecorating the master bedroom, wondering what it would be like to share it with Dominic.

And then he was there, at her side.

A blush warmed her cheeks.

He looked down at her, one brow arched.

"Hi," she said airily, eager to get out of the bed-room before he divined her thoughts. "I'm all packed and ready to go."

He glanced at her suitcases, waiting near the door. "I'll need to rent a car."

"You can, if you wish, or I can take you."

"What do you mean?"

"I will return you to your house the same way I brought you here."

"Oh."

He watched her, quietly waiting for her reply.

"How, exactly, did you bring me here?"

"Vampires are able to cross great distances rapid-ly." A faint smile tugged at his lips. "Did you not find that bit of information in the books you read?"

She shrugged. "I don't remember."

"So?"

"Well . . . it is a long way . . ."

"Is there anything you want to take with you now?"

"My bag and overnight case."

With a nod, he lifted her into his arms, then picked up the two items she had mentioned. "Are you ready?"

"I guess so."

"You are not afraid?"

"Well . . . a little, maybe. I've never done this be-fore. At least not when I was awake," she amended. "How long will it take?"

"We will be there before you know we have left."

She blinked and the next thing she knew, she was standing in the living room at Nightingale House. "Wow! That's incredible!"

"Indeed."

She frowned. "My car! I left it at the motel . . ."

"It is in the garage." He dropped a quick kiss on the tip of her nose. "I will go and get the rest of your things."

He was back in moments, empty-handed.

Tracy stared at him. "You didn't bring . . ."

"It is all upstairs."

"All of it?"

"Of course."

"You're amazing."

His smile was a trifle smug. "I am glad you think so."

"So," she mused, "what shall we do tonight?"

"I think it is time for you to see my world."

"What do you mean?"

"Sea Cliff is a haven for vampires."

She blinked up at him. In the back of her mind, she heard Bryan asking her if she thought there was anything strange about the village. "A haven? You mean . . "

Dominic nodded. "There are perhaps a dozen or so who live here."

"But . . . I thought, that is, all the books I read said vampires couldn't live together."

"We do not hunt the same territory," Dominic said, "nor do we hunt where we live. As for living together, there is safety in numbers."

"All those people in black . . . I thought they were just Goths . . ."

"Some are."

"And the rest?"

"Are vampires."

"I really don't think I want to meet any of them."

"It is necessary."

"Why?"

"Because you are mine. And since you will not let me bind us together, it is necessary that the others see us together, that they know you belong to me."

She lifted a hand to her throat. "And that will keep me safe?"

"Save for Kitana, I am the oldest of my kind. To violate one under my protection means death. Are you ready?"

She glanced down at her jeans and T-shirt. "Should I change?"

"You will do as you are."

She should have been afraid. She was on her way to meet a—what did one call a bunch of vampires, anyway? Inspecting her feelings as Dominic drove toward the village, she found that it wasn't fear that made her heart pound, but curiosity. Dominic would protect her. She had no doubt of that.

He parked the car in front of a bar on a quiet side street. Tracy grimaced when she saw the name of the place. The Catacombs.

With a shake of her head, she put her hand in Dominic's when he opened the door.

The inside of the bar was dim, filled with shadowy corners. Someone was playing a soft, bluesy tune on the piano in the corner. There were no mirrors; the windows were painted black. Candlelight flickered off the walls and cast shadows on the faces of the customers. She wondered what kind of drinks were served at a vampire bar, then giggled softly. Bloody Marys, no doubt.

Dominic frowned down at her. "Are you all right?"

"Fine."

The piano fell silent as they moved into the room.

Dominic led her to a small table and she sat down, aware that many pairs of eyes were focused on her. She hadn't been afraid before, but a sudden case of nerves sent a shiver down her spine.

She folded her hands in her lap to still their trembling.

Murmurs and whispers filled her ears.

A pair of women dressed in sparkly black midriff tops, short black skirts, black fishnet stockings, and short black leather boots moved up on either side of Dominic.

The blonde put her hand on his shoulder and smiled up into his eyes. "Dom." She trailed her long red fingernails down the length of his arm. "Long time, no see."

The brunette took hold of his other arm. "Who's this little mortal you've brought with you?" she asked in a sultry voice. "Have you brought us something sweet?"

With slow deliberation, Dominic lifted their hands from his arms. "This is Tracy." His voice was low, yet it carried to every corner of the room. "She is my woman, under my protection." His gaze rested meaningfully on the face of each person present. "She is not to be harmed, or toyed with in any way."

The blonde and the brunette backed away from him, then turned and disappeared into the shadows at the far end of the bar.

Tension seemed to drain out of the room.

The piano player took up where he had left off.

Dominic sat down across from Tracy. He looked relaxed, but she noted the fine lines around his mouth, the wariness in his eyes.

She leaned forward. "Brought them something sweet?" she whispered. "Did they think you'd brought me here to . . . for . . . ?"

He nodded. "It is done, from time to time."

Tracy glanced surreptitiously around the room. "Is everyone in here a vampire?"

"Just about."

"Just about?"

"There are mortals who bind themselves to vampires. The girl in the red dress at the next table. Her name is Gina. She belongs to Marcus."

"Like I belong to you?"

"In a way."

"He drinks from her, doesn't he?"

"Yes, but it is her choice."

"What happens to mortals who wander in here?"

"That rarely happens."

"Why's that?"

"There are wards set about this place . . ."

"Wards?"

"Think of them as supernatural shields. Most mortals pass by the place without ever realizing it's here.

"And those who innocently wander in? What happens to them?"

His gaze met hers. "Do you really want to know?"

Unable to speak past a throat gone suddenly dry, she nodded. She needed to know it all.

"The vampires feed on them, and then let them go."

"How can you let that happen?"

"How can I stop it?"

"I don't know. You said you were the oldest vampire around. Doesn't that make you the king, or the boss, or something?"

He smiled faintly, then shrugged. "Vampires are not ruled by kings, nor do we adhere to a democracy. There is only one thing a vampire respects, and that is power. This is my domain and they will adhere to my rules so long as I can enforce them. I have forbidden them to hunt in the village, but I cannot keep them from following their instincts. Any mortal who comes in here is considered fair game. I ask only that there be no killing."

"And those two . . ." She started to say *women*, then hesitated. "Female vampires?"

"What of them?"

"They seemed mighty chummy."

Dominic smiled. "Are you jealous, my best beloved one?"

"Of course not," she said quickly, but they both knew she was lying.

"Zarabeth and Petrina. Petrina brought Zarabeth across last year. Petrina has been vampire for five hundred years. Both have asked to be my concubines, you might say."

"Oh? And what does that mean, exactly?"

"It means they would live in my house and be under my protection."

"Both of them? At the same time?"

"Zarabeth is young in the life. It is not uncommon for new vampires to seek to align themselves with one who is strong until they gain power of their own."

"And Petrina? I'd think that after five hundred years, she would be old enough to take care of herself," Tracy remarked dryly.

Dominic laughed.

"I take it she finds you attractive."

"So she says."

"And do you find her attractive?"

"Yes, my best beloved one, but it is you, and only you, that I desire."

"Did you make her a vampire?"

"No."

Tracy glanced around the bar. Now that her eyes had adjusted to the dimness, she saw faces more

clearly. There were perhaps a dozen men and women in the room, some sitting at tables, some standing at the bar. Most were clad in black. She noticed
that they all seemed extraordinarily beautiful, with
clear skin and lustrous hair, and they all moved
with a kind of unconscious grace, almost as if they
were floating above the floor.

A few weeks ago, she hadn't believed in vam-
pires; now she was in a room surrounded by them.
She looked up at Dominic. "Who made them all?
You?"

He gazed briefly at the pulse in her throat. "I
have never brought another across."

"But, there are so many."

"There are hundreds of us," he replied. "Perhaps
thousands throughout the world. I doubt anyone
knows for sure."

Several couples moved onto the small dance area.
Tracy stared at them. It seemed incongruous, somehow, to see vampires dancing together as if they
were ordinary people.

She glanced at Dominic. He was watching her, a
faint smile playing over his lips.

"Would you care to dance?" he asked.

She shook her head.

He regarded her for several moments, then
asked, "What are you thinking?"

"It just seems weird, seeing them dance."

"Why is that?"

"I don't know, it just does."

"Because they are vampires?"

"I guess so."

"We are not, after all, that much different from
you."

"Yeah, right."

"Ah, Tracy, we were human before we were vampires. Our lifestyle may have changed but in most of us, our humanity remains."

"So, vampires are just people with a peculiar lifestyle—is that what you're saying?"

"More or less."

"Except for the blood part. And the fact that you can't go out in the sun. And that you sleep all day."

He shrugged. "You knew all this before we came here."

She looked at the dancers again. They didn't really look all that different from normal people. If she hadn't known they were vampires, she would have thought them to be just ordinary people with a penchant for wearing black.

She turned her attention back to Dominic. At first glance, there was nothing about him to suggest that he was a vampire, at least not from a distance. But, close up, she was ever aware of the aura of power that clung to him, the deep inner stillness that sometimes came over him.

Rising, he held out his hand. "Come," he said. "Dance with me."

She hesitated only a moment before she put her hand in his. He pulled her gently into his arms, his dark gaze intent upon her face as he guided her around the floor.

They danced together as though they had done it hundreds of times. His hand was cool, firm against her back. She stared up at him, once again smitten by his bold good looks. For a time, she lost herself in the joy of being in his arms. He gazed down at her, his eyes warm with affection. His breath was whisper-soft against her face.

"This is a pretty song," Tracy remarked. "I don't think I've ever heard it before."

"It is called 'Vampire's Lament'. Marcus wrote it for his mortal woman."

"Do you know the words?"

Dominic listened a moment, then began to say the words, his voice moving over her, soft and seductive as a sigh.

"Open for me, this creature of the night, let me ease my pain in the warmth of your light. Come, walk with me, share this moment in time, open your heart, your soul, now mine.

"My laugh is hollow as I walk these darkened halls, time is nothing but a tick upon the wall. I am life, eternity and forever, alone in my despair, reaching toward never.

"Shall I find the one? Is there one to find? Will I know the soft light that will flow from her soul into mine? Is it possible to feel? Is it possible to know? If her touch is the water, is my answer the flow?"

She found the words oddly touching. The lyrics could have been written for the two of them. She was sorry when the music ended.

Dominic was leading her off the floor when Petrina intercepted them. "My turn," she purred. "Dance with me, Dom."

Dominic glanced at Tracy, then shook his head.

Petrina also looked at Tracy, her cat-green eyes narrowing with disdain. Then, she smiled up at Dominic. "Surely your little mortal won't mind if you dance one dance with an old friend."

"I do mind," Tracy said, surprising all of them. "Take your hands off of him."

"Well, well, what do you know," Petrina said with a malevolent grin, "the little mortal has . . . teeth."

Dominic laughed, a deep, rich masculine sound. "Run along, Pet, before *she* takes a bite out of *you*."

Tracy had no idea that vampires could blush, but a surge of red flooded Petrina's cheeks. She glared at Tracy, then vanished from sight.

Taking her by the hand, Dominic led Tracy back to their table.

"I probably shouldn't have said that, should I?" Tracy remarked, sitting down.

"Probably not. You have made an enemy of her now."

"Well, she made me mad!"

"And a little jealous, perhaps?"

"Not a little. A lot."

He smiled, pleased. "Do not worry about Petrina. She is harmless."

"Oh, sure, a harmless vampire."

"She will not harm you, my best beloved one."

"As long as you're around," Tracy muttered. "But what if she finds me alone?"

"She knows I would destroy her if she dared lay a hand . . ." He grinned. "Or a fang, on you."

Tracy smiled at him. "I'm not afraid, not really."

But later, lying alone in her bed, she couldn't help wondering what the outcome would be if Petrina caught her alone.

Chapter 15

Petrina stalked the dark city streets, her rage growing with every step. How dare he! How dare he talk to her like that, treat her like that, sending her away as if she were some troublesome child! She was not some fledgling vampire, to be lightly dismissed! He had embarrassed her, humiliated her, not only in front of that foolish mortal female, but in front of Sea Cliff's other vampires, and that was something she could not forgive.

"Petrina?"

She turned to find Zarabeth hurrying after her.

"Go home, Bethy."

Zarabeth didn't argue. She had lived with Petrina long enough to know better.

Petrina watched her friend vanish into the darkness.

Dominic would be sorry for his lack of respect, she vowed, as she continued on her way. In five hundred years, she had never formed attachments to any place, or any one, save for Zarabeth. She had fully intended to drain the girl and cast her aside but something about Zarabeth had given her pause and she had brought her across instead. Zarabeth had become Petrina's first friend since becoming a vampire. At first, it had been strange; now the two of them were very nearly inseparable.

Aside from Zarabeth, the only thing she wanted was Sea Cliff. Petrina had hoped Dominic would accept her in his house, that they could rule Sea Cliff together. She knew now that such a thing was impossible. Dominic had rejected her for that puny mortal.

She thought briefly of destroying the woman but knew such a thing would gain her nothing but Dominic's hatred and perhaps cost her her own life.

Which left only one alternative.

She frowned as she contemplated it, and then she smiled. It was always better to rule alone.

Chapter 16

Tracy sat up, yawning. A glance at the clock showed that she had already slept most of the morning
away. Dating a vampire certainly kept her up far later
than she was accustomed to. By the time she showered and had breakfast, the day would be half gone!
Not only that, but her laundry was piling up and
she had bills to pay.

Rising, she went downstairs to put the coffee on,
then hurried back upstairs for a quick shower. She
pulled on a pair of cut-off shorts and a tank top,
then went downstairs to fix breakfast. Opening the
refrigerator, she grimaced at what she saw. Not surprisingly, all of the food she had left in the fridge
when she ran away had soured, wilted, or turned
blue with mold.

After dumping it all in the garbage and washing
out the refrigerator, she grabbed her purse and
her keys and headed for the village.

Driving down the main street, she noticed anew
how deserted the place was. Funny, she had never

paid much attention to that before. Many of the
shops didn't open until after sundown. She saw a
few tourists peering into windows. An elderly couple sat at a table at the outdoor café, sipping lattes.

Tracy pulled into the parking lot of the market
and got out of her car. Did the townspeople know
that their town was a haven for vampires? Or were
they as happily ignorant of the fact as she had
been only days ago?

Grabbing a cart, she wandered up and down the
aisles, filling her basket with whatever caught her
fancy. It occurred to her that few of the items she
bought would have even been in existence when
Dominic was mortal—things like frozen dinners,
ice cream, milk in cartons, meat in neat little packages, food in cans, sliced bread, dry cereal, candy
bars. Did he ever wonder what modern-day food
tasted like?

As she watched the clerk total up her purchases,
Tracy decided that, judging by the amount of chocolate she had bought, she was definitely feeling anxious. Dark chocolate had ever been her comfort
food of choice.

She was on her way to her car when she heard
Bryan call her name. Pausing, she glanced over
her shoulder to see him hurrying toward her.

"Hey, where've you been?" he asked. "I've been
worried sick."

"I was on a little . . . umm, holiday, I guess you
could say."

He frowned at her as he helped her put her groceries in the trunk. "Holiday? Where'd you go?"

"Maine."

"Oh. Well, I wish you'd let me know. I thought
maybe that madman had abducted you or something."

Tracy grinned. That was exactly what had happened, but she couldn't tell Bryan that. "Well, not to worry. I'm back now. How've you been, otherwise?"

"Fine." He closed the trunk. "I was really worried about you. Have you read the paper lately? Three people were found dead last week, with no apparent cause of death except they'd all lost a lot of blood. There were no signs of violence, and no signs of a struggle. The police are stumped. One of the reporters said it sounded like some kind of vampire killing." Bryan frowned at her. "Tracy? Hey, Trace, are you okay? You look as pale as a ghost."

"I'm fine. I . . . it's just hard to believe something like that could happen here." Even as she said the words, she thought it was surprising that there hadn't been more murders in the village, considering that the place was crawling with vampires. She recalled Dominic telling her that vampires didn't hunt where they lived. Obviously, he had been wrong about that.

"Can you come down to the beach later?" Bryan asked. "I've missed you."

"I'll try."

"Great." Leaning forward, he gave her a quick peck on the cheek. "See ya later."

She watched him walk away, thinking how refreshing it was to be in his company. He was so open, so honest. There was nothing dark and mysterious about Bryan.

With a sigh, she slid behind the wheel and drove home.

The mailman had come in her absence. After putting the groceries away, she sat down at her desk to read the mail and pay her bills.

The first letter was from Mr. Petersen, who repeated that he was immensely pleased with her work and enclosed a nice check as a down payment for the remaining seascapes. He also mentioned that he would like her to do a portrait of him and his children as a Christmas gift for his wife and that he would send her a photograph to work from, if that was feasible. If not, he would arrange a date and time to be at her studio with his children.

Tracy smiled as she picked up the phone to call Mr. Petersen. This was exactly the kind of break she needed. Mrs. Petersen was a wealthy woman, influential in her community. If she were pleased with the portrait of her family, she would no doubt tell all her friends. You couldn't beat word-of-mouth advertising!

Later, after the bills were paid, Tracy went upstairs to her studio. The seascape she had started in Maine had been set up near the window.

She painted for over an hour. Lost in the act of creation, she forgot everything else but the feel of the brush in her hand as she added shading and depth to the canvas. She loved the smell of the paint, the sense of fulfillment and satisfaction that engulfed her as she transferred the image in her mind to the canvas.

Stepping back, she regarded her work through a critical eye, and then nodded. One sent. One more finished. Only another ten to go.

After cleaning her brushes, she prepared a new canvas and then, on the spur of the moment, decided to take a break.

Going downstairs, she grabbed an apple from the fridge and went down to the beach.

Bryan was sitting on his lifeguard tower.

"Hey, there," she called. "Can I come up?"

He smiled down at her. "Sure."

She climbed the ladder, then sat down beside him. "So, rescued anyone today?"

"Not yet. Pretty quiet." He touched the tip of her nose with his finger. "I guess you've been painting."

"Yeah. Guess I should have looked in the mirror before I left the house."

"Well, it's pink. People will just think you're sunburned."

"Right."

"So, what did you do in Maine?"

"I was visiting a friend."

"You left kind of suddenly, didn't you?"

"Kind of."

"School will be starting soon," he remarked. "I sure hate to see summer end."

"Me, too." She gazed out at the ocean. There was something almost hypnotic about watching the waves. She had always loved the ocean. Endless and deep, sometimes calm, sometimes wild with energy, a vast, ever-changing sea that was home to thousands of creatures from tiny sea horses to gentle whales and man-eating sharks.

"Are you busy tonight?" Bryan asked.

"Yes, I'm afraid so."

"Are you seeing him?" There was no mistaking the hard edge of jealousy in Bryan's voice.

"Yes."

"He's no good for you. Why do you insist on going out with that man? There's something about him. Something not right."

"Oh, Bryan."

"Don't patronize me. Just because you're older doesn't mean you're wiser."

"I didn't say that, but Dominic's a good man."

Bryan snorted derisively.

"Maybe I'd better go."

"No!" He laid a restraining hand on her arm. "I'm sorry."

"It's okay. But I really should go. I've got work to do."

"You're not mad, are you?"

"No, of course not. See ya later."

Back home, she poured herself a glass of milk, then went upstairs. Glass in hand, she regarded the blank canvas, then, setting the glass aside, she mixed her colors and began to paint.

She had fully intended to start on another sea-scape; instead, her brush strokes sketched a tall man wandering through a moonlit garden. A man who stood beneath a lamp post and cast no shadow on the ground.

Intent upon her task, she paid no attention to the time as she carefully applied each brush stroke. His face, pale in a wash of silver moonlight, was harsh and yet beautiful. His eyes, dark and shadowed, were filled with the secrets of eternity. His mouth was well-shaped and sensual, with just a hint of a roguish grin. A long black cloak fell in graceful folds from broad shoulders. It was by far the best thing she had ever done. There was carefully leashed power in every line.

Stepping away from the canvas, she studied the portrait wrought by her hands and her heart. "Perfect," she murmured, laying her brush aside. "Absolutely perfect."

"You flatter me."

She whirled around, startled by the sound of his voice.

"Forgive me, I did not mean to frighten you."

She glanced at the window, surprised to see

that the sun was setting. "I didn't realize it was so late."

He drew her into his arms, stared at the painting over the top of her head. Again, she had captured him on canvas and he studied the image intently.

"Do you like it?" she asked.

"Very much. Is this how you see me?"

"Yes."

"And is this how I appear? Or merely an artist's interpretation?"

She looked up at him. "Both, I guess," she replied, and then frowned. "Is it true you can't see yourself in a mirror?"

"Yes."

"If I took your picture, would it come out?"

"No."

"So you haven't seen your face in over two thousand years." She shook her head. "That's incredible."

He jerked his head toward the painting. "This is better than a mirror," he said with a wry grin, "though I doubt I ever looked quite so handsome in mortality."

She glanced over her shoulder at the canvas. "It's how I see you."

He cupped her cheek in his hand. "I believe love has colored your perception," he murmured, and lowering his head, he kissed her.

She clung to him as he deepened the kiss, caught up in a maelstrom of emotion. Her eyes were closed, yet she saw colors brighter than ever before. She imagined she could feel each thread that made up the fabric of his clothing. It seemed as though she could feel each particle of air around her. She caught the scent of rain, and even as awareness crossed her mind, she heard the dull roar of thunder, the patter of drops against the window.

Overwhelmed, she drew back to stare up into Dominic's eyes.

He answered her question before she could ask.

"You are feeling what I feel," he said quietly. "Seeing things as I see them."

"But why?"

"I have taken your blood. Not enough to bind us together, but enough that, if I open my senses, you can see and experience a part of my feelings."

Well, that was a scary thought! "What would happen if I had taken *your* blood?"

"We would be forever bound. My thoughts would be yours, as yours would be mine."

"You mean you'd be able to read my mind?"

"I can do that now."

"But if we were bonded, I'd be your slave, wouldn't I, like that woman is Marcus's slave?"

"No, my best beloved one. It would be nothing like that."

She took a step away from him, suddenly frightened. "I don't believe you."

"There are many ways a vampire can possess a mortal," he said calmly, as if they were discussing nothing more important than the weather. "Ways to compel mortals to obey."

"Is that what Marcus did to that girl?"

"No. She went to him of her own free will."

"But he could have made her do it against her will?"

"Yes."

"And you could do that to me?"

Watching her carefully, he nodded. He was on dangerous ground here. A wrong word now might frighten her away.

"Why haven't you?"

"Because I do not want a slave."

"Have you ever forced anyone else to do your bidding?"

"Of course. Each time I feed."

She wrapped her arms over her breasts. "So you hypnotize them and force them to give you their blood?"

"I speak to their minds to take away their fear. It is not unpleasant for them, and when it is over, I wipe all memory of it from their minds."

"That's despicable!"

"Would you rather I took them by force and drained them of life?"

"Of course not, but . . ."

"I am what I am, *querida*. I cannot change my nature, not even for you, nor would I. I have been vampire far longer than I was human. I have survived thousands of years. I have learned patience. I have learned compassion. I have learned to take what I need without taking life. It has not been easy. Vampires are predatory by nature. The need to hunt is a part of me and will not be denied. There are those who hunt in the old way, who take a life each night. No longer human themselves, they have little regard for human life. I will not tolerate their kind here."

"Is that right? Have you read the paper lately? Bryan told me that three people have been killed in the last couple of days. Drained of blood."

Dominic's eyes narrowed. "You have seen that boy again?"

Tracy dismissed his question with a wave of her hand. "Did you hear what I said? Three people have been killed, Dominic. If you don't allow any of the Sea Cliff vampires to hunt in your territory, then who's doing it?"

Dominic shook his head. "I was not aware of any killings." It troubled him to realize he had been unaware that someone was hunting in his territory. His only excuse was that he had been so preoccupied with Tracy he had been oblivious to everything else.

"Well," Tracy remarked a trifle sharply, "maybe you should look into it before there's a fourth."

With a nod, he was gone.

Tracy stared at the place where he had been standing, wondering if she would ever grow accustomed to his ability to vanish in the blink of an eye, wondering if she truly wanted to.

Chapter 17

Dominic stalked the night, his anger as dark and thick as the clouds that scudded overhead.

Someone had dared to hunt in his territory, killing not once but three times. Even though there were a dozen other vampires in the village, he had claimed this piece of ground as his own over a century ago. He had been the first vampire to take up residence in Sea Cliff; therefore, it was his. He allowed others to dwell there but only if they agreed to abide by his law. He had told Tracy that the vampires had no democracy and no ruler and that was true, to a point. No one vampire ruled over the others. But there were a few vampires like himself, ancient vampires filled with power, who had staked out parts of the world as their own. This tiny village on the coast of California was his and he would not allow any other immortal to disrupt the peaceful atmosphere he had created.

He moved swiftly through the dark streets, his preternatural senses reaching out, searching through the night for the one who did not belong.

Each vampire resident was accounted for: Zarabeth was already at rest, her hunger sated. Nicholas, Marcus, Landau, and Magdalena were huddled together at The Catacombs, debating whether it was more fun to take their prey by surprise or seduction. Franco was hunting in the city. Laslo and Turk, the two youngest of his kind, were playing billiards in a back alley pool hall. The other four were wandering the night, oblivious to the rain. Try as he might, he could find no hint of Kitana's presence. Had she left the village?

He scoured the village and the beach from one end to the other and back again, unable to find any trace of an unknown vampire.

Pensive, he walked the dark streets that led home. Even though he had been unable to find evidence of an intruder, something was not right.

He jerked his head up as the scent of fresh blood was borne to him on the night wind.

Quickening his steps, he turned down a narrow alley that ran behind a small delicatessen. Blurred by a curtain of rain, he saw two shapes struggling in the darkness. The scent of blood grew stronger.

As he approached, one of the figures vanished from his sight. Was it Kitana?

The second figure, a mortal female, dropped to the ground. Blood oozed from her throat.

Dominic frowned thoughtfully. To his knowledge, Kitana was the only vampire in the area who had the ability to shield her presence from him. A law unto herself, she would not feel bound to abide by any rules he set forth.

But there was little time to worry about that

now. He knelt beside the woman, the scent of her life's blood strong in his nostrils, awakening his hunger even though he had fed earlier. His fangs pricked his tongue. He licked his lips as he stared at the unconscious woman. Her pulse was slow and erratic, her skin a sickly gray.

He swallowed hard, his hunger at war with his conscience. She was almost past saving. Should he let her go?

He lowered his head, his tongue flicking across her throat to taste a single crimson drop. Warmth flowed through him. What harm to take the rest when she was at death's door?

He lowered his head again, mouth watering in anticipation.

And then he thought of Tracy. He had told her he had not killed for many years. She would not approve of what he was about to do.

He reared back, his gaze narrowed as he looked at the woman lying on the ground. He had only moments to decide. She was perhaps thirty, a little on the plump side. Her hair was light brown, plastered to her head by the rain. The gold band on her left hand gleamed dully in the moonlight. He swore softly. She was married. No doubt she had children.

With a low growl, he tore open his wrist and held it to her lips. "Drink!"

It was a command, not a request.

Unable to resist the compulsion in his voice, the woman opened her mouth and swallowed.

Almost immediately, her color returned, her pulse grew stronger.

As strength returned, she clutched his wrist to her mouth with both hands and she drank as though ravenous.

With a cry, Dominic wrenched his arm away from her.

Only then did she open her eyes. She stared up at him, her expression bewildered.

Dominic stared deep into her eyes. "You will not remember any of this," he said, his voice low, hypnotic. "You will not remember me, or the one who attacked you. Is that clear?"

She nodded, the movement sluggish.

Rising, he pulled the woman to her feet. "Go home."

She blinked up at him, then turned and walked down the alley, her steps slow and unsteady. She didn't look back.

With a thought, Dominic arrived in Tracy's bedroom.

She was in bed, asleep. Her long honey-colored hair was spread out on the pillow, a splash of gold against the pale blue pillowcase.

He gazed down at her, all else forgotten as he admired the gentle curves of her figure, the perfection of her countenance, the way her lashes lay on her cheeks, the length of a long, shapely leg. He had followed her for centuries and now, at last, she was almost his. This time, he thought, this time he would have her.

Tracy woke slowly, uncertain what had awakened her. The rain, perhaps? And then, as her mind cleared, she realized she wasn't alone in the room. Panic swept through her and then, sensing his presence, her fear receded.

"Dominic?"

"I am here."

She sat up. "Is something wrong? You left so abruptly earlier."

"There is nothing wrong, my best beloved one. I wanted only to see your face before I take my rest."

Small frissons of pleasure moved through her at his words. "Oh. Aren't you going to kiss me good night?"

"Most assuredly." Sitting down on the edge of her bed, he drew her into his arms.

She snuggled against him, lifting her face for his kiss. He smelled of rain and cologne and . . . she looked up at him. "Where have you been?"

"Out."

"Were you . . . feeding?"

"Why do you ask?"

"You smell like . . . like blood."

"I found a woman earlier. She had been attacked by a vampire and was near death."

"Oh, no!"

"I revived her and sent her home."

"Will she be all right?"

He nodded.

"You said no one hunts in Sea Cliff and yet three people have been killed. How could that happen?"

"There is an interloper in the village. I saw him briefly." Dominic frowned. "He must be very old, to mask his presence from me so effectively."

"Maybe he's gone now."

"Perhaps." He stroked her hair lightly. "Let us not speak of him now."

"You said you were outside. How come you're not wet?"

"Because I do not wish to be."

"Must be nice."

"Indeed. Come to me, my best beloved one,

now, tonight. Let me show you the world as only a vampire can see it."

The thought made her stomach churn. "No. I can't. I'm not ready." She looked up at him, her expression dark and confused. "Maybe I'll never be ready. Will you find me again if we're parted in this life?"

"I will always find you, *querida,* in this life, or any other."

Once, the thought had filled her with alarm; now, it was strangely comforting.

Dominic kissed her cheeks, her brow. "I must go. Dawn approaches." He kissed her again, his lips claiming hers, hot and hungry, and then he gazed deep into her eyes.

"Dream of me, my best beloved one," he murmured. "Dream of our life together." And then, as he had so many times before, he vanished from her sight.

A moment later, the first faint rays of golden sunlight pierced the darkness.

Chapter 18

When Tracy woke later that morning, she wasn't sure if Dominic had actually been in her room in the last hour before dawn, or if she had dreamed it.

Rising, she showered and dressed, then went downstairs to put the coffee on. Feeling suddenly hungry and domestic, she mixed batter for waffles and fried a couple of strips of bacon. When that was done, she added a cup full of strawberries to her plate, poured a glass of orange juice, and for the first time since she had moved into the house, she sat down to a proper breakfast.

Savoring a bite of bacon, she thought of Dominic. Imagine, having to sustain oneself with nothing but a warm liquid diet for over two thousand years. Eating was one of life's pleasures. She couldn't imagine giving it up, and yet . . . what a marvel, never to have to worry about growing old and feeble, to always be young and vital and in perfect health, to stay forever as she was now, in the prime of her life.

She shook her head, trying to dislodge the thoughts building in her mind, but to no avail. What a blessing it would be, never to be tired or sick or have to worry about gaining weight, never having to worry about losing your sight or your hearing. Dominic said vampires saw with greater depth and clarity than mortals. What would that mean to her work?

Rising, she cleared the table, washed the dishes, and put them away. And always, in the back of her mind, was the question, *what if?*

Going upstairs, she slipped into her smock and began to work on another seascape for Mr. Petersen. She watched her brush move over the canvas, saw the picture take shape, but she worked mechanically, her mind seemingly stuck in the groove of, *what if?*

What if she let Dominic make her a vampire?

She thought of all the things she would be giving up—food, sunlight, vacations with her family, a normal life, children.

She thought of what she would gain—a love that would last forever, a life that would never end, the ability to travel great distances in the blink of an eye, eternal youth and vigor.

Would it be a fair trade?

But, what if, after it was done, she was sorry? There was no going back, no way to return to mortality if she suddenly decided she didn't want to be immortal any longer.

What would her parents say if they found out their daughter was a vampire?

Dominic made the life sound appealing, but in books and movies, there was no happiness for vampires. They were constantly being hunted, destroyed in truly horrible ways. Gruesome images of Van Helsing driving a stake through the heart of a vampire, or cutting off its head, or setting one on fire, sprang to the forefront of her mind.

Dominic said mortals were unaware that there were vampires in their midst. But what if he was wrong? What if even now there were men in the world who were hunting vampires, destroying them where they slept?

She stared at the painting she had created. To be a vampire was to live a life against nature. Would her soul be forever damned if she accepted the Dark Gift?

Dropping her brush into a jar of cleaning fluid, she put her paints away, stripped off her smock, and left the house.

She practically flew down the stairs to the beach. It was a beautiful day. Everything looked fresh and clean after last night's rain. Standing there, with the sand warm beneath her feet, she closed her eyes and lifted her face to the sun.

She didn't know how long she had been standing there when Bryan's voice sounded behind her.

"Hey, sun bunny!"

Opening her eyes, she turned to see him striding toward her. "Hi, Bry."

"Hi. How's it going?"

"Fine. I'm taking a break."

He nodded. "I'm glad you decided to take it here. Wanna come up to the tower and have a Coke?"

"Sure, thanks."

Side by side, they walked down the beach.

Tracy was keenly aware of the damp sand squishing between her toes, of the heat of the sun shining down on her head and back, of the smell of the ocean, the cry of the gulls soaring overhead. A sailboat drifted off shore. A half-dozen teenage boys were surfing, showing off for the bikini-clad girls who were pretending to be indifferent but were watching every move the boys made. An elderly man with a metal detector was walking toward them, his gaze intent upon the ground. A pair of middle-aged women sat beneath a huge umbrella; one was reading a book, the other was working a crossword puzzle. Further down the beach, a couple of kids were making sand castles while their mothers looked on.

Ordinary people doing ordinary things. Was she ready to give all that up?

"Tracy?" Bryan grabbed her arm when she started past the tower. "Hey, Tracy, we're here."

"What? Oh, sorry. I guess my mind wandered."

"You okay? You look . . . well, like you're gonna cry."

She forced a smile. "No, I'm fine."

He regarded her for a moment, then scrambled up the ladder. When he reached the top, he turned and waited for her, offering her his hand when she reached the top.

Stepping into the tower, he pulled a pair of sodas out of a cooler and handed her one.

"Thanks." She popped the top and took a long drink, then sat down.

Bryan sat beside her.

"So, have you made any rescues lately?" Tracy asked.

"Three today."

"Really?"

He nodded. "Some old guy who swam out too

far. A teenage girl who got caught in a riptide and nearly took me down with her. And a woman who panicked when the waves knocked her down. Seems she couldn't swim."

Tracy lifted her can to him in a salute. "My hero."

Bryan's cheeks turned pink. "Yeah, well . . ." He shrugged. "It's not brain surgery, but it's still saving lives."

"Life is precious, isn't it? Would you want to live forever, if you could?"

"Sure, if I could stay young. Who wouldn't?"

"Would you really? Part of what makes life precious is the knowledge that it doesn't last forever, that it could be over in the blink of an eye. Every day, every minute, is a gift. It should never be wasted, never be perverted. We're here for such a short time, we should cherish every moment we have."

He stared at her. "Geez, what brought that on?"

"Oh, I don't know. I've just been doing a lot of thinking lately, about life and death and what it means."

"Hey, that's heavy."

She looked at him and grinned. "Too heavy for such a lovely day. I think I'm going for a swim."

"Be careful out there. Lots of riptides today."

"I will. Thanks for the Coke."

He took the can from her hand. "Can I see you later tonight?"

"I'm not sure. Call me?"

"Will do."

Impulsively, she kissed him on the cheek, then scrambled down the ladder.

She was already barefooted. Clad in shorts and a T-shirt, she waded out into the ocean and began to swim. The water was cool, invigorating. She swam for a while, then turned onto her back and floated. Overhead, the sky was a bright, clear blue, as deep and wide as all eternity.

Refusing to think of anything beyond the pleasure of the moment, she let herself drift in the arms of the sea. But, in spite of her determination, troublesome thoughts crept into her mind.

She would never be able to swim on a summer day if she accepted the Dark Gift.

Dominic had not seen the sun in over two thousand years.

He would never be a father. He would never hold a precious new life in his arms, hear his child's laughter, or dry its tears.

And neither would she, if she accepted the Dark Gift.

Pushing such disturbing thoughts from her mind, she struck out for shore.

On the beach, she shook the water from her hair. She waved to Bryan, then trotted toward the steps that led toward home.

Dominic rose before the setting of the sun. Here, deep within the earth, he could rise before night spread her cloak over the land, though until the sun set, his powers were weak. Still, it afforded him an extra hour or two of awareness, of life. Even after all these years, he dreaded the approach of the Dark Sleep, hated the sudden lethargy that engulfed him, knowing he would be trapped in oblivion until sunset. And yet, since he had found Tracy, his sleep was not completely dreamless. He often dreamed of her, sometimes seeing her as she had been in ages long past, sometimes seeing her as she was now, and sometimes, best of all, dreaming that she had accepted the Dark Gift, that she shared the endless night with him.

He sensed her now in the house above, knew she was preparing her evening meal. It had been so long since he had tasted food that was not warm and liquid. He had a sudden, unexpected yearning for a slice of dark brown bread and butter and a glass of goat's milk. What would happen should he attempt to eat solid food after such a long time? Would he be able to swallow it? Would it stay on his stomach, or would he vomit it up again?

What would Tracy say if he appeared in her kitchen and asked to join her at her table?

The thought no sooner crossed his mind than he was there.

"Oh!" Tracy pressed one hand over her pounding heart as he appeared before her. "I wish you wouldn't do that!"

"Forgive me. I will come in the door next time."

"Thank you."

Dominic closed his eyes and took a deep breath, his nostrils filling with aromas he knew only from memory.

"Are you all right?"

He opened his eyes to find Tracy staring at him, her brow furrowed.

"Would you mind a guest for dinner?"

"Who?" Her eyes widened. "You?"

He nodded.

"But . . . how? I thought you could only drink . . . you know."

He shrugged. "I have a sudden craving for food."

"Really? That's odd, isn't it?"

"Yes, extremely."

With a shake of her head, she pulled another plate from the cupboard and set it on the table, along with a glass and silverware. "Sit down."

He did so, his gaze watching her avidly as she pulled pans and dishes from the oven and the cupboard.

"We're having chicken, baked potatoes, and asparagus," she told him. "What would you like to drink?"

"Goat's milk."

She bit back a smile. "I'm afraid I'm fresh out. How about just regular milk, from a cow."

"All right."

He watched her fill a glass with white liquid. Lifting it, he took a sip, and grimaced. He didn't remember goat's milk as being so cold, but of course there had been no refrigeration when he was a young man. He took another sip, then set the glass aside and stared at the silverware. He had never used a fork, only a knife and a spoon. But he had watched countless people eat, had pretended to do so on occasion.

Taking a resolute breath, he cut a piece of chicken, speared it with the fork, and put it in his mouth. He chewed carefully, his mouth filling with myriad tastes—the juice of the chicken, the meat and skin, the herbs she had cooked it with. He tasted the potato and the asparagus, conscious of Tracy's curious gaze watching his every move. He had almost forgotten how to chew food, so accustomed was he to a liquid diet.

"How is it?" she asked.

He swallowed the last bite of chicken, felt his insides begin to burn. And churn. "Very good," he said, and bolted from the table.

Outside, in the cover of darkness, he fell to his knees and retched until he was hollow inside.

And then he went hunting a meal fit for a vampire.

Tracy let out a sigh as she rose and began clearing the table. It didn't take a genius to figure out what had happened. His stomach had rebelled against ingesting solid food. Even if he hadn't been a vampire, his body probably couldn't have adjusted from a liquid diet to a solid one so quickly.

Poor Dominic. Again, she wondered what it would be like to be a vampire.

And then, while standing at the sink rinsing the dishes, she was smitten with an idea. A strange idea, to be sure. What if she pretended to be a vampire for a week or two? She wouldn't drink blood, of course. Instead, she would drink some kind of liquid protein and pretend it was blood. She wouldn't eat or drink anything else. She grinned. She would wear nothing but black. She would sleep days—in a bed, not a coffin, thank you. She would paint, shop, and clean house at night.

She frowned. How did vampires go to the post office? She could buy stamps at the market, but what about mailing packages? If she were truly a vampire, how would she mail her paintings to Mr. Petersen? How had Dominic managed it?

She wouldn't worry about that now. She could get by for one week. It was only pretend, after all.

As she put the dishes in the cupboard, she wondered what Dominic would think when she told him.

Chapter 19

"You are going to do what?" Dominic stared at her as if she had lost her mind.

"I'm going to live as a vampire for one week," Tracy replied. "Starting tonight."

He grunted softly. "Shall I find you a coffin?"

"No!" She grimaced. "Do you really sleep in one?"

"It is only a box, after all."

She stared at him. "I don't think I could sleep in one."

"It is not required."

"Well, that's a relief. But you have one. I saw it."

"It is quite comfortable, I assure you. If you wish, you can try it out."

"No, thank you!"

He laughed softly, amused by her decision to "live as a vampire" for the next seven nights.

His gaze moved over her. She wore a black tank top, black jeans, and black boots. "A new fashion statement to go with your new lifestyle?"

"I thought black was the color of choice for vampires."

"We do seem to wear it quite a lot, do we not?"

"I've hardly seen you in anything else. Except that night in Maine. Oh, and that night we walked on the beach."

"I guess I should expand my wardrobe."

"You think?"

"Come on," he said, grabbing her by the hand. "Let us go shopping."

She thought he was kidding, but the next thing she knew, they were in the city and he was pulling into the mall parking lot. Feeling suddenly lighthearted, Tracy let him lead her into the first menswear store they came to.

To her surprise, she discovered that Dominic had quite a sense of humor. He held up several gaudy Hawaiian shirts for her approval, grinned when she shook her head.

He held up golf shirts, baggy camouflage shorts, argyle socks.

Her sides were aching from laughing so hard by the time they left the store. Taking him by the hand, she led him into an exclusive men's shop.

She picked out several shirts for him. Much to her surprise, they were all in dark colors—indigo, a deep wine red, a rich chocolate brown, charcoal gray, black. And one white shirt with long sleeves that reminded her of the kind of shirt pirates once wore.

He looked at her, one brow arched. "I thought you were going to brighten my wardrobe."

Tracy shrugged. "I was wrong. These colors suit you."

With a nod of agreement, Dominic paid for the shirts and they left the store.

Hand in hand, they walked through the mall.

Tracy's mouth watered as they passed by the food court. Mrs. Field's Cookies. Haagen-Dazs Ice Cream. McDonald's French fries. Starbucks Coffee. A popcorn stand. Corn dogs. A candy store. Frozen lemonade.

Dominic looked over at her, a wry grin twitching his lips.

Tracy punched him in the arm. "Don't say a word!"

"You can always start your new life tomorrow."

It was tempting, so tempting. What had she been thinking? She should have had one last pig-out party before giving up the good things of life.

She shook her head. "No. I said I was going to start tonight, and I will."

Dominic nodded. There were so many different kinds of food these days, things unheard of back in the days when he had been a mortal man—things like ice cream, cotton candy, hot dogs, coffee that came in myriad flavors. So many new tastes in food and drink. He had savored some of them on Tracy's lips. But any desire he'd had to indulge in solid food had been thoroughly eliminated the night before. It had been foolish of him to think he could eat solid food. He was no longer human. His body could no longer tolerate such things. He was a vampire and blood was his only source of sustenance.

Leaving the mall, Dominic drove to The Catacombs.

"If you are going to live as a vampire, you might as well get acquainted with them," he remarked as he parked the car.

Entering the bar, Tracy noticed that many of the vampires who had been there the last time were there again.

Petrina sashayed up to Dominic as soon as they walked through the door.

"Dom," she purred, her voice low and sultry. "Did you come for that dance?"

Tracy smiled sweetly at the vampire. "Any dancing he does tonight will be with me."

Petrina looked up at Dominic, a pout on her pale lips. "Dom, why do you insist on bringing this mortal here? We could have so much more fun without her."

"You heard the lady, Pet," Dominic said, drawing Tracy into his arms. "I will be dancing with my woman."

"Your woman," Petrina said, a feral gleam in her eyes. "What does that mean, exactly?"

"It means she is my woman," Dominic said, his voice suddenly harsh. "Not my slave."

"She doesn't share her blood with you?"

"No." It wasn't quite the truth. He had tasted her blood, but he saw no need to share that knowledge.

A taut silence fell over the room as all conversation ceased. A moment later, the piano fell still as well.

"Why do you bring her here then?" Petrina demanded. "The Catacombs is only for our kind, or those who serve us. She is an outsider. She does not belong."

A low murmur of agreement rippled through the other vampires.

Dominic's gaze moved over the faces of the vampires in the room. "This is my territory," he said, his voice filled with quiet power. "Tracy is my woman. I have given her my protection, and offered her the Dark Gift. Whether she accepts it or not, she will remain under my protection. Anyone who harms or defiles her will answer to me."

"This may be your territory," Petrina remarked, "and you may be the oldest vampire among us, but according to the ancient laws of our kind, if she is not vampire and not a slave, she is fair game to anyone who can take her."

Petrina's gaze moved over Tracy, her narrowed eyes glowing with hunger.

"Do you wish to challenge my authority?" Dominic's voice rang out, echoing off the walls. "Any of you? If so, step forward and I will oblige."

The vampires fell back, all but Petrina. Power gathered around her like an ominous cloud.

"So be it," Dominic said.

"There is no need for a challenge," Petrina said. "You have only to drink from her. We will know then that she is truly your woman and therefore deserving of your protection, and ours."

Tracy stared up at Dominic, her heart pounding.

The other vampires closed in, their eyes glittering.

Dominic turned toward Tracy. "It must be of your own free will."

It was hard to think with all those pairs of hungry eyes staring at her. If she refused, would Petrina challenge Dominic to a battle? She was sure Dominic would win, and while she wasn't fond of Petrina, she didn't want to be responsible for any hurt done to either Petrina or Dominic. More importantly, she wanted to be accepted by the vampires for Dominic's sake. Would it shame him in some way if she refused? Would Petrina actually fight him? Would it be a fight to the death?

"Tracy?"

"Do whatever you have to do." Turning her head to one side, she closed her eyes, and waited.

Dominic's gaze rested on the face of each of the vampires that now stood in a circle around them. "The blood is the life. I take this woman's blood, freely given, and in doing so, I pledge my life to protect her from any and all who would do her harm."

Leaning forward, he swept Tracy's hair away from her neck.

Tracy's breath caught in her throat as she felt his fangs at her throat. There was no pain, just a quick heat followed by a wave of languorous pleasure.

As from far away, she heard a sudden intake of breath from the watching vampires as the scent of her blood filled the air.

She opened her eyes when Dominic's tongue laved the wounds.

"And now, to complete the ritual, she must drink from you."

Tracy stared at Petrina, unable to believe her ears. Drink from Dominic?

He was watching her, waiting.

"Dominic . . ."

His gaze held hers captive. "It will not make you vampire," he said. "It will only bind us together."

Dared she trust him? What would happen if she refused? She met Petrina's taunting gaze, knew the vampire was doing this out of spite. Determined not to give Petrina the satisfaction of knowing she was afraid, Tracy smiled at Dominic. "I'm ready."

Love and admiration shone in his eyes as he made a shallow gash in his wrist and offered it to her.

Tracy's smile faded as she stared at the bright

red blood. She had licked her own blood on more than one occasion, wiping it away with her tongue when she sustained a paper cut, or scraped her finger on a thorn. But this . . .

Leaning forward, she closed her eyes and licked a drop of blood from Dominic's skin. It was fiery hot, and sweet.

"It is done." Dominic's voice echoed off the walls like rolling thunder.

"So it is," Petrina said.

Marcus smiled at Tracy. "Welcome to The Catacombs."

"Thank you."

The other vampires drifted back to the bar or to their tables.

Dominic drew Tracy into his arms as the piano player began to play again.

When she started to speak, he shook his head. "Later."

When the song ended, he led her to the bar. He ordered "the usual" for himself and a glass of orange juice for her.

She drank it down in three long swallows and asked for more.

When she finished the second glass, Dominic took her by the hand and headed toward the door.

Tracy shivered as they stepped out onto the sidewalk. As though waking from a dream, she stared at Dominic. "How could you put me in a position like that?" she demanded. She wiped her hand across her mouth. "How could you?"

She jerked her hand from his grasp and wrapped her arms around her middle, sickened by the memory of what she had done.

"I am sorry, my best beloved one. I had no idea she would invoke such an ancient law."

"You should have known!"

"Tracy . . ."

"Don't touch me!"

"Tracy, calm yourself. No harm has been done."

"No harm? No harm! You drank my blood! You made me drink yours!"

"Was it so very unpleasant?"

"Yes!" He reached for her again, but she slapped his hand away. "Leave me alone. I'm going home."

"I will take you."

"No."

"It is not safe for you to be on the streets alone." Reaching into his pocket, he offered her the keys to his car.

"Not safe? I thought I was under your protection now," she said, her voice laced with sarcasm.

"Not every vampire in the village was in the bar tonight."

She wanted to refuse his offer but wisdom prevailed. Muttering, "Thank you," she took the keys from his hand, careful not to touch him.

"I will walk you to the car," he said, his tone indicating he would not take no for an answer.

He opened the door for her, not with the key, but with a thought.

She slid behind the wheel, shoved the key in the ignition, and drove away without a backward glance.

Once out of the parking lot, she knew she didn't want to go home, couldn't face being in that big, empty house, or wondering if he was prowling around below, listening to her every move, her every thought.

Turning off the main street, she drove to the Driftwood, anxious to surround herself with normal people doing mundane things.

"So much for my life as a vampire," she muttered.

Parking the car, she hurried into the neighbor-
hood bar.

Inside, she took a deep breath. Compared to the
murky atmosphere of The Catacombs, the Driftwood
seemed as bright as day. An upbeat tune was playing on the jukebox. There was a low hum of conversation, the sound of laughter, of ice cubes tinkling
against glassware. Even the smell was different.

She slid into a booth, ordered a virgin strawberry
daiquiri, then sat back and closed her eyes. Whatever had made her think she wanted to be a vampire? How could she have even considered it? And
Dominic. She could pretend he was human, that
he chose to live a slightly different kind of life, but
he wasn't human and never would be again.

Vampire. She shuddered as she recalled the hungry way Petrina and the others had looked at her.

She couldn't stay here. Even under Dominic's
protection, she would never feel safe in Sea Cliff
again.

She lifted a hand to her neck. He had taken her
blood, and she had tasted his. A bond, he had said,
exchanging blood would create a bond between
them.

What, she wondered, did that really mean?

It means I can find you wherever you go.

Startled, she glanced around, expecting to see
Dominic standing nearby. It took her a moment to
realize that the voice she had heard so clearly had
been in her mind.

*It means we can communicate when we are apart;
that I can read your thoughts, and you can read mine.*

Get out of my head! She silently screamed the words.

And then he was there, sitting in the booth
across from her.

She stared at him, her heart pounding. "I can't

do this anymore." She fisted her hands around her drink to keep them from trembling. "I don't want to be a vampire. I don't want to be part of your world. And I don't want you in my head."

"Tracy . . ."

"I mean it, Dominic. You said you would let me go if that was my choice. Did you mean it, or not?"

"I meant it."

"Then let me go."

"As you will," he said quietly.

She was filled with a wave of unexpected regret. He looked so stricken, so unhappy. Why couldn't she have fallen in love with an ordinary man? She had waited her whole life to fall in love and when she did, it was with a vampire.

Reaching across the table, he took one of her hands in his and kissed her palm. "Farewell, my best beloved one."

"Maybe things will work out next time," she said, hoping to erase the sorrow in his eyes.

"There will be no next time," he replied, and vanished from her sight.

Tracy sighed. Breaking up was never easy.

She finished her drink and slid out of the booth.

It wasn't until she reached home that she wondered what he had meant when he said there would be no next time.

Chapter 20

Tracy felt numb for the next few days. She went to bed early at night, spent her mornings painting, her afternoons doing housework and laundry and taking care of business.

She received a referral from Mr. Petersen and agreed to paint a country landscape for one of his clients.

She saw Bryan at the beach every afternoon. It was refreshing to be in his presence. He made no demands on her and he was fun to be with. Though she didn't really feel like going out, when he asked her to go to dinner and a movie on Friday night, she agreed.

She refused to think about Dominic. With a supreme effort of will, she put him out of her mind. There had never been any future for them. No matter that she loved him. No matter that he had followed her through time. There was no place for them to come together. An eagle might love a whale, but there was no way for them to have a life together.

She had been afraid that Dominic wouldn't leave her alone, that she would hear his thoughts, that he would ask her to reconsider, but, true to his word, he didn't try to contact her in any way.

And that worried her.

There will be no next time.

His last words played and replayed in her mind, sounding more ominous each time. Had he meant that he would not pursue her in her next life? That had to be it. Surely he would not destroy himself because of her. Would he?

Time and again she was tempted to search him out, to go to the house below and see if he was there, but that would mean starting it all over again, and she wasn't sure she could do that. Until she could tell Dominic she loved him enough to share all of his life, it seemed better for them to stay apart.

And going out with Bryan would only complicate things. She thought of calling him and telling him she couldn't make it and then decided a night out was just what she needed. There was nothing complicated about Bryan. He was fun and easy to be with. What harm could it do?

He arrived promptly at six on Friday night and they drove into the city for dinner.

"I had a call from my dad today," Bryan said. "He wants me to come home and settle down."

"Are you going?"

"I don't know. Sometimes it seems like it's inevitable that I go home and become a cop like everyone else."

"But you don't want to."

"Not really. I miss my family, though. They all live close together. My sister just had her first baby." He slammed his fist on the steering wheel. "I just wish I knew what I wanted to do."

"Do you have to decide now?"

"Well, the next academy class starts in October. If I'm going, I need to make up my mind so I can apply before the cut-off date."

"Well, I'll miss you if you decide to go."

"I'll miss you, too."

He pulled into the restaurant parking lot a few minutes later. The Blue Lantern was a popular restaurant with a bar and a dance floor on one side, and a restaurant on the other.

They ordered drinks while waiting for their table.

Bryan glanced at the couples who were dancing, then looked at Tracy. "Want to give it a go?"

"Why not?"

Somewhat tentatively, Bryan took her in his arms.

He was a pretty good dancer, though not nearly as smooth as Dominic . . . she slammed the door on that train of thought and focused on the music. The jukebox was playing an old Heatwave tune, *Always and Forever.*

Tears stung Tracy's eyes and she blinked them back. Dominic had vowed to love her forever.

Their table was ready when the song ended.

Tracy ordered shrimp. Bryan ordered steak.

Abruptly, he reached across the table and took her hand. "Tracy, you know I'm in love with you."

She blinked at him.

"If I decide to go back home, I want you to come with me. As my wife."

"Bryan."

"I know this is sudden. I don't even have a ring to offer you, but I had to tell you how I feel before I lost my nerve."

"Oh, Bryan."

"I guess that's a no."

"I don't know what to say." She had known he

thought he was in love with her, but a proposal was the last thing she had expected.

"I don't guess you need to say anything else."

"It's just so sudden."

"Maybe you could think about it?"

"I will."

He brightened a little at that.

They were walking down the street toward the theater when Tracy saw Petrina and Zarabeth coming toward them. Petrina wore a short black miniskirt, a black crop top, and knee-high black boots. Her long black hair framed her pale face. Zarabeth wore skin-tight black leather pants and a blood-red tank top. Her blond hair was cut short, dyed black on the ends.

The two vampires stopped in front of them. Petrina glanced from Bryan to Tracy, a smirk on her face. "Aren't you going to introduce us?" she asked.

"Bryan, this is Petrina and her friend, Zarabeth. Ladies," Tracy said, emphasizing the word, "this is Bryan Longstreet."

Petrina ran her fingertips down Bryan's arm. "So pleased to meet you," she purred.

"I'm happy to meet you, too," Bryan replied. "Both of you."

"Does Dominic know you're out with another man?" Petrina asked, and then answered her own question. "Of course he doesn't."

"Where are the two of you going?" Zarabeth asked.

"Uh, to the movies," Bryan said, obviously ill at ease.

"Sounds like fun," Petrina said.

"Yes," Tracy agreed, taking Bryan's hand. "Too bad you can't come with us."

"Oh, but we can." Petrina smiled. "Can't we, Bethy?"

Zarabeth nodded.

With a sigh of exasperation, Tracy pushed past the two vampires, pulling Bryan with her. "I'm sorry," she whispered.

"Who are they?" Bryan asked.

"Just a couple of . . . of girls I met. They're friends of Dominic's."

"Ah," Bryan said, as if that explained everything.

Bryan bought their tickets and they went inside to find their seats.

Moments later, Petrina and Zarabeth slid into the two seats behind them.

Tracy was glad when the lights went down and the show started, though she found it difficult to concentrate on the movie, knowing there were two vampires sitting behind her. Now that she had sent Dominic away, she was no longer under his protection, making her fair game for the vampires. The thought sent a cold shiver down her spine. Even if she was still somehow under Dominic's protection, Bryan wasn't.

Tension seeped into her and by the time the movie was over, she was ready to shatter at the slightest touch.

She clung to Bryan's hand as they left the theater, acutely aware of Petrina and Zarabeth strolling along behind them, their heads close together.

What mischief were they planning?

"Hey, Trace, you all right?" Bryan asked.

"Yes, sure, I'm fine."

"Are you cold?"

"No."

"You're shaking."

"Oh. I . . ."

Before she could come up with an explanation, Petrina and Zarabeth moved up beside them, one on either side.

"We've decided you should come to The Catacombs with us," Petrina said.

"No, thanks," Tracy said, her hand tightening on Bryan's. "We have other plans."

"We won't take no for an answer," Zarabeth said.

"Petrina," Tracy said, trying to keep her voice from shaking. "Not tonight."

"Oh, yes, tonight," the vampire insisted.

"You heard the lady," Bryan said. "We have other plans."

"And you heard Zarabeth," Petrina said, taking hold of Bryan's arm. "We won't take no for an answer."

Bryan winced as her hand closed over his arm like a vise, her fingers digging into his skin.

Tracy looked up at Bryan. "I'm sorry."

"It's okay," he said, trying to sound nonchalant about the whole thing. But Tracy saw the sweat bead on his brow.

When they reached Bryan's car, Petrina and Zarabeth climbed into the back seat.

There was no conversation on the drive to The Catacombs.

"I don't remember ever seeing this place before," Bryan remarked as they exited the car. "Is it new?"

"New?" Petrina laughed as her fingers curled possessively over Bryan's arm. "Hardly. It's been here for years."

Tracy glared at Petrina. "Bryan is *my* date."

"You can't have them all," Petrina said, pouting. "Make up your mind. Do you want Dominic or this mortal?"

"Bryan's with me." She knew instinctively that the only way to survive this night was to bluff her way through.

With more courage than she felt, Tracy peeled the vampire's fingers off Bryan's arm, then took him by the hand and walked into the bar.

Stepping through the door, she wondered if Dominic was inside.

The bar was dimly lit, as usual. A slow, sultry tune was being played on the piano. Several couples were dancing, their bodies pressed intimately together.

Tracy recognized a few of them, including Marcus and his human companion. There was no sign of Dominic.

Petrina slithered up to Bryan. "Come on, honey," she crooned, "let's dance."

Petrina led Bryan onto the dance floor. Zarabeth grinned at Tracy, silently daring her to make a scene.

Instead, Tracy moved to the bar and sat down between two vampires. She recalled Dominic had introduced them as Laslo and Turk. She nodded briefly at both of them, then turned to watch Petrina and Bryan dance.

Petrina was pressed so close to Bryan that they looked like they were joined at the hip. She was whispering in his ear; whatever she was saying brought a rosy flush to his cheeks.

Zarabeth sauntered over to stand in front of Tracy, blocking her view of the dance floor. "So tell me, where is Dominic this evening?"

Squaring her shoulders, Tracy met the vampire's gaze. "I don't know. I'm not his keeper."

Zarabeth laughed softly. "Petrina will be delighted to hear that. I must tell her, when she gets back."

"Gets back?" Tracy leaned to one side and peered around Zarabeth. There was no sign of Petrina. Or of Bryan. "Where did they go?"

Zarabeth shrugged, her eyes wide with mock innocence. "I'm not her keeper."

Tracy slid off the bar stool and pushed her way through the crowd onto the dance floor, her gaze searching for some sign of Bryan. If anything happened to him, it would be all her fault.

She was suddenly aware that all conversation had come to a halt.

The music stopped, and a heavy silence fell over the room.

Like wolves on the scent of prey, all the vampires save for Marcus moved toward Tracy until they had formed a tight circle around her. The air hummed, vibrating with preternatural power. Their eyes glowed red with their lust for blood.

Tracy broke out in a cold sweat as the vampires gathered around her. She looked over at Marcus. He was sitting in a booth, his arm around his human companion. She saw regret in his eyes before he turned away.

Pulses racing, heart pounding in her ears, she sent out a silent plea for help.

Chapter 21

Bryan opened his eyes to darkness. He blinked several times, hoping to clear his vision, but the darkness remained. Reaching out, he realized that he was lying on a bed with no memory of how he had gotten there.

Rising, he felt his way around the room, searching for the door, only to discover that he was locked in what seemed to be a small, windowless room.

Moving blindly across the floor, he made his way back to the bed and sat down.

Where was he, and how had he gotten here? The last thing he remembered was dancing with some really weird Goth chick while she whispered obscene suggestions in his ear. Bryan knew he wasn't a man of the world but he wasn't a complete innocent, either. Still, he had felt himself blushing furiously at some of the outrageously salacious things Petrina had proposed.

Too nervous to sit still, he rose and began to pace the floor beside the bed. Where was Tracy?

Was she being held here, too? How long had he been here? And where the devil was he?

He tried to tell himself there was nothing to be afraid of, that Petrina was just playing some sort of sick joke, but as the minutes passed, fear took hold of him. He broke out in a cold sweat, began to tremble convulsively as he recalled her grip on his arm. No mere woman was that strong.

He tried the door again. And again and then, in desperation, pounded his fists against it.

"Hello!" He pounded on the door again. "Is anybody out there?"

"Are you so eager, my little mortal? Then I shall not keep you waiting any longer."

The voice was low and filled with quiet menace.

Bryan stepped away from the door, his heart hammering in his chest. He took a deep breath in an effort to calm his nerves. It didn't help.

The door opened and he saw a tall, slender woman with dark red hair silhouetted in the doorway. She wore a long red gown. The skirt spread around her feet, making it look like she was standing in a pool of blood. He frowned a moment, wondering where Petrina had gone.

"I'm going home now," Bryan said. He moved forward, intending to push her out of the way and get the hell out of there.

"Are you?" She smiled, revealing a pair of gleaming fangs. "I don't think so."

Bryan took a step backward. "What are you?"

"I am vampire." Her voice was mesmerizing, seductive.

"Very funny."

"I am glad you think so."

She glided into the room, her green eyes glittering like shards of emerald glass.

Bryan tried to dart past her, but she was too fast for him. She grabbed his arm and with a twitch of her wrist, she hurled him onto the bed.

He stared up at her, terror coiling around his insides as she sat down beside him.

"Fight me, if you wish," she purred, "but it will do you no good."

He had never hit a woman in his life, but this was no time to be squeamish. Sitting up, he drew back his fist and launched a haymaker.

Her head snapped back at the force of his blow, but other than that, it didn't faze her at all.

Laughing softly, she wrapped one hand around his throat and pushed him back down on the bed. "Your puny human strength is nothing as compared to mine, you foolish creature," she chided.

"Let me go." He had meant the words to be a demand, but they emerged as little more than a whisper, the plea of a frightened child.

"Perhaps later."

He stared into her eyes, eyes now glowing and red. He swore aloud as he felt her fangs at his throat, but there was no pain, just a sudden sense of lethargy that drained him of all desire to resist.

He moaned softly, and then the world dissolved in a crimson mist.

Chapter 22

Dominic's head jerked up, his eyes narrowing as Tracy's voice echoed in his mind.

Dominic, help me! Please, come to me now.

For a small moment of time, he thought of ignoring her. He had spent the last few days pondering his past, reliving every lifetime he had spent with Tracy. He was tired, so tired of pursuing her. Tired of existing. Tomorrow, he had planned to end his existence. What would it be like to see the sun after so many years? Would his body go up in flames at the first touch of the sun on his flesh? Would it be over quickly? He was not afraid of death, but to burn . . . it was something he had feared since burning his hand when he was a young boy. He had never forgotten the excruciating pain.

"Dominic!"

The fear in her voice coiled around his heart and soul.

A moment later, he was streaking through the night, all thought of ending his existence forgotten.

Outside the doorway of The Catacombs, he dissolved into a fine mist before slipping inside.

Anger welled within him at what he saw. All the vampires in the room save for Marcus were gathered around Tracy like wolves closing in on a wounded doe. Eyes glowing, fangs extended, the vampires formed a loose circle around her. From time to time, one of them reached out to touch her, stroking her hair, dragging a fingernail over her cheek, down the length of her arm.

She stood tall and straight in their midst, her expression defiant. For all her outward show of bravado, he could smell her fear; it was a palpable presence in the room, exciting the vampires still more. She shuddered as one of the males licked the side of her neck.

Dominic sent his senses through the room. The boy's scent was strong, yet he was nowhere to be seen. Had they killed him? The boy meant nothing to him, but if they had killed the boy, then they had openly defied the law. Not only the law of the land, but the law that Dominic had set forth decreeing that there would be no blood shed within the boundaries of the village. To defy his law was to defy him.

Zarabeth began to circle Tracy, taunting her with tales of mortals she had killed. Tracy's face paled but she glared at Zarabeth, her expression filled with disdain.

Zarabeth ran her fingernail down Tracy's arm. "Have you nothing to say? We might spare you if you ask us nicely."

Zarabeth put her arms around Tracy, holding her immobile. She put her face close to Tracy's neck and took a deep breath, her eyes closing in rapture.

"Enough!"

Taking on his shape, Dominic strode across the room.

The vampires immediately drew back, leaving Tracy standing alone in the center of the floor.

Going to her side, Dominic slipped his arm around her waist and drew her up against him. "Are you all right?"

She nodded. "Bryan . . ."

Dominic glanced around the room. "Where is the boy?"

It was Marcus who answered. "Petrina took him."

Dominic's gaze settled on Zarabeth. "Is he dead?"

"I don't know."

"Would she take him home?"

"I don't know."

Dominic looked at Tracy, then back at the vampires. "To harm what is mine is to harm me." His voice was mild, but Tracy heard the steel beneath. "To defy my law is to defy me, and the penalty is death."

Zarabeth shook her head. "No!"

"Petrina has openly defied me."

"Vampire does not kill vampire."

"Be still else I destroy you, as well."

A low murmur of consternation ran through the room.

Dominic silenced them with a look. "This is my chosen territory and my law prevails. When I allowed you to share this place with me, you agreed, one and all, to abide by my law. We have peace here because we do not feed on the villagers. We give them no reason to suspect our presence. The boy Petrina has taken has family. He has a job. He will be missed."

Dominic looked down at Tracy, his expression softening. "Come, I will take you home."

"What about Bryan?"

"I will find him," he said, and with that, he swept her into his arms.

A moment later, they were in her bedroom at Nightingale House.

Slowly, he lowered her to her feet.

"The lights," she said. "Put on the lights."

He waved his hand and the lamps beside her bed sprang to life, chasing the darkness from the room.

"Are you all right?" he asked.

"Fine," she said, and dissolved into tears.

"Tracy!" He pulled her into his arms, raining kisses on her brow, the crown of her head. "Do not weep, my best beloved one."

"Find Bryan," she said. "Please."

"I do not want to leave you alone."

"I'll . . . I'll be . . . all right. Please . . . hurry!"

"As you wish," he said, and vanished from her sight.

Tracy crawled into bed, fully dressed, and drew the covers up to her chin. Never in all her life had she been so frightened. Trembling uncontrollably, she closed her eyes. Into her mind came images of the vampires as they had closed in around her, their eyes glowing with a lust for blood. Her blood. If Dominic had not arrived when he did . . .

She opened her eyes and the images vanished. She was never going to be able to go to sleep, doubted she would ever feel comfortable alone in the dark again.

And what about Bryan? Would Dominic find him in time, or was it already too late? How would she ever live with herself if anything happened to Bryan? Oh, Lord, he could be dead, or worse. What if Petrina had turned him into a vampire?

He had done nothing to deserve such a horrible fate. Nothing but be her friend.

With a low groan, she doubled over, her arms wrapped around her middle, and rocked back and forth.

"I'm sorry, Bryan," she sobbed. "So sorry."

Reality returned slowly. He was aware of being cold. And thirsty. Opening his eyes, Bryan was grateful to see that he was no longer in the dark. A single candle burned on the table beside the bed. There was a bowl of fruit, a hunk of cheese, a pitcher of orange juice.

Sitting up, he ate ravenously, drained the pitcher of juice and wished for more.

Rising, he began to pace the floor. Where was she?

He tried the door again even though he was certain it would be locked. To his surprise, it swung open. He stood there a moment, wondering if it was some kind of trick.

Heart pounding, he took a step forward, his whole body tensed for an attack that did not come.

As far as he could tell, he was in an abandoned warehouse. A faint gleam of moonlight offered the only illumination and he moved toward it. He had gone about a dozen steps when he saw a door.

He was hurrying toward it when Dominic St. John suddenly materialized in front of him.

With a startled cry, Bryan skidded to a stop.

For a long moment, he stared at Dominic, who stared at him in return.

"You," Bryan gasped. "You're one of them."

Dominic lifted one brow. "Indeed." His nostrils flared. "And you are not. Yet."

"What do you mean, yet?"

"You are her creature now. It is only a matter of time until she brings you across."

"What are you talking about?"

"She has taken your blood, has she not?"

Bryan nodded, his expression filled with revulsion.

"And she has given you hers in return."

Bryan shook his head. "No, I didn't . . . I wouldn't . . . it was just a nightmare . . . wasn't it?"

"I am sorry. She has marked you now and there is no way for you to escape her so long as she exists."

Bryan stared at Dominic. "What are you saying?"

"You need not worry. She has defied me and for that, she must be destroyed. When she is no more, you will be free of her."

"I don't believe any of this," Bryan said, his voice rising. "It can't be true."

"Come," Dominic said. "I will take you home."

"Where's Tracy? Is she all right?"

"She is no concern of yours."

"I asked her to marry me tonight. I think that makes her my concern."

Hands clenched at his sides to keep from reaching for the boy's throat, Dominic stared at Bryan. "What was her answer?"

"She said no, but I'm hoping she'll change her mind."

"I could destroy you with a thought," Dominic remarked. "And it would please me to do so."

"Just tell me if she's all right."

"She is home," Dominic said.

"You haven't done to her what that woman did to me, have you?"

"No. Give me your hand."

Bryan took a step backward. "No way."

The words had barely left his lips when Dominic was beside him, grasping his forearm. A moment later, feeling slightly dizzy, Bryan opened his eyes and found himself standing outside his apartment. "How did you do that? How do you know where I live?"

"It does not matter. If you are wise, you will not leave your house after sunset. If Petrina comes here, do not invite her in."

"It wasn't Petrina."

"What?"

"It wasn't Petrina who . . . who took my blood."

"Who was it?"

"I don't know. I never saw her before."

"What did she look like?"

"She was beautiful, with dark red hair and the coldest, greenest eyes I've ever seen . . ."

"Kitana." Of course. It was Kitana he had seen in the alley. She was the only immortal strong enough to cloak her presence.

"You know her?"

Dominic nodded. "She is the oldest of our kind."

"It's true, then? You're a vampire, aren't you? And so is she?"

Dominic nodded. "She has taken your blood and given you hers in return. She will be able to speak to your mind. She will hear your thoughts and if she wishes it, you will hear hers."

"Are you going to kill her?"

"That was my intent when I thought it was Petrina who had taken you."

"And now?"

"I do not know if Kitana can be destroyed. Go inside now," Dominic said. "You will not be safe after dark so long as she survives."

With a hand that shook, Bryan unlocked the door and quickly stepped across the threshold. "You can't come in, but thank you," he said, and slammed the door.

With a wry grin, Dominic willed himself back to Nightingale House, and Tracy's side.

He found her asleep in her bed, the covers drawn up to her chin. She looked young and vulnerable lying there, and more beautiful than any other woman he had ever known.

He had hoped to show her the wonders of vampire life, to make her see that even though there was much to give up when one accepted the Dark Gift, there was also much to gain. Though he could not walk in the sunlight, he had walked through centuries of time. The only thing he truly lamented was his inability to father a child. The undead could not create life. Was it selfish of him to want Tracy to join him in his unnatural life, to ask her to give up the joys of motherhood to spend eternity at his side?

Turning away from the bed, he went to stare out into the night. Selfish or not, it no longer mattered. He would destroy Petrina and Kitana and if he survived, he would greet the dawn and Tracy would be forever free of him. He wondered fleetingly what, if anything, awaited him on the other side. There were those who believed that vampires had no soul. If that was true, then only oblivion awaited him. And if he still had a soul, would he burn in hell for all eternity?

"Dominic?"

He turned at the sound of her voice.

"Did you find him?"

"Yes."

"Is he . . . ?"

"He is alive."

"Thank goodness you found him in time!"

"He is alive, but he is still in danger."

She sat up, clutching the covers to her breasts. "What do you mean?"

"A vampire has taken his blood and given him her blood in return. He is her creature now."

"But he's not a vampire?"

"Not yet."

"This is all my fault!"

Crossing the room, he sat down on the edge of the bed and drew her into his arms. Ah, the wonder of holding her again. For a moment, he closed his eyes and drank in her nearness, the warmth of her, the sweet smell of her hair and skin, the sheer pleasure of holding her in his arms.

"It is not your fault," he said, stroking her hair. "Do not worry about the boy. I will not let her bring him across."

"Thank you for helping us. I wasn't sure you would."

"I will always answer your call," he replied quietly. "If I am able."

She drew back a little so she could see his face. "What do you mean, if you're able?"

"The boy proposed to you tonight."

"How do you know that?"

"He told me." Dominic took a deep breath. "Do you care for him?"

"Yes."

"Do you love him?"

"I turned him down."

"That is not what I asked. Do you love him?"

"No."

"Perhaps you should."

Tracy stared at him. "Do you want me to marry him?"

"I want to know you have someone to look after you when . . ."

"When what?"

"Nothing." Rising, he went to stand at the window again. It would be dawn soon.

"Dominic, what are talking about?"

"I am going away, and I do not want you to be alone."

"Where are you going?"

"It does not matter."

"It matters to me."

"Does it?" He turned away from the window to face her. "You told me you wanted me out of your life. I am only doing what you asked."

"What did you mean when you said there would be no next time? Dominic? Answer me."

"Only that I would not pursue you any longer, in this life or any other."

"That's all you meant?"

"What did you think I meant?"

"I thought maybe you were thinking of doing something like . . . you know."

"I am not thinking of destroying myself." It was not a lie, he thought, not exactly. He was no longer thinking of it. The decision had been made. Of course, Kitana might end his existence for him.

Moving toward the bed, he sat beside Tracy once more. "Sleep now, my best beloved one." He smoothed the hair from her brow, ran his knuckles over her cheek, leaned forward to kiss her gently. "I will stay by your side until dawn. There is nothing for you to fear."

Soothed by the sound of his voice, she slid under the covers and closed her eyes. "I wish things were different," she murmured drowsily. "I do love you, you know."

"And I love you more than my life, my best beloved one," he replied, but she was already asleep.

Chapter 23

Tracy woke early after a restless night. Staring out the window, she tried to convince herself it had all been a bad dream. The sun was shining brightly. Birds were singing outside her bedroom window. On such a morning, it was almost impossible to believe there were vampires sleeping the day away, waiting only for the night to emerge from their lairs to prey upon the innocent.

Dominic. Was he resting in the house below? She went over their conversation of the night before. What had he been holding back? Try as she might, she couldn't shake off the feeling that he meant to destroy himself because of her, because she wasn't brave enough to accept him for what he was, because she wasn't strong enough to share her life with him.

Sitting up, she dialed Bryan's number. It was a little early to be making phone calls, but she needed to hear his voice, needed to know he was all right.

He answered on the third ring. "Hello."

"Hi, Bry. It's Tracy. Did I wake you?"

"No. Are you all right?"

"I'm fine. Are you?"

"I don't know." He was silent for a long moment. "I feel sort of . . . strange."

"What do you mean?"

"I don't know how to explain it. I don't have any appetite, and the sun hurts my eyes."

Tracy felt suddenly sick to her stomach. Was he turning? She refused to consider such a thing. Dominic had said Bryan would be all right. Had he only said that to calm her the night before?

"Trace?"

"I'm here."

"He's one of them," Bryan said. "A vampire."

"Who?"

"Dominic."

"Oh. Yes, I know."

"You know? You know, and you went out with him? Are you crazy?"

"Bryan . . ."

"Vampires in Sea Cliff." He laughed, though there was no humor in it. "Who would believe it?"

"What did Dominic tell you?"

"He told me he was going to try and destroy that creature and that I shouldn't go out after dark until she was dead. Dead. Hah. She's already dead."

Tracy's fingers tightened on the telephone. Dominic was going to destroy Petrina. Could he? He was older and stronger. Surely it would be easy for him to destroy a younger vampire. But what if the impossible happened? What if she destroyed him instead? Feeling suddenly restless, she told Bryan goodbye and hung up the phone.

Rising, she showered and dressed and then went downstairs. She put on a fresh pot of coffee and then, feeling suddenly famished, she fixed breakfast. Bacon and scrambled eggs and fried potatoes, orange juice and coffee and toast, and a slice of melon.

Sitting at the table, she stared at the food on her plate. She never ate this much. What on earth had possessed her to prepare such an enormous meal? Even as she asked the question, she knew the answer. She was eating it because she could and, as foolish as it sounded, she was eating it for Dominic because he couldn't.

She savored every bite as if it were the last morsel she would ever consume.

After clearing the table, she washed and dried the dishes and then went outside. She'd forgotten how big the yard was. It was enclosed by a high brick wall that insured her privacy. There were a couple of peach trees near the back wall, a gazebo in the middle of the yard, a small, man-made pond in one corner.

Hands on her hips, she tried to decide where to start. There was, after all, much to be done. The gazebo needed painting, the flower beds needed weeding, the lawn needed to be mowed, the pond needed to be drained and filled with fresh water.

She grunted softly. She had no paint and no lawn mower. She didn't know how to drain the pond, so she spent the next hour and a half pulling weeds, her gaze constantly straying to the path that led to Dominic's lair.

Gaining her feet, she dusted off her jeans, then walked down the path, finally admitting to herself that this was the reason she had come outside in the first place.

When she reached the door, she placed her hand on it. The iron was cold beneath her palm.

"Dominic, are you down there?"

There was no answer, but she hadn't really expected one. With the sun up, he would be sleeping the sleep of the undead.

With a sigh, she laid her cheek against the door. "Oh, Dominic, what are we going to do?"

Tracy . . .

Startled, she backed away from the door, only to realize that the voice, his voice, had been in her mind.

Pressing her cheek against the door again, she whispered, "I'm here."

Come to me.

Her heart seemed to turn over in her chest as the door swung open.

She took a step forward, and several candles sprang to life to light her way.

She hesitated a moment, then crossed the threshold.

The door closed behind her. There was no turning back now.

Filled with apprehension, she slowly descended the passageway. The door at the bottom opened as she approached.

She moved into the room with great trepidation, not certain what she would find. Would he be in his coffin? She was afraid she would run screaming from the room if he were.

Her relief was almost palpable when she saw him sitting in the easy chair in front of the fireplace.

He looked up at her, a faint smile playing over his lips. "You came. I did not think you would."

She sat down on the ottoman. "Why did you call me?"

"To warn you to be careful."

"Bryan said you're going to destroy Petrina. Can you?"

"Yes, but there is a new complication."

"Won't it cause trouble with the other vampires if you kill one of them?"

"Perhaps. But Petrina is not the only problem now."

"What do you mean?"

"It was not Petrina who took Bryan's blood. It was Kitana."

"Who's that?"

"She is the vampire who made me."

"I don't understand. What does she have to do with Bryan and Petrina?"

"This is my chosen territory. Petrina has long desired to have it as her own. I think she has brought Kitana here to fight her battle for her."

"Why have you let Petrina stay?"

"She was turned by the same vampire who brought me across. I suppose I have been lenient with her because of my affection for Kitana."

"And now?"

"The next move is Kitana's. I do not want to fight her, but I will if I must."

"What about Bryan? Is he turning?"

"No. Becoming a vampire is not a gradual thing."

"Then why has he lost his appetite? And he says the sun hurts his eyes."

"She must have given him a good deal of her blood. He is feeling what she feels."

"Will he be all right?"

"If she does not drink from him again, he will be as he was before, in time."

"Dominic, what's wrong?"

"What do you mean?"

"Something's wrong. I can feel it. Tell me."

"There is nothing wrong, my best beloved one. I only wanted to see you one last time."

"Don't talk like that!"

"Is that not what you wish, to be free of me?"

"Yes. No. I don't know." Was it really what she wanted, never to see him again? What would her life have been like if she had let him bring her across centuries ago? How did one know if one would be happy living as a vampire? If she accepted the Dark Gift, would she come to regret it?

He smiled wistfully as he reached for her hand. "You have given me much joy throughout the centuries," he said quietly. "Promise me that you will be happy in this life."

"How can I promise such a thing?"

"Leave this place. Marry your young man. Have children. Grow old together."

Tracy stared at him. "You want me to marry Bryan?"

"He loves you."

"I thought you loved me."

"With all my heart. Never doubt it for a minute."

She shook her head. "I know what you're planning." She blinked back the tears that burned her eyes. "You're going to destroy Petrina and Kitana, and then yourself, aren't you? Aren't you? Because of me."

"Tracy . . ."

"Aren't you? Don't lie to me, Dominic. Tell me the truth."

"I have waited for you for centuries," he said heavily. "Waited to make you mine. I grow weary of waiting."

"No!" She threw herself into his arms. "I can't imagine my life without you in it. Please, Dominic, don't leave me."

"Tracy!" He gathered her into his arms and held her tight, cursing as the lethargy of his kind began to steal over him. "I must rest, my best beloved one. I will come to you tonight."

She nodded, then, cupping his face in her hands, she kissed him. "I love you, Dominic."

He kissed her, then set her on her feet. Rising, he drew her into his arms again. "Until tonight," he murmured. "Go now."

She smiled at him, then hurried toward the passageway. Pausing at the door, she turned in time to see him disappear into his bedroom. With a shiver of revulsion at the thought of him climbing into the casket, she ran up the passageway and out into the light of a new day.

Outside, she wandered around the yard for a while. Relishing the feel of the sun on her face, she grabbed a blanket from the house and went down to the beach. Hardly aware of what she was doing, she found herself at Tower Ten. Shading her eyes with her hand, she looked up to see if Bryan was there. She didn't see anyone at first, and then she saw him come out of the glassed-in booth. The first thing she noticed was that he was wearing a pair of dark—very dark—sunglasses.

"Hey, Bry!"

Moving to the edge of the tower, he looked down at her and waved. "Be right down."

With a nod, she spread her blanket on the sand and sat down. He joined her a few minutes later. Handing her a soda, he dropped down on the blanket across from her.

Tracy held the can up. "Thanks. How are you feeling?"

"I don't know. Strange." He dropped a small sack on the blanket beside him and rolled his shoulders, flexed his hands. "I feel like I'm in somebody else's skin. And . . ." He leaned toward her and lowered his voice, "I have this awful craving for blood."

Tracy's eyes widened in horror. "You're not serious?"

"'Fraid so. I think I'm becoming a . . . you know."

"No! Dominic told me that's not possible. He said it happened all at once, not a little at a time."

"Then why do I feel like this?"

"He said it's because she gave you so much of her blood. He said you're feeling what she feels."

Bryan groaned low in his throat, his expression tortured. "I can't believe this is happening."

Tracy laid her hand on his forearm. "Just do whatever he told you. I'm sure everything will be all right."

"Do you really think so?"

"Sure," she said with forced cheerfulness. "What's in the sack?"

"Oh, I almost forgot. I made you something."

"Really? What?"

An odd expression crossed his face as he picked up the drawstring bag and handed it to her.

More than a little curious, Tracy opened the bag and reached inside. "What on earth?" she muttered as she withdrew her hand. "What is this?"

A flush rose in Bryan's cheeks. "It's a wooden stake—what do you think it is?"

It was perhaps three inches thick and about a foot long, with a wicked-looking point on one end.

She looked up at him, a question in her eyes.

Bryan grinned sheepishly. "I went to the library

and did some reading this morning. The book I read said that the most common ways to destroy a vampire were staking and beheading. Beheading sounds really messy. Drenching them with holy water is supposed to work, too, but . . ." He shrugged. "I'm not Catholic so I didn't think I could get hold of that much holy water. Anyway, ash is supposed to make the best stakes. Took me a while to find some. Bet you didn't know that the Norse god, Odin, used ash to make mankind."

"No, I didn't know that. You really did do a lot of reading, didn't you?"

"Well, it was really interesting once I got started. Hawthorne is good for stakes, too. Did you know that every culture in the known world has some kind of vampire legend? Even the American Indians."

"Anything else?"

"Lots of things, but I can't remember them all now. Seems like every country has its own myths. Anyway, keep that stake close by," Bryan said, tapping the point. "You never know when you might need it."

"Did you make one for yourself?"

He nodded. "Darn right! They won't take me without a fight."

Bryan finished his soda in two long swallows, then crushed the can in his hand. "I'm thirsty all the time! Nothing satisfies me."

Tracy squeezed his arm sympathetically. "Bry, I'm so sorry. If it wasn't for me, you wouldn't be in this mess."

"It's not your fault."

"Of course it is!" She shook her head in exasperation. "I just don't know what to do."

"About what?"

"About Dominic."

Bryan swore softly. "That should be the easiest

decision you have to make. Dump him. He's a monster."

"He is not!"

"You're in love with him, aren't you?"

She blew out a sigh, and then nodded. "Yes."

"I don't understand it."

"Maybe I can explain it," she replied. Plopping down on her stomach, she proceeded to tell him the story Dominic had told her, of how he had followed her through the centuries, hoping to make her his.

Bryan whistled softly when she finished. "That's some story."

"I don't blame you for not believing it."

"But I do."

"You do?"

He shrugged. "I've always believed in reincarnation. I believe that we come in contact with the same people over and over again until things work out the way they're meant to. I was even hypnotized a couple of times. Did the whole past lives thing."

She stared at him, suddenly afraid of what he was going to say next.

"I think we probably knew each other in a past life. Maybe more than one. In fact, I'm positive I was your son, the one who died in the war."

Chapter 24

Tracy shook her head. "No, it can't be." Yet even as she denied it, she knew in her heart that it was true. It explained why she had always felt so protective of Bryan, why she felt so at ease with him. Why she worried about him so.

Scrambling to her feet, she ran a hand through her hair. "Listen, I've got to go."

"Tracy, wait." Rising, he grabbed her arm. "I didn't mean to upset you."

"Upset? Why should I be upset?" She laughed. "I'm living some kind of nightmare."

"Welcome to the club."

"I'm sorry, Bryan, but I've really got to go. I need time to think." She gestured at the people splashing in the water. "And you're supposed to be working." She forced a smile. "Call me later, okay?"

"Sure. Here, don't forget this." He dropped the stake into the sack and tossed it to her.

She caught it one-handed. "Thanks. And don't worry, everything will be all right."

At home, she took the stake out of the sack and hefted it in her hand, trying to imagine what it would be like to use it. With a shudder, she dropped it on her dresser. There was no way she would ever be able to use such a thing, but it made her feel better somehow, just having it there.

Going into the bathroom, she took a quick shower, pulled on a pair of sweats and a tank top, then went downstairs and fixed herself an avocado, Swiss cheese, and tomato sandwich, and then, not wanting to think about Dominic or Bryan or vampires, she turned on the TV and lost herself in an old Robert Mitchum movie.

Two hours later, she put a load of clothes in the washer, then went upstairs to paint, determined that, for the rest of the day, she would pretend that there was nothing unusual about her life. There was no vampire sleeping in the house below. There was nothing wrong with Bryan. There were no vampires in Sea Cliff Village.

Shutting everything else from her mind, she focused on the work at hand and when she called it a day several hours later, she knew Mr. Petersen would be pleased. It was far and away the best seascape she had ever done.

She glanced out the window, felt a flutter in her stomach when she saw the sun was going down.

Dominic would be rising soon, and bringing reality with him.

Keeping her mind blank, she cleaned her brushes, wiped her hands, took off her smock and hung it up.

Night was coming and the vampires of Sea Cliff would be stirring.

She was fixing dinner when the phone rang. She caught it on the second ring.

"Hello?"

"Tracy? It's Bry. Can I come over?"

She started to say sure, then hesitated. Dominic would be there soon.

"Tracy? I don't want to be alone."

"Sure, Bryan. Hurry."

"Thanks, Trace," he said, and hung up.

Replacing the receiver, she went back into the kitchen, only then wondering if Bryan had had dinner. Assuming he hadn't, she put another couple of pork chops in the pan.

He was at her front door before the chops had finished cooking.

"That was quick," she said, closing the door behind him.

"Yeah." He followed her into the kitchen. "I feel like such a coward, afraid to be home alone after dark."

"Well, you've got good reason to be afraid. Have you had dinner?"

He shook his head. "Food's the last thing on my mind."

"Doesn't matter, you've got to eat. Sit down—it's almost ready."

Bryan dropped into a chair and stared at his hands. "She's coming for me."

Tracy glanced at him over her shoulder. "How do you know?"

"She told me so."

With hands that trembled, Tracy filled a plate for Bryan and set it on the table. "What do you want to drink?"

He looked up at her, his eyes haunted. "You don't want to know."

"Bryan, you're scaring me."

"How do you think *I* feel?" He looked at her throat, then jerked his gaze away.

After filling her own plate, Tracy sat down at the table across from Bryan. "You've got to get hold of yourself. You've got to fight her. Block her from your mind. You can do it if you try."

"Yeah."

"Don't think about it now." She gestured at his plate with her fork. "Eat. I'm a good cook."

Forcing a smile, he began to cut one of the chops.

"So, is she as good a cook as she claims?"

Bryan's face paled as Dominic appeared in the kitchen doorway.

"You should know," Tracy said. "You ate some of it once."

Dominic grunted. He remembered that night, and its consequences, all too well. Without waiting to be asked, he sat down at the table.

If possible, Bryan's complexion paled even more.

Dominic regarded him coolly. "You should eat something."

Tracy could see Bryan gathering his courage in the way he sat up straighter and squared his shoulders.

"I suppose you've already eaten," Bryan remarked.

A faint smile twitched the corners of Dominic's lips. "Indeed."

"Stop it, both of you," Tracy said. "Bryan, eat your dinner. Dominic, leave him alone."

Bryan looked sheepish; Dominic lifted one brow.

"Dominic, he needs help. He . . . he's . . ."

"What she's trying to say is that I've been craving blood," Bryan said curtly.

"What else?"

"I can hear her thoughts. She's coming for me.

Soon. And she gave me a message for you just before I got here."

Dominic leaned forward. "Tell me."

Bryan glanced at Tracy and quickly looked away. "She said if you destroy Petrina, she will destroy whoever is closest to you."

"I guess that means me," Tracy said, her voice little more than a squeak.

Dominic nodded, his attention still focused on Bryan. "Did she say anything else?"

"Only that she will see you at The Catacombs tonight, if you are not afraid to meet her."

Tracy pushed her plate away, her appetite gone. "You're not going?"

"I must."

"Why?"

"This is my territory."

"So?"

"It is mine because I am powerful enough to keep it. Those who have challenged me in the past have been defeated. If I want to keep the respect of the vampires among us, I cannot show weakness now."

Bryan pushed his own plate away. "That makes sense." Slamming his fist down on the table, he stood and began to pace the floor. "Dammit, I can't live like this!"

Rising to his feet in a single lithe movement, Dominic laid his hand on Bryan's shoulder. "Look at me."

Bryan stared into Dominic's eyes, whatever objections he'd been about to voice dying on his lips.

"You will go into the living room and lie down on the sofa," Dominic said, his voice low and hypnotic. "You will close your eyes and go to sleep, and you will not awake until tomorrow morning. Your mind will be calm and you will dream about walls. High walls that will allow nothing inside."

"Sleep," Bryan repeated.

"Yes. Go now."

Yawning, Bryan walked into the living room.

Tracy stared at Dominic. "You're just full of tricks, aren't you?"

He shrugged. "He needs the rest." Moving up beside her, Dominic lifted her to her feet. "And I wanted to be alone with you for a little while."

All thought of Bryan fled her mind when she saw the look smoldering in Dominic's eyes.

Slowly, so there could be no mistaking his intent, he lowered his head and claimed her lips with his. She leaned into him, her eyelids fluttering down as his mouth covered hers. His tongue teased her lips. His hands skimmed over her back, cupped her buttocks to draw her body closer to his until they stood heat to heat, mouths and bodies fused together.

Somehow, they were in her room, stretched out on the bed. She was melting, her body aching with need, yearning for something only he could give her.

"Dominic . . ." She moaned his name.

Groaning softly, he drew away from her and sat up.

She put her hand on his arm. "What's wrong?"

He shook his head, but did not look at her.

"Dominic?"

He stood, his back to her. "I need to go."

"Go?" She sat up. "Where? Why?"

"You are far too tempting in far too many ways."

"And that's bad?"

His hands clenched at his sides. "Right now, yes. It is difficult to separate my desire from my need. I do not trust myself to satisfy one without the other."

"But . . ."

"And I must feed."

Before she could say anything else, he was gone.

"Dominic! Dominic, wait!"

But she was talking to the air.

Pounding her fist against the pillow, she rose and went downstairs. Stalking into the kitchen, she opened the fridge and poured herself a glass of ice water, but it didn't help. She doubted if even standing under a shower of ice water would cool her off now. Her whole body burned for his touch. How could he leave her like that?

Putting the glass in the sink, she cleared away the meal no one had eaten, put the dishes in the dishwasher, washed the pans, then went into the living room. Bryan was asleep on the sofa. Sitting in one of the chairs, she studied him while he slept. Once he had been her son.

"Mama, look at me!"

How often had Jacob called to her, wanting her to watch him? He was her only child and she loved him beyond words. He was a clever boy, always eager to learn, anxious for her approval. She had watched him grow from boyhood to manhood, proud of his accomplishments. In spite of his own grief when his father died, Jacob had tried to comfort her, though it had been Dominic in whose arms she had poured out her grief. And when the South went to war, Jacob had been eager to go, eager to fight the Yankees. She had begged him to stay home, pleading that she needed him, that she could not run the farm without his help, but he would not be deterred. . . .

And now he was in her life again, this time as a

friend. And she felt responsible for him again. And, once again, his life was in danger. And, this time, perhaps his soul.

Going to the window, she drew back the curtains and stared out into the night. A full yellow moon shone down on the ocean, painting the tips of the waves with gold and casting long, golden shadows on the face of the water.

Standing there, she felt a sudden uneasiness. Dropping the curtains back into place, she went through the house, making sure all the doors and windows were closed and locked even though Dominic had told her vampires could not enter a dwelling uninvited.

Going upstairs, she slipped into her smock, put a new canvas on one of the easels, mixed her colors, and began to paint.

Slowly, the image on the canvas took form. It was a young man with dark blond hair and brown eyes. A man wearing the proud gray uniform of a Confederate soldier. A house with four white columns rose to his left. Fields planted in cotton could be seen stretching away on his right. There was a woman in the painting, too. She stood on the porch, one hand pressed to her heart, a bittersweet smile on her lips. A tear glistened in her eye.

Taking a step back, Tracy stared at the painting of Jacob and Libby and felt again her anguish as she bid her son farewell for the last time.

"It is a powerful piece."

Warmth flooded her being at the sound of his voice. Contentment washed through her as he came up behind her and slipped his arms around her waist.

She leaned against him, reveling in his strength. "I'm glad you came back."

"I cannot stay." He kissed her cheek. "I must go to meet Kitana."

"Don't go, please. I'm afraid."

"You and Bryan will be safe here."

"I'm not afraid for us." She turned in his arms so she could see his face. "Please don't go."

"I cannot be less than I am. If I do not meet with Kitana, the others will see it as weakness on my part. I cannot afford to be weak, not even for you." He kissed her again. "Promise me you will not leave the house until the sun is up."

"I promise. Promise you'll come back to me as soon as you can."

"I promise."

She stared up at him, wishing she had the words to make him stay.

"Do not be afraid, my best beloved one."

Nodding, she blinked back the tears stinging her eyes. "Kiss me."

His arms tightened around her, drawing her body close to his as his mouth covered hers.

For that moment, she forgot everything else except how much she had grown to love him.

She felt bereft when he drew away. "Be careful."

His gaze moved over her, warming her, and then he was gone.

Judging by the crowd inside The Catacombs when he arrived, Dominic figured that word of his meeting with Kitana must have spread like wildfire through the community of vampires. There was an air of tension in the room when he stepped inside as all eyes swung in his direction. He nodded to those gathered in the room as he made his way toward the bar.

He had dressed with care for this meeting. He wore a blindingly white shirt, black trousers and boots, and, for effect, a long black cloak.

The crowd parted for him as though he were Moses crossing the Red Sea.

At the bar, he asked for a glass of wine, fully aware of the conversations going on around him as the vampires speculated on the outcome of the meeting between Dominic and the oldest of their kind.

He knew the moment Kitana entered the room. A rush of preternatural power moved over him, tickling the hair on his arms, raising the hair at his nape.

Slowly, he put his glass down on the bar.

Slowly, he turned to face her.

She was as beautiful as he remembered. Slight in build, no more than five feet tall, she was nevertheless a commanding presence. She wore a long white gown and a cloak of midnight blue velvet lined in blood-red silk. Her hair fell over her shoulders in a fall of bright auburn that shimmered in the candlelight.

She smiled when she saw him. "Dominic. It has been too long."

He closed the distance between them and kissed her cheek. "I bid you welcome, Kitana."

"Such a quaint little place that you have chosen for your own. I would have thought the cities of Europe would have been more to your . . ." She smiled broadly. "Taste."

Taking her hand, he led her to a booth in the back of the room, sat down only after she was seated.

For a moment, they regarded each other across the table. Dominic wondered if she was remembering the years they had spent together, as he was. So many good years. She had taught him the ways of the Undead, and so much more. She had taught him to read and write, given him an appreciation for art and music, schooled him in deportment and etiquette, turned him from an ill-mannered lout into a gentleman. For better or worse, she had truly made him the creature he was tonight.

"They were good times, were they not?" she remarked.

Dominic nodded, wondering if she had also been reminiscing, or merely reading his mind.

"And so, we meet again. I wish it could be under more favorable circumstances."

"Indeed."

"I cannot let you destroy Petrina. She is mine, and I protect what is mine."

"She has hunted in my territory. She has broken my law."

"She did not feed on the boy."

"No," Dominic said, his voice hard. "You did."

"And very sweet he was, too," she said with a wolfish grin. And then she grew serious once more. "I have also broken your law. Will you destroy me as well?"

"Could I?"

A slow smile spread over her lips. Her green eyes glinted like emeralds touched with hellfire. "No. But then, you are mine, as she is mine."

It had been years since he had known fear. It crawled over him now. "You cannot protect us both."

Dominic watched her carefully, wondering which of her fledglings she would choose to defend. All too clearly, he recalled her threat of long ago to bring him to his knees and though she seemed friendly enough now, he wondered if he dared trust her, or if she was just toying with him, hoping to catch him off guard.

"We can end this amicably enough," she remarked. "You have only to send Petrina and her cohorts away."

"Then you have not come here to help her seize my territory?"

Kitana laughed softly. "Is that what you thought?"

"It crossed my mind."

"Foolish creature. I came here to make sure you did not destroy each other. So, *mon ami*, will banishing her from this place be punishment enough?"

Though it wasn't what he wanted, it was a decision he could live with. And the sooner it was over, the sooner he could return to Tracy.

He nodded his assent.

"You have chosen wisely," Kitana said. "I will summon Petrina."

All eyes were on the door when Petrina and Zarabeth entered the room.

Dominic slid out of the booth, his cloak flowing behind him. "You have broken my law," he said. "Because you are favored of my Maker, I have decided to be lenient with you. From this night forward, you are no longer welcome in this place." He looked at Zarabeth. "Do you stand with her?"

Zarabeth nodded.

"So be it," Dominic declared.

Petrina glanced at Kitana, who was standing beside the booth Dominic had vacated. "You are going to let him do this?"

Kitana nodded. "It is my wish that you do as he says."

Petrina looked back at Dominic, defiance blazing in her eyes. Three of the vampires sitting at the bar rose and went to stand behind her.

"Franco. Laslo. Turk." Dominic's gaze settled on each one as he spoke their names. "Do not let me find you in my territory again. Be gone now, all of you."

Zarabeth and the three male vampires vanished in a swirl of thick black smoke, leaving Petrina standing alone in the center of the room.

She lifted her arm and with a steady hand, pointed a finger at Dominic. "You will regret this night," she hissed, and then she, too, was gone.

At her going, the tension bled out of the room and the remaining vampires resumed what they had been doing before Dominic arrived.

Kitana approached Dominic, smiling faintly. "Peace has been restored." She placed her hand on his arm. "It was good to see you again."

"And you."

"Are you happy with your little mortal?"

The question sent a chill down his spine. Kitana was a female and like all females, could be given to jealousy. "Very happy."

"Will you bring her across?"

"That decision is hers, not mine."

Standing on tiptoe, Kitana kissed him, first on one cheek, then the other. "I hope we will meet again soon."

"I would like that."

With a smile and a wave of her hand, she dissolved into a sparkling red mist and was gone.

Dominic blew out a deep breath, relieved that the matter had been settled without violence or destruction.

It was still early. If he hurried, he could spend a few hours with Tracy before sunrise.

Chapter 25

Upon leaving The Catacombs, Dominic stood outside for a moment. Though he had seen nothing but the night for centuries, he still found enjoyment in the dark. He glanced up at the vast blue sky, his gaze tracking the path of the Milky Way. Mortals saw so little with their limited vision. With his vampire sight, he saw the heavens in all their glory. It was a miraculous display, a manifestation of such boundless power that it made his own abilities seem infantile in comparison.

Lost in thought, he walked away from The Catacombs and into the night. He had told Tracy he believed his soul was lost, but was it? Would a Being who could create worlds without number and all the forces of life and nature condemn him for what he was? Could he yet find forgiveness?

Shaking such serious matters from his mind, he hurried his footsteps as he turned his thoughts toward Tracy.

Perhaps if he had not been thinking of her, he

might have sensed their presence before it was too late.

They sprang at him from the mouth of an alley. Silently and without warning, the five of them drove him backward, pinning him to the ground as they savaged him with their fangs. Driven by hatred, filled with the blood of those they had preyed upon earlier, they were at their most powerful. He felt Petrina's fangs dig deep into his throat. Franco and Turk, each holding an arm, slashed at the veins in his wrists. He felt the blood flow from his body as he fought to throw them off.

Zarabeth dragged her fingers down his chest. Her nails, as sharp as claws, ripped through flesh and muscle.

With a mighty roar, he summoned his power, gathered it to him, and threw the two male vampires away from him.

Like cats, they landed on their feet. Surrounding him, they darted in, but he was ready for them now. Grabbing Zarabeth by the neck, Dominic hurled her into a pile of wooden boxes. Zarabeth shrieked as a box broke beneath her weight, driving a sharp piece of wood into her back and through her heart. It was a death blow. Dark red blood spurted from the wound.

Petrina screamed in rage as her fledgling breathed her last.

Laslo and Franco rushed him from either side. He grasped each of them by the collar and slammed their heads together in a satisfying crack. They fell to the ground, momentarily stunned.

And now Petrina and Turk circled him, their fangs gleaming in the moonlight.

Panting, his strength ebbing like the outgoing tide, Dominic faced them, his fangs bared.

Young and foolish, Turk lunged forward. Summoning the last of his strength, Dominic grabbed Turk by the neck. With a cry, he ripped out the other vampire's throat, then tossed him aside. The vampire sprawled on the pavement like a broken doll.

Standing alone now, Petrina screamed again.

Drawing himself up to his full height, Dominic beckoned to her. "Come," he said, "let us end it now."

Laslo staggered to his feet and grabbed Petrina by the arm. "Let's go," he urged. "He's too strong for us."

"No!"

Laslo tugged on her arm again. "Someone's coming!"

With a wordless cry of frustration, Petrina glared at Dominic as she lifted the lifeless Zarabeth into her arms and then melted into the shadows. Franco lurched to his feet, picked up Turk, and followed Petrina and Franco down the street.

Dominic staggered into the alley, hiding in the shadows as a patrol car passed by.

He stood there, panting heavily, while blood flowed from his wounds.

He needed to find shelter.

He needed blood.

He needed Tracy.

Tracy sat in the living room, a blanket drawn over her legs. Earlier, she had turned on the TV for company, but she was only vaguely aware of what was going on. She'd had a feeling of impending doom ever since Dominic left the house. Time and again she stared at the clock on the mantel, willing the minutes to hurry by, willing him to return to her.

Something had gone wrong. She knew it without knowing how she knew, knew it with such certainty it made her sick to her stomach.

She glanced at Bryan, sleeping soundly on the sofa. Once, she had tried to wake him up, but, caught in whatever spell Dominic had put on him, he had mumbled something about walls and turned over, oblivious to her presence.

"Dominic."

She fell asleep with his name on her lips.

She woke with a start. Frowning, she opened her eyes and glanced around, wondering what it was that had awakened her. Bryan was still asleep on the sofa. The voice of an early morning talk show host droned from the television set. Thinking it must have been the TV that awakened her, she closed her eyes, only to open them again as a faint scratching sound reached her ears. At first, she thought it was only the leaves brushing against the side of the house. And then it came again, louder this time. Someone, or something, was scratching at the front door.

Filled with trepidation, she rose to her feet and padded barefoot toward the foyer. "Is someone there?"

Tracy. Dominic's voice sounded in her mind.

"Dominic? Is that you?"

I need your help.

Pushing the curtains aside, she peered through the front window, gasped when she saw him sprawled out on the floor of the porch.

Turning the lock, she opened the door. "Dominic!"

He reached for her hand and she grasped it in

her own. Lifting him to his feet, she helped him into the house, closed and locked the door behind them.

Once inside, he sagged against her. It took all her strength to help him into the kitchen. He sank down in a chair, squinting against the light as she removed his blood-soaked shirt and trousers. Even his socks were drenched with blood.

Tracy stared at him in horror. His face and hands were badly burned. The skin on his chest was deathly pale, his eyes were red and sunken.

"What happened to you? Did Kitana do this?"

"No."

Pulling a dish towel from a drawer, she wet it in the sink and as gently as she could, began to wipe the blood from his face. He winced and jerked away from her touch.

"I'm sorry," she murmured, and ministered to the wounds in his chest. So much blood. The towel soaked it up and she tossed it in the sink and wet another one. "How did this happen?"

"Petrina."

"She did this?" Tracy asked in disbelief.

"She had help."

"Why didn't you?" The second towel was thrown into the sink with the first.

"This is my territory. If I am to hold it, I must be strong enough to do it alone."

She pulled another towel from the drawer and wiped the blood from his legs. "You could have bled to death."

"No. They were clumsy in their haste." He looked down at his wounds. Though he had bled a great deal, none of the wounds was deep enough to be life-threatening.

With a shake of her head, Tracy wiped the last

of the blood away, then tossed the third towel into the sink with the others. She looked back at him, wondering what else she could do.

He put his hand on her arm. "Tracy . . ."

"What? Did I hurt you?"

"I need . . . blood."

The way he said it, the expression in his eyes, told her he needed much more than the small amounts he had taken before.

When she had him cleaned up, she slipped an arm under his shoulders and helped him to his feet. Step by slow step, they made it up the stairs to the guest bedroom she had recently redecorated.

He groaned softly as she lowered him onto the mattress.

She hovered over him, clutching one of his hands in hers. His skin was almost as white as the sheets.

"Tracy . . ."

"I . . ."

Murmuring "It is all right," he closed his eyes

She stared down at him, stricken by his appearance, by the horrible thought that he might die. She shook her head. He couldn't die. Could he?

She chewed on her lower lip, wanting to give him what he needed, yet afraid. What if he took too much? What if he took it all? What if he turned her into a vampire?

Dared she take the risk?

How could she not?

Her decision made, she stretched out on the bed beside him. "Dominic?"

His eyes opened, dark and filled with pain she could not imagine.

"Take what you need." She turned her head to the side, giving him access to her neck. "But, please, don't take too much."

His lips were cold against her skin. The hands that held her trembled. She felt the prick of his fangs and then closed her eyes as pleasure spread through her. The movies always made it look so painful, she thought drowsily, when it was really quite pleasant.

Fragmented images of Dominic drifted through her mind—a young Dominic riding a horse through a field of tall grass, a newly made vampire on the trail of prey, being burned by the sun when he failed to reach his lair in time.

She moaned softly, then began trying to free herself from his embrace as her instinct for survival surged to the fore.

"Dominic!"

He drew back, his eyes glittering, a drop of blood—her blood—on his lips.

Lifting a hand to her neck, she stared at him. There was color in his cheeks again, his eyes were no longer sunken.

She had done that for him. It was her last conscious thought before she pitched headlong into oblivion.

"Tracy! Tracy, wake up! Good Lord, what has he done to you?"

The sound of Bryan's voice pulled her out of the darkness. She swam upward, upward, following the sound of his voice. She squinted, shading her eyes against the morning light.

Bryan blew out a sigh. "I thought you were a goner."

She stared at him a moment; then, realizing she was wearing nothing but her bra and panties, she drew the covers up to her chin. "What time is it?"

"Almost noon."

"How are you feeling?"

"I'm fine. How are *you* feeling?"

"Okay." She glanced beside her. "Where's Dominic?"

Bryan shrugged. "How should I know?"

"He was here last night. He was badly hurt . . ." She looked up at Bryan, and then at the window. The curtains were open. "You don't think . . . ?"

"Think what?"

"That he died? In the movies, when vampires are exposed to the sun, they burn up and . . . and just disappear."

"Good riddance."

"How can you say that? He saved your life!"

"Yeah, and I'm grateful, but dammit, he's a monster. I hope he is dead. Hell, he's already dead. They all are."

Tracy glared at him, angered by his words. But worse than her anger was her concern for Dominic. Where was he? Had he managed to get to his lair below before it was too late?

Bryan shook his head in exasperation. "Stop worrying. He couldn't have burned up or your bed would be a pile of ashes. And so would you."

She considered that a moment, hoping he was right. "I'm going to get up now," she said.

Bryan stared at her a moment, then a flush rose in his cheeks. "Oh, sure. I'll see you downstairs." He made a hasty retreat, closing the door behind him.

Rising, she went into the bathroom and turned on the shower. She felt a little light-headed, a little unsteady on her feet, but, other than that, seemed to have no ill effects from last night.

She took a quick shower, then made her way downstairs.

She found Bryan sitting at the table in the kitchen, a cup of coffee clutched in his hands. He looked up as she entered the room. "There's fresh coffee in the pot."

"Thanks." She poured herself a cup, then sat down across from him. "Do you have to work today?"

"Yeah. I start at one. Will you be all right?"

"I'm fine—don't worry about me. Just remember, don't stay out after dark."

"That's good advice for both of us," he reminded her.

"Are you hungry?"

"I fixed myself a peanut butter and jelly sandwich earlier—hope you don't mind."

"Of course not."

Bryan drummed his fingers on the edge of the table. "So, what do you think happened to him last night?"

"Petrina and some of the other vampires attacked him. I'm not sure why. Revenge, I guess."

"Well, I hope she's dead." Finishing his coffee, Bryan carried his cup to the sink and rinsed it out. "I need to go home and change. I'll call you later, okay?"

Tracy nodded.

After Bryan left, she fixed herself a bowl of cereal and a slice of buttered toast, poured a second cup of coffee, and sat down at the table again. She ate as though she hadn't eaten in days and when she was done, she was still hungry. She fixed another piece of toast and slathered it with jelly. And then, unable to stand it any longer, she went outside and followed the path to his lair.

She put her hand on the door. It was cold to her touch. "Dominic? Are you down there?"

Her voice penetrated the black sea of pain and lethargy that held him fast. He yearned to answer her, to give her the reassurance she craved, but he was too weak to reply, too weary in mind and body to summon the energy to unlock the door.

Last night, too weak to call on his preternatural powers, he had been forced to drag himself inch by agonizingly slow inch through the night. He could have taken refuge in an abandoned building that he passed, could have tried burrowing into the earth to avoid the rising sun, but he'd had only one thought in mind—to reach Tracy, to see her one last time before he succumbed to the pain of his burns and the weakness that grew worse with every passing moment.

With the heat of the rising sun searing his flesh, he had pulled himself up the stairs to her front porch. Feeling like a pilgrim who had finally reached Mecca, he collapsed against the door and with his last ounce of strength, he had spoken to her mind.

She had taken him to her bed, nourished him with her blood, and then fallen asleep. Knowing the sun would soon flood her room, he had made his way down to his lair and collapsed on the floor in front of the fireplace.

Now, utterly exhausted, helpless as a newborn babe, he closed his eyes and surrendered to the dark peace of oblivion.

She stood there for several minutes, hoping to hear his voice, hoping the door would open, but nothing happened. For a second there, she had imagined she felt something, but then it was gone.

Discouraged and afraid, she went back to the house.

Needing something to occupy her time, she went up to her studio to work on another seascape for Mr. Petersen.

And all the while she wondered where Dominic had gone and if he was all right.

She worked relentlessly. She finished one painting and started a second. Her seascapes were usually light and bright, mild waves beneath bright blue skies, sometimes with dolphins or killer whales cavorting in the background. Today, her oceans were dark, filled with storm-tossed whitecaps and leaden skies ripped apart by jagged bolts of lightning.

Standing back to study her work, Tracy realized she was somehow tuned in to Dominic's pain, that she was painting what he was feeling. She had never realized that vampires could feel pain. Being undead, she had assumed they were immune to pain, and even as the thought crossed her mind, she realized that made no sense at all. If he could feel pleasure, it stood to reason he could also feel pain.

Closing her eyes, she focused all her energy and concentration on Dominic. She pictured him lying in his satin-lined casket, his eyes closed. Did he find relief from his pain while he slept the Dark Sleep?

Dominic, I'm here. Ready to do whatever I can, whatever you need.

There was no answer. She tried again, and again, and each passing second of silence only served to increase her sense of helplessness, her growing fear that he could no longer respond. That he was . . . She couldn't say the word.

And then, when she had given up hope, his voice whispered in her mind.

Come to me at dusk.

I will.

Filled with excitement and anticipation, she put the finishing touches to her second painting, cleaned her brushes, and tidied up the studio.

Removing her smock, she hung it up, then left the room. She had just enough time to take a quick shower and grab a bite to eat before sunset.

Chapter 26

Bryan sat on the bench of Tower Ten, his gaze sweeping the ocean, the beach. The water, a deep blue-green, was calm, so calm even the diehard surfers had abandoned their boards in favor of a rousing game of volleyball. The rest of the beach was nearly deserted since most of the summer people had closed up their houses and gone back to the city. Only a dozen or so people lived here year-round.

Soon this job would be over until next summer and he'd be back at the Y, teaching kids how to swim in the big indoor pool on weekends and giving classes in self-defense to rich young women during the week. He hoped there would be some interest in his tai chi class.

Turning his head, he glanced up at the bluff, his thoughts naturally turning toward Tracy. He wondered what she was doing and what the devil she saw in that vampire creep. Sure, the guy was good-looking and he drove a great car and seemed to have a lot of money, but he was dead, for crying out loud!

Frowning, Bryan recalled that Petrina had put some sort of spell on him there in the vampire bar. Had Dominic put some sort of hex on Tracy? Was that why she was so crazy about the guy, because he'd hypnotized her or something like that? The more he thought about it, the more sense it made. No woman in her right mind would be so enamored of a ghoul if he hadn't worked some kind of witchcraft on her.

How to break the devil's enchantment, that was the question. And he was afraid the only answer was to destroy the vampire. He grunted softly. How best to accomplish the deed? A wooden stake through the heart seemed to be the method preferred by Hollywood. He grunted softly. Well, he had a stake. All he needed now was a good, strong hammer. And, just to be on the safe side, maybe he'd better take along an axe to cut off the head.

But first, he had to find out where the bloodsucker slept during the day.

Chapter 27

Tracy's excitement slowly turned to trepidation as she dressed to go to Dominic's side. She loved him. She wanted to be with him, to comfort him. But she wasn't sure she wanted to be dinner.

Will you walk into my parlour, said the spider to the fly . . .

Shaking such thoughts from her mind, she opened her dresser drawer. She glanced over the contents and grabbed a dark green turtleneck sweater she rarely wore. After pulling it over her head, she ran a brush through her hair, and slipped into a pair of sandals. A quick look in the mirror showed that her eyes were fever-bright.

She was about to leave the house when the phone rang. She picked up the receiver. "Hello?"

"Hey, Tracy."

"Hi, Bry, I was just on my way out."

"Oh? Want some company?"

"Not tonight."

"You're going to see him, aren't you?"

She wound the cord around her finger. "He needs me."

"Uh-huh. Where does he stay, anyway?"

"I . . . he . . . I don't know."

"You're a terrible liar, you know that?"

Before she could form an answer, he'd hung up on her.

She stared at the phone in her hand, then gently put it back on the kitchen counter and went out the back door.

Outside, she walked slowly down the path that led to the house below. "Dominic?"

She took a deep breath as the door swung open. There was no turning back now.

She found Dominic sitting in the chair in front of a roaring fire. He wore a black velvet robe over a pair of black sweatpants. She couldn't help thinking that it was a very sexy outfit.

"Hi," she said softly. "How are you feeling?"

"Better, now that you are here."

She knelt beside his chair, her gaze running over him. The burns on his face and hands looked red and ugly. And painful. Still, he looked much better than he had last night, though he still looked a trifle pale, even for a vampire.

She looked up to find him watching her intently.

As though it were a great effort, he lifted his hand and ran his fingers over the edge of her turtleneck. "Is this to keep me out?"

Tracy stared at him. Was that why she had chosen this particular sweater? Had she subconsciously seen it as some sort of barrier?

She read the yearning in his eyes, knew the decision was wholly hers.

"Relax, my best beloved one. I will not force you.

I will not even ask." Placing his hands on the arms of the chair, he levered up to his feet.

Tracy stood. "Where are you going?"

It was a foolish question, one he did not bother to answer.

She bit down on the corner of her lower lip. If she wouldn't oblige him, then he would find someone who would. "Should you go out? I mean . . . is it safe?"

"I have no choice."

"Can't you wait until you're stronger?"

"I will not get stronger unless I feed."

"But . . ."

"Tracy, *mi mejor querida*, if we are to have any life together, you must accept me for what I am. You need not join me if you cannot, but I cannot change what I am, nor would I."

"I don't want you to go out. Not tonight. Not until you're stronger."

His gaze narrowed on her face. "Are you saying what I think you are?"

In lieu of an answer, she drew the neck of her sweater down, then turned her head away, giving him access to her throat.

Taking her by the hand, Dominic led her to the sofa. Sitting, he drew her down beside him and slipped his arm around her shoulders.

"Relax, *querida*. You know I will not hurt you." He placed a finger over her lips. "Do not worry, I will take only a little."

She turned to face him again. "Will a little make you stronger? As strong as you were?"

"No, but it will ease the pain."

"I never knew vampires could feel pain."

"Vampire senses are more intense than those of

mortals. We feel everything more keenly. Pleasure. And pain."

"Take what you need, Dominic."

"Tracy, I do not want to force you."

"You're not." Leaning toward him, she turned her head to the side and gazed at the fire in the hearth. "I want to do this for you."

Murmuring to her in a language that sounded familiar even though she did not understand the words, he stroked her cheek with the back of his hand. She felt his lips against her throat as he kissed the sensitive skin behind her ear, felt the heat of his breath as his mouth trailed moist kisses down her neck. Her heart was beating wildly when she felt his fangs at her throat.

She could not believe she was doing this. Never, in any other life, had she permitted him to take her blood. Floating on a sensual sea, she wondered what was different now. Why was she letting him do this when she never had before?

Her skin grew warm and she closed her eyes, surrendering to the pleasure that flooded through her. No wonder Dracula had been able to seduce so many women. How could anyone resist his Dark Kiss? She was boneless, weightless, floating in a sea of molten crimson, sinking blissfully deeper and deeper into velvet darkness. . . .

With a wordless cry, Dominic jerked his head back, his gaze moving anxiously over Tracy's face. Her skin was pale, almost translucent, and he swore under his breath. By the fates, had he taken too much?

He whispered her name, his heart pounding with fear. He should have stopped long ago, but her life's blood tasted like the sweetest nectar, her life-force so potent, he could feel his wounds healing, feel his strength returning. Each time he had been about to draw away, he promised himself that he would take only a little more . . . and a little more. . . .

He stared down at her, hating himself for his weakness. He knew she would hate him if he had to bring her across. But he could not let her die. Not this time. Not when she had accepted him for who and what he was, not when she was so close to accepting the Dark Gift that he had offered and she had rejected so many times in the past.

"Tracy!"

She stirred in his arms. Her eyelids fluttered open. For an endless moment, she stared up at him without recognition.

"*Querida?*" He shook her gently, frightened by the blank look in her eyes. "Speak to me."

She blinked at him. Took a deep breath. And then smiled. "Dominic."

Her voice, though weak, was the most welcome sound he had ever heard.

With a glad cry, he gathered her into his arms and held her close, felt tears sting his eyes as he stroked her back, her hair. Weeping softly, he offered a prayer of thanksgiving even though he had lost the right to pray long ago.

"Dominic? Why are you crying?"

"I feared I had taken too much. I thought I had lost you again." He drew back, his gaze searching her face. "How do you feel?"

"Sleepy." She frowned as she lifted one hand to stroke his cheek. "The burns . . . they're almost gone. How is that possible?"

He covered her hand with his and held it to his cheek. "Because of you," he said. "Because of your sweetness, your generosity."

And he had very nearly killed her because of it.

He felt a rush of panic as her eyelids fluttered down and her head lolled forward against his chest.

Holding her in his arms, Dominic gained his feet and followed the passage that led outside, then took the path to her house. She needed nourishment, and she needed it now.

Leaning forward, Bryan adjusted his binoculars. Was he seeing things, or was that Dominic carrying Tracy out of the bushes and up the path toward the back door? His heart skipped a beat as the image through the glass grew closer. Damn, it looked like she was dead.

Had the vampire killed her? Damn bloodsucking fiend!

Or, worse yet, brought her across?

And what had they been doing in the bushes in Tracy's backyard?

He stayed where he was, unmoving, until the back door closed.

And then he left his hiding place and made his way toward the side gate. It opened on well-oiled hinges and he slipped inside, his black clothing making him practically invisible in the darkness as he crept soundlessly across the yard.

Dominic moved unerringly through the dark house. Making his way into the living room, he laid Tracy down on the sofa and covered her with the afghan that was folded over the back of the couch.

Going into the kitchen, he opened the refrigerator. He stared at the contents for a moment, amazed anew at the wonders of modern technology. The refrigerator itself was a miracle. Did the people of today have any idea how easy their lives were? In his day, meat did not come in neat little packages, milk did not come in cartons, there were no such things as potato chips or donuts or soda or any of the other sweets that he had tasted on Tracy's lips from time to time. If a man wanted meat, he hunted for it. If he wanted vegetables or fruit, he tilled the ground, planted seeds, and prayed for a good harvest. Clothing did not come ready-made. There were no toothbrushes, no toothpaste, no such things as flush toilets and indoor plumbing.

He pulled out a carton of orange juice and filled a tall glass, and then filled a second glass with water. Hot and cold running water was another modern luxury. In his day, the only running water was in the river.

Going back to the refrigerator, he pulled out a steak. Never, in all his life, had he cooked on a stove but he had watched Tracy. He unwrapped the steak and dropped it in a skillet, placed it on the stove, and turned on the burner. He added salt and pepper, turned it while it was still red in the middle.

When both sides were browned, he put the steak on a plate, plucked a knife and a fork from a drawer, and carried everything into the living room.

Placing the plate and glasses on the end table, he knelt beside the sofa and kissed her cheek. "Wake up, my best beloved one."

She made a sleepy sound as she opened her eyes.

He smiled at her. "Sit up, *querida*. You must eat."

"I'm not hungry." She frowned. "Why is it so dark in here?"

With a negligent wave of his hand, the lights came on. "You must eat," he repeated, and his voice brooked no argument this time.

Helping her sit up, he cut the steak into bite size pieces and offered her one.

She grimaced. "Did you even cook that? It's practically raw inside."

"It will do you good."

"But I don't like it that rare."

His gaze met and held hers. "Tracy. You will eat it. All of it. And enjoy it. Here now, take a bite."

She opened her mouth and took a bite. She drank the orange juice. She drank the water. She ate all the steak.

"Sleep now, my best beloved one."

"Stay with me?"

He brushed a lock of hair from her brow. "So long as I draw breath."

With a sigh, she clasped his hand in hers and closed her eyes.

And slept.

Dominic stretched out beside her, his hand still in hers. Now that he had fed well, the only thing he needed to regain his strength was rest and he could think of nothing better than sleeping beside his best beloved one until it was time for him to return to his own lodgings.

For a few moments, he knew nothing but utter peace. His wounds were almost healed. Tracy was beside him.

And then he felt it, a sharp jolt of awareness that told him someone had invaded his lair.

A thought took him to the door that led to the house below. He sniffed the air, swore a vile oath as the boy's scent filled his nostrils.

He swore again, cursing his own negligence in not securing the door to his lair behind him, and then he grinned as he imagined Longstreet's horror when he discovered that he was no longer alone.

Bryan moved stealthily down the passageway, a flashlight illuminating the way ahead of him. Every instinct he possessed screamed at him to turn around and get the hell out of there but he kept going forward, one slow step at a time. This was the vampire's resting place, he was sure of it. He needed to get the lay of the land so he could find his way when he returned in the daylight with stake and mallet in hand, and there was no better time to scout around than now, when the vampire was away.

He was in the living quarters now. He glanced around quickly, then went through the door, felt his heart skip a beat when he saw the casket in the center of the room. Even though he'd known Dominic was a vampire, seeing the coffin made it all the more real. All the more frightening.

He looked around, noting there was only one way in, and one way out. And he was suddenly anxious to be out. Who knew how long the vampire would stay up at the house, or what he had done to Tracy?

His hand tightened around the flashlight. By damn, if that bloodsucker had hurt her . . .

The thought died, unfinished, as all the candles in the room sprang to life.

Chapter 28

Standing in the doorway of his bedroom, Dominic bowed from the waist. "Good evening, Mr. Longstreet."

Bryan swallowed past the lump of fear in his throat. He had been afraid before, he thought. There was that time when he'd been a kid and he got caught in a riptide. And the time he was in that car wreck. He'd been shit-scared when Petrina whisked him out of The Catacombs. And terrified when Kitana had bent him over her arm with all the strength of a pro linebacker and sank her fangs into his neck. But he had never, ever, been as afraid as he was now.

"One should not come calling without an invitation," Dominic remarked quietly.

Bryan tried to speak, but no words would come. And even if he'd been able to form the words, what could he say? He could feel the vampire moving through his mind, sifting his thoughts.

"Save for my best beloved one, no one who has

unearthed my resting place has ever lived to tell of it."

Fear flowed through Bryan's veins like ice water, horror so overpowering he was afraid he was going to disgrace himself by wetting his trousers. The vampire's eyes bored into his like burning bits of ice. Try as he might, Bryan could not drag his gaze away, could not stop looking into those hellishly red eyes. Sweat oozed from every pore, trickled down his neck, his back.

Please. The word formed in his mind, a desperate cry for mercy, but try as he might, he could not get the word past the lump in his throat. Couldn't do anything but stare into the vampire's depthless eyes and pray that death would come quickly.

"Did I not warn you to stay home after dark?" Dominic asked.

From somewhere deep inside, Bryan found the strength to nod.

Dominic took a step forward. "You would have been wise to heed my advice."

"I . . . I . . ."

Dominic took another step forward. "So young," he mused. "So foolish." He smiled, revealing his fangs. "So very tasty."

"No!" Bryan tried to draw his gaze from the vampire's, tried to move, but his limbs refused to obey. He could only stand there, helpless, while the vampire circled him.

"Until tonight, you were only a nuisance," Dominic remarked. "Now, you are a threat."

"No. No, I'm not. I won't . . . won't tell . . . anyone. I swear."

Dominic laughed softly. "I have never known a mortal who could be trusted."

"Stop it!"

Bryan's eyes widened at the sound of Kitana's voice.

"Shame on you, Dominic. There is no need to frighten the boy. In another moment, he will wet himself."

"In another moment, he would have been a midnight snack."

Again, her voice moved through the room. "He is mine. Have you forgotten that?"

"I have forgotten nothing."

"Then release him and send him out to me."

It was then, with one vampire staring at him like he was nice, juicy steak and another waiting outside to slake her hellish thirst, that Bryan disgraced himself.

Dominic grimaced as the scent of urine filled the air. "Take him and welcome," he muttered, and with a wave of his hand, he released his hold on the boy. "Go," he said. "She is waiting for you."

Bryan shook his head. "No. If I'm . . ." He swallowed hard. "If someone's gonna kill me, then I'd rather it was you."

Dominic lifted one brow. "Indeed? And why is that?"

Bryan's cheeks turned a brighter shade of red. "I don't want to die at the hands of a woman."

Kitana's laughter echoed off the walls. "Fear not, young man, I am not going to kill you."

"There are worse things than death!" Bryan shouted. "Go away and leave me alone, you ghoul!"

Dominic snorted softly. "Make up your mind, young man. Do you want to die, or not?" Dominic lowered his voice. "But before you decide, you might think on this. Kitana is a lover without equal."

"Lover?" Bryan exclaimed. "She's not looking for a lover. She's looking for a meal."

"You can be both," Dominic said. "Now, go."

Bryan stared at him, his expression one of resignation. "Wait. What did you do to Tracy? Is she . . . ?"

"She is well."

"But I saw you . . ."

"She is not your concern."

Bryan glanced at the doorway, and at the vampire standing in front of him, as still as . . . death. Taking a deep breath, Bryan summoned what courage he could, squared his shoulders, and walked past Dominic and up the passageway to meet his destiny.

With a shake of his head, Dominic glanced around the room. He would either have to find a new place to spend the day, or wipe the memory of this place from the boy's mind. The latter would be the easiest, but probably not the safest. What the boy knew, Kitana now knew, and while she could not cross his threshold without being invited, that would not stop her from sending others to destroy him when he was at his weakest should she take the notion into her head. When he had told Bryan that, save for Tracy, there was no one alive who knew where he rested, he had spoken the truth.

But he would worry about that later. For now, he needed to look in on Tracy.

He willed himself outside, surprised to find that Kitana and Bryan were still there. The boy's eyes were slightly unfocused, evidence that he was under Kitana's spell.

Dominic lifted one brow. "Did you want to see me?"

"Yes." Her gaze moved over him, as tangible as a touch, and then she made a soft sound that could have been compassion. "I am sorry for what happened with Petrina and the others."

"You know what this means. On whose side will you stand?"

A faint smile flirted with the corners of her mouth. "What do you think?"

He shook his head. "If I knew, I would not ask."

"Ah, Dominic, if I intended to destroy you, you would be dust by now. As always, I stand with you." She raked her fingernails lightly over his cheek. "There is none other like you, *mi amor*. Of all those I have brought across through the years, there has been no one like you." She glanced up at the house. "If you had not been so determined to pursue that pretty little mortal through the ages, we might have spent the last few centuries together, you and I."

He nodded. "I would have liked that," he replied, "if it were not for her."

"Keep a close watch on her. Petrina is determined to destroy you. She knows of your affection for your little pet. The mortal woman is the chink in your armor now. Take your own advice, and be careful after dark."

She kissed him then, a quick brush of her cool lips across his own and then, with a wave of her hand, she vanished from his sight, taking the boy with her.

He stared at the spot where she had stood, wondering if he dared trust her. Still, she had spoken the truth. If she had wanted him dead, he would indeed be dust by now. He didn't doubt for a minute that she had the power to destroy him.

Dominic wandered through the backyard for a few moments, enjoying the weight of the night around him, breathing in the myriad scents that drifted through the air. There were many vampires who mourned the loss of the sun and grieved for the daylight they had forever lost. He had never been one of them. He had taken to the Dark Gift like a hound to the hunt and never once looked back. He reveled in his preternatural powers and if, in the beginning, he had been foolish and arrogant, he had soon outgrown it. He made no apologies for what he was. As a vampire, he had killed mortals to preserve his own life when necessary. He had done the same when he was human and he made no distinction between one lifestyle and the other. He wondered briefly if Kitana would bring the boy across, or merely amuse herself with him for a time and then let him go. Ordinarily, Dominic would have had no interest in Bryan's fate. Whether the boy lived or not was of little importance to him save for the fact that Tracy was fond of him.

Dominic drew in a lung full of air. It would be winter soon. He loved the cold months, when the nights were longer and the sun less bright.

The sound of Tracy's sigh was borne to him on the breeze. Hearing it, he put all other thoughts from his mind. She was waking, and he wanted to be at her side.

Tracy opened her eyes slowly, stretched and yawned. A glance at the clock showed that it was still early. She didn't remember falling asleep on the sofa, didn't seem to remember anything . . . and then it all came rushing back.

"Dominic? Dominic, are you here?"

He materialized out of the shadows to kneel in front of her. "Forgive me?"

"For what?"

He stroked the side of her neck with his fingertips. "I might have killed you."

"But you didn't." She smiled at him. "You look much better. Did Bryan call? I'm worried about him."

"He was here."

"He was? Why didn't you wake me?"

"He found his way into my resting place."

Her eyes widened. "Oh, no. You didn't . . ."

"No."

"Where is he now? Dominic? Tell me."

"He is with Kitana."

"You let her take him? How could you?"

"He is hers, by right of blood."

Throwing off the blanket, she surged to her feet and began to pace the floor "How could you let her have him? You know what she'll do to him!"

Dominic watched her for a moment. How like a warrior woman of old she was! Her eyes sparkled with anger. "Calm yourself, *querida*. She will not hurt him."

She rounded on him like a mother bear defending her cub. "You don't know that!"

Dominic rose to tower over her. "She is not cruel. She will play with him a while and when she loses interest, she will find another."

"What if she makes him a vampire? Can you guarantee me that she won't turn him?"

He shook his head. "No. Should she decide to bring him across, there is nothing I can do to prevent it, *querida*. I am sorry."

"I couldn't bear it if anything happened to him."

"I know." He blew out a sigh that came from the depths of his soul. "I am sorry, my best beloved one. It is my fault this has happened."

"No . . ."

"Had I stayed out of your life, his would not now be in danger."

"It's not your fault. You're not responsible for Kitana, or Petrina."

He held out his arms and she went to him, resting her cheek against his chest.

His lips moved over the back of her neck. His tongue laved the sensitive place behind her ear. "Sweet," he murmured. "So very, very sweet."

She lifted her face for his kiss.

His arms tightened around her, his dark eyes burning into her own. "Tracy, do you know what you do to me? Do you know how much I want you? How often I have dreamed of possessing you?"

She stared up at him, certain she would melt from the heat in his eyes.

"Marry me."

Her eyes widened. "You want us to get married?"

"Yes. Now. Tonight. Say yes."

"But . . . marriage." She thought of what it would mean to be married to him. She would never see him during the day. Never have a normal life. Never have children. And yet, how could she deny him again? He had loved her, waited for her, for centuries.

Closing his eyes, he rested his forehead against hers. "I cannot go on without you. The future means nothing to me if you are not there to share it with me. I want to hold you in my arms when the sun goes down, and make love to you until it comes up again."

"We don't have to get married . . ."

Lifting his head, he opened his eyes and gazed down at her. "I am an honorable man." A wry grin touched his lips. "Or I was, when I was alive. I will not make you mine unless we are wed."

She smiled up at him, touched by his words.

"Say yes."

He looked down at her, a silent entreaty in his eyes. How could she deny him again?

"Yes, Dominic, I'll marry you."

He stared at her for several moments, then crushed her in his arms, his lips moving in her hair.

Tracy closed her eyes, a sense of peace enveloping her.

After a moment, he drew away. "Do you want to change your clothes?"

"You really mean for us to get married tonight? But how? We need a marriage license." She paused. "Blood tests."

He waved his hand in a gesture of dismissal. "I will take care of all that."

Tracy glanced down at her jeans and T-shirt. "I always wanted to get married in a long white gown. . . ."

Dominic took her hand. There was a rushing sound in her ears, a sense of disorientation, and when she opened her eyes again, she was in a bridal shop in the city.

"I wish you'd give me some warning before you do that," she said.

"Time is of the essence."

Tracy looked through the gowns, choosing three she liked. Carrying them into the dressing room, she tried them on. The first was sleeveless with a square neck and a straight skirt. It looked very modern and fit beautifully, but it didn't feel like a wedding dress. The second had short puffy sleeves, a high neck, and a poofy skirt. She looked at her reflection in the mirror . . . and shook her head.

The third dress was perfect. It had a round neck,

long sleeves, a full skirt with a short train, and it fit as though it had been made for her. She picked out a shoulder-length veil to go with it.

When a saleslady came to check on her, Tracy said she would take the dress and the veil.

They made several other stops.

Dominic bought a tuxedo.

They both bought new shoes.

Tracy bought new underwear.

Standing outside the last store, her arms full of packages, she looked up at Dominic and grinned. "Well, all we need now is someone to marry us."

With a nod, Dominic took her hand again; when she opened her eyes, they were standing in front of a wedding chapel in Las Vegas.

Hand in hand, they went inside. Tracy glanced around while Dominic spoke to the woman behind the desk. A few moments later, she was being escorted to a dressing room by a rather buxom woman with dyed blond hair.

"Need any help, honey?" the woman asked.

"No, thank you."

The woman laughed, a deep, throaty laugh. "No doubt that man of yours will give you all the help you need."

"No doubt," Tracy replied, and shut the door.

She changed out of her clothes and into her gown, unable to believe they were actually in Vegas, about to be married.

She studied herself in the mirror for a moment. Maybe it was the dress, maybe there was something magical about wedding gowns that made all brides beautiful, but that was how she felt. Beautiful.

She shoved her jeans, T-shirt, and old underwear into one of the other sacks, ran a hand over her hair, took a deep breath, and left the dressing room.

Dominic was waiting for her. He was a man born to wear a tuxedo. His white shirt and black coat were the perfect complement to his dark hair and gray eyes. *James Bond, eat your heart out,* she thought, biting back a grin.

The buxom blonde entered the room. "This way," she said.

Dominic slipped his arm around Tracy's waist and they followed the blonde into a large chapel. The pews were of dark oak—a white runner covered the middle aisle. There were bouquets of white silk roses on the altar; white candles burned in gold sconces on the walls.

The blonde smiled up at Dominic. "Good luck, honey," she purred, and sashayed out of the chapel.

A tall man with a shock of thick white hair passed the blonde on his way into the room, followed by two witnesses.

He glanced down at a paper in his hand. "Dominic St. John? Tracy Ann Warner?"

"Yes," Dominic said.

Nodding, the minister took his place at the altar. "Join hands, please."

Dominic took Tracy's hand in his. His gaze never left her face as she said the words that made her his wife "until death do you part."

"And now, you may kiss the bride."

Dominic lifted her veil and then, gazing deep into her eyes, he whispered, "I will love and protect you so long as you draw breath."

And then he kissed her.

Chapter 29

"Where would you like to spend your honeymoon?"

Tracy looked up at her new husband. They were standing outside the chapel, shopping bags in hand. "Anywhere you want, so long as they have a great big bed."

Dominic hailed a cab and after a wild ride though traffic worse than anything she had ever encountered on the freeways of California, they arrived at Caesar's Palace. With a name like that, it wasn't surprising that the motif was Roman. There was a large pool outside, with fountains and statues everywhere.

She wasn't sure what magic Dominic worked at the desk. Probably the same sort of enchantment he had worked at the wedding chapel, she decided. Whatever spell he used, it worked and the next thing she knew, they were being led to a suite in the Palace Towers and Dominic was carrying her across the threshold.

He kicked the door closed with his heel; then, letting her body slide down the front of his, he set her on her feet, his dark eyes glowing. Whispering, "Mine at last," he captured her lips with his.

It was a kiss like no other she had ever known. Tender yet possessive, gentle yet ardent, it went through her like wildfire, making her heart pound and her blood run hot.

His hands moved over her, his nimble fingers unfastening her gown, lifting it over her head. Her shoes and stockings followed, leaving her clad in only her bra and panties.

She shivered as he stroked her bared flesh, all her senses coming vibrantly alive.

Murmuring "My turn," she slipped his jacket off his shoulders and down his arms and tossed it aside. His white silk shirt quickly followed. She noted, in passing, that he didn't wear a T-shirt.

Her fingers were trembling as she removed his belt, unzipped his trousers to reveal a pair of black bikini briefs. She removed his shoes and socks and he stepped out of his trousers.

Pausing, she drew back to look at him. He was beautifully made, from his broad shoulders and trim waist to his long legs. She had expected his body to be pale, though she wasn't sure why. Instead, his body and legs were the same warm, golden shade of brown as his face and arms.

She felt her cheeks grow hot under his regard.

"You are lovely," he murmured. "More lovely than I have ever seen you."

His fingertips traced the curve of her breast, slid down her belly, sending shivers in their wake.

His gaze met hers. "Mine," he said, his voice husky. "Mine, at last."

And sweeping her into his arms, he carried her

into the bedroom, placed her on the bed, and stretched out beside her.

Tracy ran her hands over his shoulders. "Tell me."

"I love you, my best beloved one," he said, his voice thick, "as I have always loved you. As I will always love you."

Warmth filled her heart. "I love you, too. So much."

He drew her close, raining kisses over her face, her breasts. Her bra and panties and his briefs seemed to disappear as if by magic and she reveled in the sensory pleasure of bare skin against bare skin. His was cool beneath her palms. She tested the strength of his arms, measured the width of his shoulders, ran her fingertips over his muscular chest and hard, flat belly. He gasped as her exploration continued downward, and then he was rising over her, his dark gray eyes glowing with desire as he claimed the prize he had won time and again throughout the centuries; a prize that had never been sweeter than it was now, when she knew the truth of their past lives together, when she knew everything there was to know about him, and loved him anyway.

She cried out in mingled pain and pleasure as their bodies came together. It was everything she had ever dreamed of, more than she had ever imagined. Surely no mortal man could have lifted her to such lofty heights, brought her such soul-shattering delight.

She stilled as she felt his teeth at her throat.

Dominic drew back, his body trembling with a need that went beyond hunger, beyond pain.

She read the question in his eyes and after a moment of indecision, she nodded.

He kissed her deeply and then she felt his teeth at her throat again. There was no discomfort, no fear, only a rush of sensual pleasure that built and built until she was mindless, breathless. She clutched him to her, reaching for something that was just out of reach.

His voice whispered in her ear, urging her on, crying her name, until the world shattered around her, left her floating in a pool of such exquisite pleasure she was certain she had passed beyond the veil of mortality. And there, locked in his arms, she felt his tortured soul brush hers as he found peace and acceptance in her arms.

Slowly, slowly, she drifted down to earth. Dominic rolled onto his side, carrying her with him, so that they lay face to face. She had often heard the expression "forever in his eyes," but in Dominic's case, she really could see forever in his eyes—*her* forever, if she only had the courage to ask for it.

She sighed with pleasure as his hand lightly stroked her back, her hair. Their bodies were pressed intimately together from chest to ankle. She imagined she could feel his heart beating in time with her own.

He brushed a lock of hair from her brow. "Tell me you have no regrets."

"Of course I don't. Why would I?"

"You have given up much to be my wife."

She caressed his cheek. "And gained much in return."

"I hope you will always feel that way."

"Right now I just feel . . . sticky."

With a hearty chuckle, he lifted her from the bed and carried her into one of the two adjoining bathrooms—one for him, one for her. This one had a light gray marble floor, a glass-enclosed marble shower, a separate whirlpool bathtub, a gray marble vanity with a round sink and brass fixtures, and a hair dryer. The toilet and bidet were enclosed. She grinned when she saw there was a phone within easy reach of the commode.

Her cheeks turned pink when she saw herself in the mirror, her lips swollen from his kisses, her skin flushed.

She frowned at her reflection, saw her eyes widen as she realized what was bothering her. Dominic cast no reflection in the mirror.

"Bath or shower?" he asked.

She looked at her image in the mirror again, then turned to look at him, at his arms holding her.

"Tracy?"

She stared at the mirror again and then looked up at him. "You're not there. In the mirror."

"No." A muscle worked in his jaw. "I told you before, vampires cast no reflection."

"Why not?"

He lifted one shoulder in a negligent shrug. "Kitana said it was because vampires have no souls."

"Is that what you believe?"

"Perhaps it is true."

"I don't believe that!" She looked in the mirror again, accepted what she saw, and put it from her mind, determined not to let it spoil this moment. "I must be getting heavy."

He lifted one brow, dismissing the notion. "So," he said, "what will it be? Bath or shower?"

"Shower."

He opened the door, reached inside, and turned on the water. When it was just right, they stepped inside. It wasn't one large shower, as she'd thought, but two showers that met in the middle. Each bathroom had its own separate entrance from the main room and met in the middle, in the shower.

For a moment, he held her in his arms. And then, picking up the soap, he washed her from neck to toes, sending shivers of delight coursing through her as his hands moved over her.

And then he handed her the soap.

Feeling deliciously wicked, she returned the favor.

And then they made love with the water running over them, and washed again.

It was, without a doubt, the best shower she'd ever had.

Getting dressed later, Tracy got her first good look at their suite. Done in rich earth tones, it was the most luxurious room she had ever seen. There was a full-sized desk and chair in front of the windows, which stretched across most of one wall. The entertainment center located across from the bed held a 27-inch TV, complete with remote and cable. There were tables with lamps on either side of the bed, a large mirror on the wall. There were lights in the closet, even an iron and ironing board.

"Wow, I've never seen anything like this except in the movies," she muttered. "How much is this costing you?"

Dominic moved up behind her and slipped his arms around her waist. "Three hundred dollars."

She glanced over her shoulder. "Three hundred dollars? For one night?"

He chuckled. "It is worth it just to see the look on your face."

She stuck her tongue out at him.

"I was going to get the Rain Man Suite."

She giggled. "The Rain Man Suite? You mean, like from the movie? How much was that?"

"Thirty-five hundred dollars."

"A night? Wow, I'd like to see that."

"I can arrange it, if you like."

"That's all right. This one is fine."

"I am glad you like it. I thought it would be more intimate." He nuzzled her neck. "More romantic."

"I don't think you need a setting to be romantic," she remarked dryly. "It seems to come to you naturally."

He laughed out loud. "Are you ready?"

She nodded. She had never been to Las Vegas and she was eager to see the casinos and try her hand at the slot machines. Looking in the mirror, she frowned, wishing Dominic had given her time to pack. She only had two choices—her wedding gown or the jeans and T-shirt she had been wearing at home.

"They have shops in the hotel," Dominic said, reading her mind.

She couldn't stop looking at him as they rode down in the elevator. Each time his shoulder brushed hers, each time their eyes met, she recalled what it had been like to be in his arms. Warmth flowed through her body as she anticipated what would happen when they returned to their room.

Dominic caught her gaze. Grinning, he leaned down to whisper in her ear. "If you do not stop looking at me like that, I will take you here, now."

She felt a rush of heat flood her cheeks. A moment later, the elevator door opened.

She was overwhelmed by the number of stores located inside the hotel. A brochure told her that there were more than a hundred shops and restaurants, including Gucci, Versace, Abercrombie and Fitch, Ann Taylor, Just For Feet, FAO Schwarz, Spago, and Planet Hollywood.

The domed ceiling was painted to look like the sky, complete with fluffy clouds; the buildings had a Roman motif, with lots of marble and statues.

Spying a simple black sheath in a window, she went inside to try it on and bought it, along with a pair of black, low-heeled sandals.

Dominic also picked black, of course, and when she complained, he bought a powder blue shirt instead. Black slacks, black loafers. The store assured them that their old clothing would be sent up to their room.

When they passed The Cheesecake Factory, she bought a slice of chocolate cheesecake and ate it as they walked along.

Dominic smiled indulgently while she ate, laughed softly as she licked her fingers. Unable to resist, he pulled her into his arms and kissed her. She smelled of soap and toothpaste and rich, dark chocolate. It was an intoxicating combination.

Walking along The Appian Way, they wandered down corridors filled with marble and an exact replica of Michelangelo's David. They passed Bernini's and Cartier's and a shop that sold Italian ceramics and dinnerware.

He stopped automatically when they came to a Godiva chocolate shop.

Tracy grinned up at him. "Think you know me pretty well, don't you?"

He didn't say anything, only pulled a twenty-dollar bill out of his pocket and handed it to her.

She bought a bag of assorted dark chocolates.

"Some for now," she said, popping one into her mouth. "And some for later."

Tracy couldn't help staring when they entered the casino. There was an impressive gold statue of a man she assumed was Caesar sitting on a horse. Lights flashed, bells and whistles and the sound of music and laughter filled the air. There were Roman statues and columns and rows and rows of slot machines, from regular slots to video Poker, Keno, and Twenty-one. And there were people everywhere clad in everything from jeans and T-shirts to floor-length gowns and tuxedos.

Tracy stopped in front of an unoccupied slot machine. "Do you have a quarter?"

"I think so," Dominic replied dryly, and fished a quarter out of his pocket.

Filled with excitement, Tracy dropped the quarter in the slot and pulled the handle. Bars and sevens flashed in front of her eyes as the wheels spun and when they finally stopped, there were three sevens in a row.

Several quarters dropped into the tray.

"I won!"

"Beginner's luck," Dominic said.

"You think so?" Scooping a quarter from the tray, she fed it into the machine and pulled the handle.

And lost.

"Come on," Dominic said.

Tracy scooped her winnings up and dropped them in a plastic cup she found beside the machine. "Where are we going?"

He led her to an unoccupied machine that was third from the aisle near the entrance to the casino.

Tracy looked up at him. "Why here?"

"It's a busy aisle near a busy entrance. It's been my experience that most of the so-called loose machines are up front." He called an attendant and got fifty dollars worth of quarters. "Here you go." He tapped the machine. "Always play the maximum number of coins."

With a nod, she put five quarters in the machine. And won again.

She spent the next hour playing the machine, winning more than she lost.

Dominic stood behind her, amused by her excitement, content to simply watch her.

After an hour, she was thirty dollars ahead and ready to try something else. Going to the cashier, she exchanged her quarters for dollars, which she offered to Dominic.

"Keep it," he said.

"I don't have any place to put it."

Grunting softly, he folded the bills in half and placed them in the right pocket of his trousers. "The right is yours, the left is mine."

Moving through the casino, Tracy couldn't help but notice the way women turned to look at Dominic. Not that she could blame them. He was easily the most handsome man in the place. Not only that, but he exuded an air of mystery and sensuality that was impossible for any female over thirteen to ignore.

Dominic stopped at one of the craps tables and Tracy moved up beside him. She watched the game for a few minutes, completely baffled by what was going on. Dice and money seemed to change hands at an alarming rate and she had no idea how the players knew who was winning and who was losing. The man next to her had a row of one-hundred-dollar chips in front of him.

She wondered how the men who worked at the table remembered who had made which bets, and whose money to take and who to pay off.

She heard calls of "Eight the hard way" and "Any craps" and "Come on, seven" and "Twenty on big six" from the players and wondered what it all meant.

Tracy looked up at Dominic. "I'd ask you to explain it to me, but I don't think it would help."

Dominic pulled a roll of bills from the left-hand pocket of his trousers, peeled off five twenties, and handed them to her.

"That's your money," she said, noting which pocket he had reached into, "not mine."

"I have more money to lose than you do."

She couldn't argue with that.

"The easiest thing to do is play the field," he said. "It is one bet on one roll of the dice. If a shooter rolls a three, four, nine, ten, or eleven, you win. If they roll a two or a twelve, you win double. A five, six, seven, or eight means you lose."

"That sounds simple enough."

"You can also play any craps, which means if a shooter rolls a two, three, or a twelve, you win seven to one."

"Oh, I like that!"

Dominic grinned at her. "Or you can play any seven, which pays four to one, or ace-deuce, which means you win if a shooter rolls a three. The odds are fifteen to one."

"I get the feeling you've been here before."

"A time or two."

She felt a twinge of jealousy. "Did you come with someone?"

"No, *querida.* I would not have brought you here if I had."

Pleased, she decided to play the field and placed a twenty on the table.

She was having a good time when she felt someone watching her. Glancing up, she saw a tall, painfully thin man staring at her through hooded brown eyes.

When she met his gaze, he smiled at her. The look sent a shiver down her spine and she tapped Dominic on the arm.

When he didn't look at her right away, she tugged on his hand. "Dominic, that man is giving me the creeps."

That got his attention. "What man?"

"Over there. In the gray sweater."

Dominic found the man in question. Their gazes locked for stretched seconds, then the man in the gray sweater left the table.

"Who was that?" Tracy asked.

"An old acquaintance."

Her eyes widened. "You mean he's a vamp—"

"Yes."

"Vampires in Vegas," she murmured. "Sounds like a movie title."

"It is a favorite hunting ground."

Glancing at all the people milling around, Tracy found that easy to believe. Gamblers, transients, tourists who'd had too much to drink—they would be easy prey.

"Are there others here now?"

He nodded. "The man in the flowered tie. The woman in the sequined dress. The stickman at the next table. The attendant making change at the slot machine in the corner. The lady in the cashier's cage."

Tracy moved closer to Dominic, all thought of gambling forgotten as she tried to pick out the vampires among the people moving through the casino. She looked at the woman in the sequined dress, trying to see what it was that set her apart from the other women at the craps table. Her skin was pale and flawless and though she wasn't really pretty, there was something different about her, something intangible yet undeniable. The same was true of the man in the flowered tie. He looked rather ordinary and yet there was something about him that set him apart from the others. She noticed that the other people at the table clustered around them, seeming to be eager for their attention.

Dominic leaned down to whisper in her ear. "It is the glamour of being vampire that sets them apart."

Tracy frowned at him. "Is that why I invited you to dinner that first night? Because I was mesmerized by you?"

"No, though that might have been a part of it. We share the bond of eternity, my best beloved one." He looked down at her, his dark eyes hot. "We will always find each other."

She whispered his name, hoping he could hear the longing in her voice.

His gaze moved over her face and then, abruptly, he scooped up his chips and dropped them into his coat pocket. Taking her by the hand, he led her out of the casino to the elevators.

Desire hummed and flared between them as the car climbed the floors.

He was undressing her almost before the door to their room closed behind them and by the time they reached the bedroom, she was naked. Lying in bed, she watched him undress, admiring anew the width of his shoulders, the way his muscles rippled under his skin as he stripped off his trousers, the latent power evident in every move.

He looked at her, and she thought she would melt from the heat of his gaze. And then he was there on the bed beside her, drawing her into his arms, murmuring that he adored her, worshipped her, could not exist without her.

Caught up in the wonder and the magic that was Dominic, she welcomed the touch of his fangs at her throat, pleased that he desired her, that she could give him that which he needed to survive.

The second time they made love was as soul-shattering and pleasurable as the first. Exhausted mentally and physically by the events of the day, she fell asleep in his arms.

She woke with the sun shining brightly in her face. Eyes closed, she smiled and stretched as she remembered the night past and then, with a cry, her gaze darted to the pillow beside hers, afraid of what she would find.

But Dominic was gone.

Relief swept through her. For a moment, she had been afraid she might find a pile of ashes on the pillow.

Piling the pillows behind her, she sat up and stared out the window.

A moment later, there was a knock at the door.

Wrapping a sheet around her nakedness, she padded across the thick carpet. "Yes?"

"I've brought your breakfast, Mrs. St. John."

She smiled at the sound of her married name as she opened the door a crack and peered out. "I didn't order any breakfast."

"Mr. St. John ordered it last night, ma'am."

Tracy opened the door and stepped back and a young man wheeled a cart into the room. A second young man followed the first. He was carrying a vase filled with red roses, which he placed on the desk, and then he handed her an envelope.

"Will there be anything else, ma'am?" the first young man asked.

"No, thank you." She glanced around the room. "I'm afraid I don't have any . . ."

The boy smiled at her. "It's been taken care of," he said, and the two young men left the room, closing the door behind them.

Tracy opened the envelope and withdrew a sheet of hotel stationery and five one-hundred-dollar bills. Laying the cash on the desk, she read the note:

> *My best beloved one, I have gone to seek my rest. I will come to you at sunset. Use the money to buy whatever you wish, whatever you need. Know that I am dreaming of you and exist only to be in your arms again.*
>
> *DSJ*

She read the note again, kissed his initials, and then sat down at the desk to eat. Unrolling the napkin, she found another note. She grinned as she read it.

"I wasn't sure what you liked for breakfast. I hope something here will appeal to you. Love, Dom."

One by one, she uncovered the trays, revealing a strawberry waffle, chocolate chip pancakes dusted with powdered sugar, scrambled eggs, two poached eggs, and eggs over easy. Another tray held hash browns, fried potatoes, bacon, and sausage. There was a cup of fruit, three kinds of muffins, a blueberry tart, two slices of French toast, a single-size serving of Rice Krispies, a carton of milk, a glass of orange juice, and a cup of coffee.

For a moment, she stared at all the dishes spread before her, and then she burst out laughing. One thing was for certain. Life with Dominic would never be ordinary!

Filled with the warmth of his love and caring, she ate a bite of everything, then went into the bathroom and luxuriated in a hot bubble bath.

Later, she went shopping, buying whatever caught her eye. Something for her. Something for him. Something for her. Something for her that was also for him.

She sent her purchases up to their room and then left Caesar's Palace, deciding she might as well go sightseeing while she could. She wandered through the other casinos, overwhelmed by their opulence. They were all so gorgeous, both inside and out.

She ate lunch at the MGM Grand, stopped at The Mirage to wander through Siegfried and Roy's Secret Garden and Dolphin Habitat, spent a few moments playing Blackjack at the Excalibur. And yet, no matter where she was or what she was doing, she couldn't help wishing Dominic were with her, couldn't help wishing she could hurry the sun across the sky.

How many vampires were there in Vegas? In the world?

Where had Dominic gone to spend the day?

Where did the others go?

In the movie *Dracula*, the vampire had been required to sleep on his native soil. Obviously that was Hollywood fiction since Dominic hadn't mentioned such a thing, but thinking about it made her wonder how many other vampire myths were fantasy and how many were fact. Would he be repelled by garlic? A cross? Would pure silver or holy water burn him? She would have to ask him later.

She was crossing the lobby of Caesar's Palace when she suddenly remembered Bryan. Hurrying up to her room, she dropped her packages on the bed, which had been made in her absence, and quickly dialed his number.

He didn't answer, so she left a message, telling him where she was and giving him her room number. It was only when she hung up the receiver that she realized he was probably down at the beach.

At least she hoped that's where he was. She couldn't shake the feeling that something horrible had happened. She couldn't help worrying that Kitana might have brought Bryan across, or that he was helplessly in thrall to her. She shook off a quick mental image of Bryan lying in a coffin beside Kitana, his lips stained with blood. If anything happened to him, it would be all her fault. Knowing how Bryan felt about vampires, how would she live with herself if Kitana forced the Dark Gift on him?

As much as she wanted to spend another night here, it was time to go home. She had to get in touch with Bryan, had to know that he was safe.

She glanced out the window, her heart skipping a beat when she saw the sun was low in the sky.

Dominic would be rising soon.

Chapter 30

Kitana came awake the moment the sun began its slow descent below the horizon. Instantly alert, she sat up and stretched her arms over her head. As always, she was filled with a sense of indomitable power and well-being. She had been a sickly child. While her brothers and sisters were outside playing in the sun, she spent her days indoors, staring out the window. Unable to run and play with the others, she had been confined to her bed. Any exertion wearied her. Sometimes the mere act of eating had exhausted her.

She was nineteen years old the night the stranger came to her parents' inn. She had been sitting on a chair in the common room in front of the fire, blankets swathed around her. Summer or winter, she was always cold.

The man's gaze had settled on her face for a long time. His eyes had been a blue so pale they seemed almost colorless. But, for all that, they mesmerized her with their intensity. When he looked away, she felt as though she had lost something precious.

She had risen early the next morning, hoping to see him again. She had waited in the common room all day, but he had never made an appearance. And then, just when she was beginning to think she would never see him again, he had glided into the room. She couldn't help staring. Never before had she seen a man like him. His clothing—fawn-colored breeches, a white lawn shirt, soft leather boots—was impeccable. Unlike the people of her small village, his skin was clear and smooth. His pale blond hair fell to his shoulders.

She stared at him, hoping to be noticed, and when he looked her way, a rush of warmth flooded through her, chasing away the cold that was ever a part of her.

Her eyes had widened as the stranger moved toward her.

When he reached her side, he inclined his head. "Good evening, my pretty one."

Pleasure filled her at his words. "Good evening, kind sir."

"Will you walk with me?"

She had swallowed hard. "Me? You want me to walk with you?"

He held out his hand. "Will you do me that honor?"

She hadn't known what to say. No man had ever noticed her before. She glanced around the common room, looking for her mother but, for once, there was no one else in sight.

Filled with a sudden sense of adventure, she had thrown back the quilt that covered her and placed her hand in his.

With easy strength, he had helped her to her feet. Placing her hand on his arm, he had escorted her from the inn.

Outside, night had fallen. A slice of butter-yellow moon kept company with the stars.

Kitana shivered, though she wasn't sure if it was her illness or the cool air that made her tremble. The stranger seemed to tower above her though he was only a few inches taller than she.

"How long have you been ill?" he asked.

"All my life, sir."

"Have you seen a physician?"

"Yes. None of them has been able to help."

"I can help you."

Pausing, she had peered up at him. He looked back at her, his eyes glowing like pale sapphires in the darkness. "Are you a doctor, sir?"

"No."

She shivered again, frightened now without knowing why. "I think I should go back. My mother . . ."

"Do not be afraid, *mein kleines.*"

She drew her hand from his arm and backed away. "Good night, sir."

She didn't see him move, but the next thing she knew, his fingers were digging into her forearm and he was dragging her into the trees. She struggled in his grasp, kicking and scratching. Her nails raked his face, but to no avail.

When they were well away from the inn, he came to a stop.

Kitana looked up at him, her heart drumming in her ears. "What . . . what are you going to do to me?"

"I am going to give you a gift that was given to me centuries ago."

"A gift?" she asked skeptically. "What kind of gift?"

He looked past her into the distance. "I am the last of my kind."

"Your kind?" Some of her fear dissipated in the face of her curiosity.

"I am *Vampyr.*"

"*Vampyr?*" She repeated the word, then gasped. "You mean vampire? You're a vampire?"

He nodded. "All the others are gone. Those who were not destroyed by the hunters have taken their own lives."

She tugged against his hold, her gaze darting from side to side. "But I have no wish to be a vampire."

"I have never brought anyone across. My blood is pure, my powers strong." His gaze settled on her face again. "I have what you need," he said quietly. "But be warned, the gift I am about to give you carries great risk and great responsibility."

She stared up at him, the taste of fear bitter on her tongue, as he lowered his head toward her. She tried to fight him, her struggles increasing when she felt his teeth at her throat. And then, abruptly, she was filled with a sense of warmth and well-being. She closed her eyes and leaned into him, all thought of resistance swallowed up in the sense of euphoria that engulfed her.

"Kitana. Kitana, child, you must drink."

Feeling drugged, she blinked up at him.

He thrust his wrist in front of her, pushed it against her lips. "Drink!"

Staring into the endless depths of his eyes, she did as she was told. And when he tried to draw his arm away, she clung to him, hungry for more. Strength flowed into her with every swallow. Energy pulsed through her with every breath. For the first time that she could remember, she felt healthy and strong, felt as though she could run and never grow weary, climb a tree, swim the river.

Muttering an oath, he wrested his arm from her grasp.

She stood on her own, looking up at him, her brow furrowed in confusion. Though it was late night, she could see clearly. The veins in the leaves on the trees. The individual threads in the stranger's coat. The thin plume of smoke rising from the inn.

She looked at him and laughed out loud; then, extending her arms out to her sides, she twirled around and around.

"Vampire!" She shouted it to the stars. "I am vampire!"

That night, the stranger, whose name was Wolfric, told her all she needed to know to survive. She listened intently, though now and then her attention was drawn away. It was difficult to concentrate on one thing when there was so much to see, to hear. Every sense was heightened, sharpened.

When, near dawn, he rose to leave her, she clung to his hand, begging him not to go.

He had smiled down at her and for the first time she noted how very weary he looked.

"Enjoy your new life, *mein kleines*," he had said kindly.

Tears filled her eyes, dripped onto her hand, as red as blood.

Tenderly, he had stroked her cheek. "Remember me."

"Please do not leave me. I am afraid."

"There is nothing to fear."

"Where are you going? Will I ever see you again?"

Rising, he had drawn her up against him and kissed her cheek. "*Auf wiedersehen.*"

"Wait!"

Even before the word left her lips, he was gone in a twinkling of silver mist.

And she had known, on some deep instinctive level, that he had gone to meet the sun.

Rising, she bathed, then dressed with care. Like many newly made vampires, the lust for blood had been overpowering. In the beginning, the hunger had been unbearable and she had taken lives, perhaps more than necessary. Back then, she had lacked the patience to feed slowly and in her haste and hunger, she had killed indiscriminately. In time, she had learned to control the hunger, to feed at her leisure. She had learned it was not necessary to kill to survive, that she could leave her prey alive, if she chose, though she rarely did so.

There was, after all, no end of handsome young men to feast upon. Though she had bewitched many of them through the years, she had bequeathed the Dark Gift to but a few. Like Dominic. Even after all these centuries, she regretted her foolishness in letting him get away. But she had still been a young vampire then, easily amused, quickly bored.

Of the mortals she had turned, Petrina was the most like Kitana. Not every mortal could handle immortality, but Petrina had been a vampire at heart even before the change. She was a relentless hunter. She delighted in keeping her prey alive, toying with them as a cat played with a mouse, taking the blood of her victims a little at a time, all the while letting them know that death awaited them.

Ah, Petrina. She far excelled Kitana in cruelty and blood-letting. And she had set herself against Dominic. Kitana frowned. Sooner or later, her two fledglings would again seek to destroy one another. And while she was fond of Petrina, it was Dominic who had ever been her favorite. Perhaps she could find a way to arrange a peace between them before they destroyed each other. She did not wish to lose them both.

Long ago she had vowed to bring Dominic to his knees, but they had been words spoken in anger. Though she had told him she could destroy him, she was no longer certain it was true. Power radiated from him, power perhaps equal to her own. And while she would have enjoyed his company through the ages, she was no longer certain of her ability to control him. He was a proud man, arrogant in his preternatural strength,

But tonight was not a night for thinking of the past. Tonight was a night for romance.

Smiling, she ran a hand through her hair, filled with an almost girlish excitement at the prospect of seeing the boy, Bryan, again.

Chapter 31

Tracy knew the moment he entered the room. One minute she was alone, staring out at the lights that lit up the city, and the next, she was aware of a subtle shift in the atmosphere and Dominic was standing behind her, his arms around her waist, his lips nuzzling her neck.

She leaned against his chest, overcome by a sense of completeness now that he was there.

It had been in her mind to ask him to take her home but now she wanted nothing more than to be in his arms. Just for a little while, she told herself. The night was young. They had plenty of time.

His tongue laved the sensitive skin behind her ear. "Did you miss me, my best beloved one?"

"Of course." She turned in his embrace and smiled up at him. "I even bought you a present."

"Indeed?"

She nodded. "Two, actually." Standing on tiptoe, she kissed him, then slipped out of his arms.

Going into the closet, she withdrew a shopping bag and handed it to him.

Dominic looked at her, then delved into the bag and withdrew a midnight blue robe with black silk piping.

"Do you like it?" she asked.

He ran his hand over the velvet, then reached out to cup her cheek. "Thank you, *querida*," he said, then frowned. "It must have cost a great deal."

"Almost as much as this room," she said, grinning, "but it was worth it."

His gaze caressed her face and then he drew her into his arms once more. "I love you, my wife, more than you will ever know."

"Oh, Dominic," she murmured. "I love you, too."

"You mentioned two presents," he reminded her.

A faint blush pinked her cheeks. "So I did. I'll be right back."

"Where are you going?"

"Just into the bathroom for a minute."

Going to the closet, she picked up a bag, then went into the bathroom and closed the door.

Dominic stared after her, then, after removing his shirt, he put on the robe. It was a luxurious garment, he thought, fit for a king.

He looked at the bathroom door, wondering what she was doing in there, felt his breath catch in his throat when the door opened and she stepped out clad in a diaphanous white nightgown that was so light, so sheer, it looked as though it had been fashioned of dreams and moonbeams. Her glorious honey-gold hair fell down her back and over her shoulders in soft waves.

She blushed under his frankly admiring gaze.

"You bought that for me?" he asked with a faint grin.

"Do you like it?"

"Very much. And it is just my size."

Soft laughter filled the room as she walked toward him. He could see the faint outline of her figure beneath the whisper-soft silk. The scent of her perfume trailed behind her but it was the scent of the woman that intoxicated him. Desire swelled within him. She was his. He could scarcely believe it. After countless years, she was in his arms, warm and willing. The wonder of it, the reality of it, was almost more than he could bear.

With a low cry, he swept her into his arms. Trembling with need, he carried her to bed and laid her on the mattress. Stretching out beside her, he drew her into his arms. With an air of reverence, like a supplicant at the altar, he worshipped her with his hands and his lips, whispering that he loved her, had always loved her.

And she caressed him in return, telling him with every touch, every kiss, that she was his, would always be his.

Her nearness, the intensity of their lovemaking, intensified his power. It swelled within him, cocooning them in a world of preternatural sensations.

Tracy moaned softly as her senses grew and expanded. His feelings, his pleasure, were tangled up with her own until she couldn't tell one from the other. She felt his hunger, as well, and when his fangs grazed her neck, she turned her head to the side, a wordless sound of acquiescence rising in her throat.

Her eyelids fluttered down as his body merged with hers and then she was lost—wonderfully, deliciously lost in Dominic's embrace.

* * *

Dominic held Tracy close, her back tucked against his chest, his arms tight around her, their legs entwined. He had waited centuries for this woman, he thought, and would willingly endure them all again for this moment.

She was his woman now, his wife, at last.

Her scent filled his nostrils. The sweetness of her essence lingered on his tongue.

Only one thing remained, he thought, and wondered if, in this life, she would accept the gift he had offered her countless times before.

He loosened his hold when she stirred in his arms. "Is something wrong?"

"No, but . . ." She rolled over and smiled at him. "I didn't have dinner and I'm hungry. And I'm worried about Bryan."

"I do not understand why you worry so over that boy."

"I can't help it. He was my son in a past life, I'm sure of it."

"Ah, Jacob."

"Yes. Would you mind terribly if we went home?"

"Whatever you wish, *querida.*"

"I hate to leave, but . . ."

He placed one finger over her lips. "It is all right, my best beloved one." He kissed her tenderly. "We can go home whenever you like."

Tracy ordered room service and while they waited for it to arrive, they made love again, then showered together.

She laughed as she washed Dominic's back. "It never occurred to me that vampires bathed."

He glanced over his shoulder, one brow arched in wry amusement. "Indeed?"

She shrugged. "I guess I just never thought of vampires doing normal things, you know?"

"Just skulking around in the shadows, preying on innocent women?"

"Well, something like that. Of course, I never really believed in vampires, either, until I met you. Now I'm wondering if there are really ghosts and werewolves." She frowned at him, irritated by the amusement in his eyes. "Are there?"

"Not that I know of."

"Well, that's a relief."

They were drying each other off when there was a knock at the door.

"I will get it," Dominic said. Wrapping a towel around his middle, he went to answer the door.

He dressed while she ate, prowled the room restlessly while she dressed and got her things together.

She took a last look around the room to make sure she hadn't forgotten anything.

"Ready?" he asked.

She nodded. "Thank you for a wonderful honeymoon."

"Thank you," he said quietly, "for marrying me."

They were the sweetest words she had ever heard.

Dominic held out his hand. "Ready?" he asked again, and she put her hand in his.

A moment later, they were back in Nightingale House.

Tracy put her bags down on the floor inside the door, then moved through the downstairs rooms, turning on the lights.

When she returned to the living room, Dominic was standing where she had left him.

"I need to find Bryan," she said.

He nodded.

"I guess we should start at his place, but I don't know where he lives."

"Kitana will know where he is."

"How do we find her?"

Dominic stared into the distance a moment. "She is at The Catacombs. The boy is with her."

"Is he all right?"

Dominic stilled for a moment, then crossed the distance between them and took her in his arms. "She has brought him across."

"No!" She pounded her fists against his chest, tears streaming down her cheeks. "No, no!"

"I am sorry, *querida*. I did not think she would act so swiftly."

"You knew she'd do it? You knew, and didn't tell me?" She pounded her fists against his chest again. "Why didn't you tell me? Why didn't you stop her?"

"I could do nothing to stop her."

Tracy collapsed against him, sobbing, "Poor Bryan."

Dominic held her while she cried, one hand lightly stroking her hair, until her tears subsided.

Moving out of his arms, she went into the kitchen, wet a dish towel, and wiped her face. Bryan, a vampire.

Dominic's voice sounded behind her. "Perhaps it was his idea."

"No. He loved being a lifeguard. He loved the sun, the outdoors." She turned to face him. "And he hated vampires. Why would he become one?"

"Kitana can be very persuasive. Do you still wish to go?"

"I don't know. Maybe he wouldn't want me to see him . . . that way."

Dominic smiled faintly. "It is nothing shameful, *querida*, only a different way of being."

"Isn't there some way to undo it?"

"No."

Tracy sighed. "Let's go." She had to see Bryan, had to talk to him, ask him if he was all right. "I hope he's all right."

The Catacombs was in full swing when they arrived. Tracy saw Marcus and his human companion sitting at a table in the back. Landau and Magdalena were standing at the bar. There were others she recognized but had no names for.

And then she saw Bryan.

He was standing at the end of the bar beside the most beautiful woman Tracy had ever seen.

As though feeling her gaze, the vampire turned to look at her and Tracy knew immediately that this was Kitana, the vampire who had made Bryan. The vampire who had made Petrina.

The vampire who had made Dominic.

Bryan turned then, his gaze meeting hers across the room.

She was suddenly sorry she had come here. What could she say to him?

Bryan smiled at her and then, apparently seeing the horror in her eyes, the smile died away. He spoke to Kitana, then started toward Tracy.

She took a step backward, only to be brought up short when she ran into Dominic. He put his hands on her shoulders to steady her.

"He is still Bryan," Dominic said quietly.

She forced a smile as Bryan drew closer. "Hi, Bry."

"Hi, Tracy."

An awkward silence fell between them.

Tracy's gaze moved over Bryan. He looked the same, and yet he didn't. She tried to put her finger on what was different. The changes were subtle. His hair seemed fuller, darker. His skin was flawless. And even though he was a new vampire, his power danced over her skin.

She looked up into his eyes. "Did you want this, Bryan? Was it your choice?" She glanced at Kitana. "Or hers?"

"It was hers, but now that it's done . . ." He shrugged. "It's not so bad."

"Did you . . . have you . . . ?"

He nodded.

"Bry, I'm so sorry."

"It's not your fault. And it's not bad, really."

"Not bad? How can you say that? You hated vampires! You called them . . ." She paused, acutely aware that she was surrounded by vampires.

"I know," Bryan said, smiling sheepishly. "But Tracy, you can't believe the power! It's amazing, the things I can do. I'll bet I could swim from here to Catalina and back again. And colors . . . you've never seen such colors. Kitana said she'll take me to Europe once . . ." He paused and glanced over his shoulder.

"Once what?" Tracy asked.

"Nothing."

"I think he means once things are settled between me and Petrina," Dominic remarked. "Isn't that right?"

Bryan shifted from one foot to the other, but said nothing.

Tracy looked over at Kitana again, only to find the vampire regarding her through cold, calculating eyes. She was glad to feel Dominic's arm slide possessively around her waist as the other vampire glided across the room toward them.

"Dominic," Kitana said, inclining her head in his direction.

"Kitana. I see you have brought your new play-mate with you."

She slid her arm through Bryan's and smiled up at him. "Yes. He pleases me very well."

"For how long, I wonder."

"For as long as I desire," she retorted, then turned her attention to Tracy. "I wonder how soon you will tire of this one, now that she no longer resists you. It was always the chase that thrilled you."

"She is my wife now," Dominic said.

"Your wife!" Kitana exclaimed, her eyes narrowing. "You married a mortal? Why?"

"My business is no longer your business," Dominic replied, his voice cool. "Except where Petrina is concerned. Where is she hiding?"

"Surely you don't think I will tell you."

"She cannot hide from me forever."

"Is this bit of ground worth fighting over?"

"It is to me, but she has more to answer for than that."

Kitana nodded. "She was wrong to attack you in such a cowardly fashion."

"She paid for it. Zarabeth and Turk are no more."

"Petrina will never forgive you for that."

Dominic snorted. "If not for Petrina, they would still be among us. She has no one to blame but herself."

"She does not see it that way."

He shrugged. "She does not worry me. But you do."

"You have nothing to fear from me."

"And when I destroy Petrina?"

"I would rather you didn't."

"And when I do, will I have to fight you as well?"

Kitana shrugged. "Who can predict the future?"

"If you still have any power over her, tell her to leave this place. The next time we meet, I will destroy her."

Chapter 32

Tracy looked up at Dominic, alarmed by the quiet menace in his tone.

Kitana heard it, too.

Bryan shifted restlessly, obviously upset by all the talk of killing. Tracy didn't blame him. She was feeling more than a little unsettled herself.

Kitana smiled reassuringly at Bryan. "Do not let such talk bother you." She turned to Dominic once more. "Remember what I told you," she said, and glanced pointedly in Tracy's direction.

"I remember."

Kitana laid her hand on Dominic's arm. "Take care of yourself."

Tracy looked up at Dominic as Kitana led Bryan away. "What did she mean? What did she tell you?"

"Not now," Dominic said.

"All right, but we're going to talk about it later."

Dominic guided Tracy to a table and ordered her a drink, then moved through the room, speaking to each of the vampires. It reminded her of the way candidates running for public office shmoozed with the common folk, garnering votes and good will. Was Dominic asking for the support of the vampires in the coming battle with Petrina? Would they give it to him? Was Petrina so strong he needed help to defeat her?

She tapped her fingernails on the table, took a sip of her drink. There was something in the air, something that made the hair raise along the back of her neck, something that made it impossible to sit still.

Frowning, she gazed around the room again. Was it her imagination, or were there fewer vampires than before? She hadn't seen any of them leave, but Marcus and his companion were gone. So were Magdalena and Landau and Nicholas and some of the others she had seen earlier.

With a start, she realized there were only a handful of vampires left in the room, and that they were all standing with their backs to the bar. Five males and one female. She knew somehow that they had sided with Petrina. But why had the others gone and left Dominic alone? And even as she asked herself that question, she heard Dominic's voice in the back of her mind. *This is my territory. If I am to hold it, I must be strong enough to do it alone.* She knew then that he had sent the others away.

She looked at the vampires again. Was he strong enough to fight them all?

A sudden stillness fell over the room. Power shimmered in the air, crawling over her skin like ants.

There was a faint sound, like static in the air, and Petrina materialized in the center of the room.

Dominic turned away from the bar to face her. "So," he said quietly. "It begins."

"We don't have to fight," she said. "You could leave."

"I will not."

"Nor will I."

Dominic glanced at Tracy. "Go home, *querida*, and lock the doors."

She shook her head. "I'm not leaving you."

Dominic nodded. She would be as safe here as anywhere else so long as he survived.

Blocking everything from his mind, he gathered his power around him.

There was no warning, no signal.

Energy flamed through the air as Petrina launched herself at him, her hands like claws, her fangs bared.

The other vampires formed a loose circle around them, their eyes glittering, their nostrils flaring as Petrina drew first blood.

A slow smile spread over Dominic's face as the hand he lifted to his cheek came away bloody. It was a foolish thing to do, letting her draw first blood, but some latent sense of honor rebelled at the thought of fighting a woman, even a woman who was determined to see him dead.

With a cry, she sprang at him again but he was ready for her now. She was an old vampire. She carried the blood of ancients in her veins, but she was no match for him. He was older, stronger, and carried the same blood in his veins.

She shrieked in outrage as he pinned her against the wall, his fangs at her throat.

"You are beaten. Admit it and leave this place."

She shook her head, and smiled at him.

Tracy screamed, "Dominic, look out!"

He turned, but it was already too late. The vampires closed in on him, their nails and fangs savaging his flesh.

With a roar, he struck out at his attackers. Save

for Petrina, they were all young vampires, over-confident of their powers, and yet they were strong and determined. He wondered what Petrina had promised them in return for their treachery. One on one, he could have destroyed them without effort. But the five of them circled him like angry gnats, darting in and out, giving almost as much damage as they received. He was vaguely aware that Petrina had slipped away.

And then he heard Tracy cry out.

Over the heads of the vampires trying to wrestle him to the ground, he saw Franco and Laslo grab Tracy. They forced her back into the booth until she was lost from his sight beneath the two of them.

Her fear drove straight to his heart. With a mighty surge, he turned on the vampires, flinging them aside the way a horse shook water from its coat.

Heedless of the blood flowing from his arms and legs, he battled the other vampires. Hatred fueled his anger, making him oblivious to the wounds they inflicted on him. One of the younger vampires turned and ran from his rage.

He tore out the throat of the second, ripped the heart out of the third.

In the lull that followed, he heard a harsh cry of pain, turned to see Laslo and Franco reeling backward, their faces contorted with anguish as they clawed at their eyes.

Tracy sat up, a small brown bottle in one hand. "Holy water."

Dominic grinned at her, and then felt a new wave of fear as Petrina rose up behind Tracy and wrapped the fingers of one hand around Tracy's throat.

"Your little bottle is empty," Petrina said with a sneer. "And you are mine."

"No!" Dominic started forward, but Petrina held out her free hand. "Another step and I will tear out her heart."

"No!"

Petrina glanced at Franco and Laslo. "We are going to go now, and we will take your little mortal with us, to make sure you don't follow."

"Petrina, wait . . ."

"You took Zarabeth and Turk from me," Petrina said. "Now it is my turn to take something from you."

"If you kill her, I will hunt you down. There will be no place where you can hide, no place where I will not find you."

Something that might have been fear flickered in Petrina's eyes and was quickly gone. "I will make you a deal then," she said, her hand tightening on Tracy's throat. "I will not kill her, and you will leave Sea Cliff to me."

"You will not turn her?"

"No."

Dominic stared at Petrina for a long moment, as though weighing her words, and then sighed in resignation. "Very well. Leave her and go."

Petrina shook her head. "I do not trust you. We will take her with us, and leave her where you can find her."

Dominic's gaze rested on Tracy's face. "Do not be afraid, my best beloved one. I will find you." He looked at Petrina again. "Do not betray me."

"I have your word that you will not follow us?"

He nodded.

"And your word that you will wait until tomorrow to find her, that you will not use the bond between you before that time?"

He nodded again. "Have I your word that you will not kill her and you will not turn her?"

"Yes, my word."

Dominic grunted softly, wondering what Petrina's word was worth.

"Franco, Laslo, come."

The two vampires went to stand beside Petrina. The skin on their faces was red and scorched. In some places, it hung in lacy tatters, like bloody cobwebs.

Dominic looked at Tracy again. "I will find you, *querida*. I will always find you."

Eyes wide with fear, she nodded.

And then Petrina took her away.

Dominic stood in the middle of the room, his mental anguish far greater than the pain of his wounds, which continued to bleed profusely.

He had gambled everything he loved, everything he held dear, on Petrina's promise. His only hope was that she wanted Sea Cliff bad enough to keep her word. If she betrayed him, he would not rest until he had cut her heart from her body and flung it into the sea.

Suddenly overcome with the loss of blood, he left The Catacombs. He lacked the energy to will himself home. Instead, he slid behind the wheel of one of the cars parked outside, started the engine with a thought, and drove to Nightingale House.

Leaving the car in the driveway, he went up the porch stairs. He stood on the verandah for several minutes looking out over the ocean. The water was like a great black mirror reflecting the light of the moon. He looked skyward, his gaze tracing the outline of the Big Dipper, following the path of the Milky Way. He would miss this place but it was a small price to pay for Tracy's life. Perhaps they would go back to his house in Maine. She had been happy there. As for himself, he could be happy anywhere, so long as she was there beside him.

Tracy. He clenched his hands at his sides. He could find her with a thought but he had promised not to do so. Was he being a fool to wait, a fool to trust Petrina? He knew without doubt that if he broke his word, she would kill Tracy without a qualm. And yet his apprehension grew with every passing moment.

Opening the front door, he stepped inside.

And knew immediately that Petrina had been there.

"Tracy!"

Calling her name, he followed Petrina's scent up the stairs, down the hall to Tracy's bedroom.

He came to an abrupt halt when he opened the door, his gaze taking it all in in a single glance. Franco and Laslo stood on either side of the bed. Petrina knelt on the mattress. Her head jerked around as he opened the door. There was a smear of blood on her lips.

Tracy's blood. She was lying on the bed, her eyes closed, her face as pale as death itself.

Rage rose up within him as he met Petrina's gaze.

Defiantly, she returned his stare.

"You gave me your word," Dominic said coldly.

"You gave me your word you would not follow me."

"I did not follow you. This is where I live." His eyes narrowed. "And where you will die."

He was moving as he spoke, his hands reaching for Petrina. But she was moving, too, and when he reached the foot of the bed, she disappeared in a swirling black mist.

Undaunted, Franco and Laslo attacked him, one from each side, bearing him down to the ground.

Dominic was feeling weak and light-headed from the amount of blood he had lost earlier, but his rage, combined with his soul-deep concern for Tracy, fueled his flagging strength. With a roar, he surged to his feet. The two vampires flew after him, but he was too quick for them. Pivoting on his heel, he broke the mirror over Tracy's dresser. Grabbing two long shards of glass, he whirled around, slashing first Laslo and then Franco across the throat, slicing their jugular veins. Blood fountained from the killing wounds. Both vampires fell back, their hands clutching at their throats, screams issuing from their lips as the mirror's silver backing scorched their preternatural flesh.

Dominic saw a flash of movement out of the corner of his eye and Petrina materialized in front of him. He ducked just in time to avoid the brunt of her attack. Nevertheless, her nails, as sharp as a raptor's claws, raked his cheek as she hurtled past him. He felt a sudden wetness on his skin and knew she had drawn blood.

She caught herself and whirled around, her fangs bared.

Dominic faced her, his feet spread wide, waiting.

She sprang at him again, her face contorted with hatred.

Dominic waited until the last second, then, darting backward, he grabbed the stake from the dresser and drove it into her breast.

She shrieked as the wood pierced her heart. Eyes wide, she stared at the blood spreading over the front of her dress, then slowly sank to the floor where she twitched once, then lay still.

Panting heavily, Dominic spared hardly a glance for the bodies on the floor as he hurried to Tracy's side. She was still alive, but close to death.

Two tiny drops of blood stood out in stark relief against her throat.

"Tracy! *Querida*, can you hear me?"

She didn't respond, only lay there unmoving, her breathing growing more shallow by the moment.

A low groan rose in his throat. He couldn't let her go, couldn't lose her now, couldn't endure the thought of waiting, searching, perhaps for centuries, to find her again.

"Tracy." He stroked her cheek, then shook her shoulder gently. "Tracy, *querida*, wake up."

Slowly, her eyelids fluttered open. She stared at him blankly a moment, and then a faint smile touched her lips. "Dominic . . "

"*Querida*, do not leave me again."

"I don't want to . . ."

"Then take what I have to offer."

Her eyes widened. "No."

"Forgive me, my best beloved one, I cannot lose you again."

She stared up at him, too weak to resist as he bent over her. She felt the slight prick of his fangs, followed by the familiar sense of euphoria. Petrina's bite had not been so pleasant. She closed her eyes, let herself drift away on a sensual sea of pleasure.

She was drowning, sinking into oblivion, when she heard Dominic's voice calling her name.

"Tracy. Tracy! Come back to me."

It took every scrap of energy that remained to her to open her eyes.

"You must drink, my best beloved one."

"Drink . . ." She was thirsty, so thirsty. She opened her mouth, felt it fill with warm, salty liquid. She drank until he took it from her and then she closed her eyes and tumbled into the comforting abyss of slumber.

Dominic knelt beside her, watching the color return to her face. Her breathing grew stronger, steadier.

What had he done?

Throughout centuries of time she had refused the Dark Gift. Would she hate him for what he had done? How would he survive her hatred? But survive he must. He had brought her across—he could not leave her now.

Nor could he leave her here.

Gathering her into his arms, he willed them across the country to his house on the coast of Maine. He placed her on the sofa, then went upstairs to the master bedroom and opened the door that led into a hidden room behind the fireplace.

Knowing it would frighten her to wake in a casket, he took the mattress and bedding from the bed and carried it into his lair. He turned on the light so she would not awake in darkness, and then he went downstairs for Tracy.

He put her to bed, fully clothed, removed her shoes, covered her with the blankets, and then went through the house, securing it against intruders.

He stayed by her side, watching her throughout the night, and when he sensed the dawn's approach, he took off his shirt and boots and then, stretching out on the mattress beside the woman he loved, he gathered her into his arms.

For the first time in his life, he would pass the daylight hours lying beside the woman he loved.

For the first time in his life, he would awake from the Dark Sleep with her beside him.

Chapter 33

Kitana slipped her arm around Bryan's shoulders, felt him stiffen in response to her touch. "Are you still angry with me, *mon amour?*"

He lifted one shoulder in a negligent shrug. "What difference does it make? It's done now, and it can't be undone."

"Ah, my sweet, do not be sad or angry." She made a broad gesture with her hand. "The world awaits us. You have only to tell me where you wish to go."

"Anywhere?"

"Anywhere."

He grunted softly. "I always wanted to go surfing in Australia."

"We can leave tomorrow, if you like."

"Yeah, and I can ride the waves at midnight." He turned to face her. "You've taken the sun away from me."

She ran her finger over his cheek. "Have I given you nothing in return?"

"A lust for blood?" He stared into the ashes of

the fire. "I know too well the addict's curse—undying, infernal, unholy thirst. Swear to dawn, 'Never again!' yet come the night, another sin. Once so proud, now Hunger's Whore, hunting, seeking, drinking more . . ."

She laughed softly, a rich, deep sound that had the unexpected power to arouse him. "I've made a poet of you."

He grimaced.

"Complain all you want, *mon amour*, but you can't fool me. You may miss the sunlight, but you revel in the power that is now yours."

He stared into her eyes. Once, those eyes had filled him with dread, but no more. She had said she loved him. Perhaps she did. He had tried to resist her, tried to hate her, but it was impossible. When they were alone together, she was the most enchanting creature he had ever known. She was warm and playful and, as Dominic had said, the most incredible lover a man could wish for.

He was about to tell her he wasn't angry anymore when she went suddenly still.

"What is it?" he asked.

"He's done it at last."

Bryan frowned at her, wondering what she was talking about, and then swore under his breath. "No."

"Yes. After all these centuries, Dominic has made a fledgling of his own."

Chapter 34

She woke slowly, eager to leave the dark dreams
that had plagued her through the night. Eyes still
closed, she stretched. And frowned when her hand
encountered someone in the bed beside her.

Fully awake now, she turned to find Dominic
lying beside her, his gaze intent upon her face.

"Dominic, what are you doing in my ..." She
paused when she realized she wasn't in her bedroom, or in any other room of her house. "Where
are we?"

"How do you feel, my best beloved one?"

"I feel fine. Where are we?"

"At my house in Maine."

"What are we doing here?" She frowned as she
gazed around the room. The colors in the wall-
paper seemed to vibrate with life. She could hear
the rustle of the leaves from outside. Though there
were no windows in the room, she knew that night
had fallen.

She looked at Dominic again. "What happened?"

she asked, and then her eyes widened as memory returned. "Petrina!" Her hand flew to her throat. "She bit me. She drank from me . . ."

She stared into Dominic's eyes, searching for answers and yet afraid of what she might see. "You didn't!" She recoiled in horror. "Tell me you didn't."

"*Querida* . . ."

"How could you do such a thing?" She was on her feet almost before she realized she wanted to rise. "You knew how I felt!"

Dominic sat up. The blankets pooled in his lap.

Tracy stared at him. He looked the same as always, yet different somehow. Even as angry as she was, she couldn't help admiring the width of his shoulders, his broad chest, the latent strength in his well-muscled arms, or the narrow line of black hair that started at his waist and disappeared beneath the blankets. She had a sudden, inexplicable urge to find her paints and draw him as he looked now. She would call it *Vampire at Dusk.* . . .

She looked up at his face again. He was still watching her, his expression guarded.

She held out her hands, turning them this way and that, wiggling her fingers as if she had never seen them before.

She was a vampire. She said the words in her mind, trying to determine what she was feeling. Every sense she owned was alert and alive.

"I'm a vampire." She said the words aloud, surprised to find that the idea was not as shocking or abhorrent as she had expected.

Dominic rose and held out his hand. "Come with me."

She hesitated a moment and then put her hand in his. Wordlessly, he led her outside and into the gardens.

He made a gesture that encompassed the yard. "It is beautiful, yes?"

Slowly, she perused the grounds. Though it was dark, she could see colors as clearly as if it were midday. The bright pinks and reds and yellows of the roses were vibrant and alive in a way she had never seen before. She could see every thorn, the delicate veins in each leaf, in stark detail. The lawn was a deep emerald green. Each blade of grass was clearly defined.

And sounds. She heard the soft sighing of the wind though it was not strong enough to stir the leaves of the trees, the faint croaking of a frog, the flutter of a moth's wings, the shifting of a bird in its nest overhead.

She ran her hand over the back of one of the stone benches, her fingers suddenly sensitive to each tiny groove.

She twirled around. She felt better than she had ever felt in her life, knew that she could run or swim for miles and never tire. Knew if she but willed herself to do so, she could fly over the high wall that surrounded the estate.

Bemused, she stopped twirling to look at Dominic and found him watching her, his expression that of a proud father watching a child take its first steps. And that was what she was doing, she mused, taking her first steps toward a new life.

He was waiting, she realized, waiting for her reaction to her changed condition, waiting to see if she would forgive him for what he had done, or curse him and flee his presence.

Head tilted to one side, she regarded her husband as though seeing him for the first time. With her vampire sight, he was more handsome than ever. His black hair gleamed like polished ebony.

His eyes, as gray as storm clouds, were filled with apprehension.

She loved him too much to let him go on suffering, wondering if she hated him for what he had done.

But how could she hate him? She had vowed to love him until death parted them. In mortal time, that might have meant twenty or thirty years, perhaps forty, if they were lucky. But now . . .

A slow smile spread over her face. Deep down, in spite of everything she had said to the contrary, hadn't she always wanted to be what he was? To live forever? It was only her own cowardice, her fear of the unknown, that had kept her from making the decision. Subconsciously, hadn't she always hoped that Dominic would make the decision for her?

"*Querida.*" He took a hesitant step toward her.

"I'm a vampire," she said again.

He nodded, his expression uncertain.

She closed the distance between them and placed her hands on his chest, loving the feel of his skin beneath her palms, the way the hair on his chest coiled around her fingers, the way he quivered at her touch.

She tilted her head back to better see his face. "We're alike now, you and I."

He said nothing, only watched her, his expression wary, as she ran her hands over the width of his shoulders.

Tracy laughed softly. "Are *you* afraid of *me* now?"

He nodded again. "More than you can imagine."

His answer surprised her. "What are you afraid of?"

"I am afraid of your hatred."

"Hate you?" She raked her nails lightly over his bare chest, slowly moving down, down, running her hands sensuously over his flat belly and up to his chest again.

He shuddered at her touch, but made no move to touch her in return.

"I could never hate you, Dominic."

"You forgive me then?"

Rising on tiptoe, she kissed him, first one cheek and then the other. "I feel as though I've been dreaming my whole life, waiting for you to wake me up, and now it's happened." Her gaze searched his face. "Am I dreaming again?"

He drew her into his arms then, one hand caressing her cheek as he molded her body to his. She had ever been beautiful to him but never more so than now, with her eyes shining with love and acceptance.

"No, my best beloved one," he murmured, his voice husky with desire, "you are not dreaming. Tonight, our real life together begins."

Epilogue

Tracy stirred with the setting of the sun, stretched, then turned on her side to gaze down at Dominic. His eyes were closed but she knew he was awake, awaiting her kiss. She never tired of looking at him, touching him. She loved the shape of his brows, the curve of his lips, the silky texture of his hair, his high cheekbones and fine, square chin. She blew a strand of hair from his brow, licked the hollow of his throat.

And still he did not move.

Smiling faintly, she leaned forward and brushed her lips across his. His response was immediate. He lifted her onto his chest and they spent several moments kissing and caressing.

Six months had passed since Dominic had brought her across. Six months, and she had no regrets. There had been adjustments to make, of course, but they had come about gradually. She had completed her order for Mr. Petersen, painted his family's portrait—at night, of course—and closed her studio. She hadn't given up painting, but now she painted mainly for her own pleasure, though she occasionally sold a painting to one of their friends, and had a few pieces on consignment at the local art gallery. Nightingale House was filled with her art.

Sea Cliff was again a quiet haven for vampires, a small town that attracted a good number of tourists in the summer but gained few permanent new residents.

She and Bryan remained good friends, often laughing about how strangely their lives had turned out. Tracy continued to be amazed that, in many ways, vampires lived ordinary lives. She and Dominic often went dancing or to the movies with Bryan and Kitana. Marcus had brought his human companion, Gina, across and she and Tracy became close friends, often going shopping together. At night, of course.

When Gina and Marcus were married, Tracy and Dominic stood up with them.

The wedding made such an impression on Kitana that she decided to marry Bryan. It was a wedding unlike any Tracy had ever seen. The bride and groom, the wedding party, and all the guests wore black. The bride carried a bouquet of blood-red roses; the bride and groom toasted each other with red wine.

Tracy moaned softly as Dominic nibbled on her neck. She had given up much, she thought, as her fingertips caressed his broad back, but she had gained so much more.

Dominic. A man unlike any other. One who had vowed to love her forever, and given her forever in return.